Echo of Wings

ECHO SERIES

SOPHIA ST. GERMAIN

To Michael—

My real-life hero.

Contents

Chapter One

Someone followed her.

Lillian angled her head when a twig snapped in the dark forest. Not letting her steps falter, she continued walking toward the town, her eyes fixed on the thinning tree line ahead. Her follower was right behind her; his careless steps echoed between the tall trees.

She rolled her eyes—as if she wouldn't have picked up on his advance. With no magic, she'd sharpened her senses into weapons and wielded them with deadly precision. Being caught by surprise in a world where magic ruled just wouldn't do. Her father had drilled this into her since she was a child. And at eighteen, it had saved her more times than she cared to count.

The forest went silent. Lillian brushed her hand against her thigh, felt the hilt of her dagger, and slowly wrapped her hand around it. She smiled at the thrill of adrenaline that rushed into her blood as the shadow leaped out from behind a tree. Many underestimated her slight frame. But she'd trained her whole life for this.

When his arm wrapped around her, she twisted and threw her elbow up into his face. It connected with his nose with a crunch, and she swiftly crouched down to sweep out a leg, sending her attacker sprawling. Lillian used the momentum to pin him down, locking his arms under her knees.

She placed the dagger at his throat and snorted, "Well, that wasn't very nice, was it?"

"Lil, you broke my nose," the man groaned from underneath the hood.

Her breath hitched in her throat, and Lillian pulled at the dark cloak to reveal her attacker's face. A man with blue eyes and unruly auburn hair glared at her, and her heart skipped a beat.

"Eli! I wasn't expecting you back until tomorrow."

"Well, I missed you. Although now I'm not entirely sure why."

She hungrily took in his familiar face, the strong jaw and high cheekbones, and the burned copper hair that shimmered in the moonlight streaming through the trees.

It'd been over a month since she'd seen him last. Lillian had counted each day. Like she counted every day nowadays, since she didn't know how many she had left. Lillian forced the thoughts deep inside her when a knot formed in her chest. She needed to keep them far from Eli—she didn't want to look into his blue eyes and find the same sorrow that laced her father's eyes lately.

Flipping her white hair over her shoulder, she winked, "Oh, come on, Eli, I thought violence was part of my allure." She removed the dagger but kept her hold on his arms, drinking in his familiar scent.

"While it's certainly alluring, I could have done without the broken nose." Pride glimmered in his eyes. He'd taught her that trick, after all.

"Well, I'd say I was sorry, but since you're the one who sneaked up on me, I'm really not." She grinned at him.

Her best friend, and since last year, lover, grinned right back before he freed his arms and sat up. Warmth spread inside her as Eli's smile lit up his whole face and the dimples she loved formed in his cheeks. Lillian's pulse quickened when he shifted her so her legs wrapped around him.

Laughing softly, he whispered, "I think you missed me as well, Lil."

When her smile widened, he kissed her. Eli kissed her gently like he was afraid of breaking her, and she slid her arms around his neck to pull him closer, needing to feel that he was truly there.

It took Eli a long time to break down the walls she'd put up to stop herself from falling for him. Since her time was running out, she kept almost everyone at arm's length. It was easier that way. She swallowed; her sickness had nearly broken her father, and she didn't wish that fate upon anyone—least of all Eli.

As if he could sense her thoughts, Eli finally deepened the kiss, sliding his hands into her hair. She wrapped her legs tighter around his waist, her breathing becoming uneven as the heat from his body enveloped her. It wasn't until she tasted something coppery on her tongue that she pulled back.

"While I'd be happy to continue this, we should probably get you to a healer."

"Such care for me. I'd believe you, but this is what? The *third* time you've broken my nose?" Eli winked at her.

She stuck out her bottom lip. "Ah. But you deserved each one, did you not?"

He did. The first time, she'd finally bested him during training, although since he'd managed to disarm her, she'd had no choice but to use brute force to get him to yield. The second time... Well, he shouldn't have flirted with that woman right in front of her. He did have that one coming. Her nostrils flared just thinking of it.

Eli shook his head and smiled, blood from his nose dripping down his brown leather tunic. Lillian started to get up, but Eli was faster, lifting her effortlessly to set her on her feet. When she scowled, Eli just grinned and held out his hand.

"Let's go home, Lil; I'm sure your father can't wait to lecture you about being out alone at night again."

Chapter Two

They were quiet as they walked out of the forest and onto the moonlit path into the town that was their home. Lillian smiled at the comfort of Eli's warm hand, marking the new calluses that lined them. Wondering how many fights he'd gotten into this time, she opened her mouth. But before she could ask, his eyes went vacant, and he squeezed her hand as he stopped in his tracks.

She eyed him curiously as he communicated through the familiar bond with her father. When he turned away from her, she rolled her eyes. The mind speaking was one of the perks of the familiar bond, but for her, it wasn't much of a perk, only wildly frustrating. It was *very* challenging to eavesdrop when you couldn't actually hear them.

Sighing, she thought about that day ten years ago when Eli shifted into his fox for the first time, and the bond with her father instantly snapped into place. While it pushed her patience to the limit when they used it to keep information from her, Lillian had to admit it was helpful in their work as rebels.

The gods bestowed the original familiar bonds during the War of Gods to make the shifters and humans who fought alongside them more coordinated and better fighters. The bond allowed the shifters and magic wielders to share their powers, and communicate without enemy gods hearing.

Nowadays, the familiar bond between a shifter and a magic wielder was rare, but they weren't surprised to find Eli was her father's familiar. The shifter typically sensed the bond even before their first shift, and Eli had been pulled to their house when he was only eight.

Eli's grip on her hand tightened, and Lillian was ripped from her thoughts.

"No," he whispered.

"What's happening?" Eli shook his head, but she asked again as soon as his eyes focused.

He tried to smile, but the warmth didn't reach his blue eyes. "Nothing happened, Lil." Eli lowered his voice. "Sentries looking for rebels are in town, so we need to lay low. They also found a few children with magic who hadn't reported to the king, and none of your father's men could stop them."

She clenched her fists, staring intently at the weathered stone wall marking the entrance to their town, where plumes of smoke from the chimneys twirled toward the night sky.

"We need to do something more, Eli. Figure out how to stop King Alek." Lillian shook her head. "My father has to give me a better mission—not just ask me to spy on the few sentries that happen to stroll by in case they let slip what Alek is doing with the children."

"Hush. You know better than to talk about this here." Eli's voice was barely a whisper as he scanned the darkness around them. "You know Atli is just worried about you; he isn't keeping you at home because you're not ready. But I agree with you—it's time."

Lillian smiled gratefully. Ever since she'd been old enough to understand what her father did on his travels, that he wasn't merely a merchant traveling to find goods to barter, but a rebel looking to find ways to undermine the crown, she'd known she wanted in.

Even if he'd trained her as a rebel and she'd been successful with the missions he'd allowed, her father held her back, always worried for her health. Lillian blew out a frustrated breath. He didn't understand that it was her sickness that made her ache to help. She craved to leave an imprint on this world before she died. Make it a better place for those who would stay behind. Do *something* for which she might be remembered. Eli understood, perhaps the only one who knew it wasn't just something she wanted. It was something she needed.

"Before we go home, let's drop by Edla so she can fix you up. I truly don't want to be staring at a crooked nose for the rest of my life," she joked, trying to lighten the mood.

But when sadness flashed in Eli's eyes, she cursed herself silently. She knew better than to mention her looming death. Lillian started to speak but quieted when Eli pulled her into his arms and nodded into her hair.

The moonlight bathed their small town in a silvery glow when they entered through the stonewall encasing it, illuminating the rugged stone buildings and the cloaked people walking on the narrow cobblestone streets. They stopped by a small house with a blood-red door, signaling the healer's residence, and Lillian knocked softly.

Edla often let patients recovering from more severe illnesses or injuries stay in her spare room, arguing she needed to keep an eye on them. But everyone in town knew she did it to keep them fed enough not to counteract her healing. Even the best healer could not cure hunger. And there was a lot of hunger in Echo.

The door opened, and a small, blonde woman waved them into the softly lit house. Heat washed over them from the crackling fire in the back of the room, and the smell of herbs from a steaming pot resting beside the fireplace filled Lillian's nostrils.

Edla looked pointedly at them with her brown eyes. "Another broken nose, Eli? I thought you two had stopped beating each other up."

Eli offered the healer a crooked smile. "My own fault this time, Edla."

Edla shook her head and gestured for them to sit on the worn couch by the fire, its leather creaking as Lillian eagerly slipped onto it. She released a soft breath, her energy almost drained from the night's long walk, but quickly straightened her back when Eli and Edla studied her.

"I'm going to have to set it first."

Eli nodded, and Edla got right to work. She gently gripped his nose and, without warning, pulled it into place. Eli, to his credit, barely winced and only winked when Lillian shuddered. Edla cupped his cheek with her hand; a subtle glow radiated from it as she healed him, and Eli sighed when he drew a full breath through his nose.

"All better. Now, please sit still for a minute. Lillian, if you could come with me to grab a cloth and some water from the kitchen?"

Lillian knew it was only an excuse to speak to her alone, but she nodded and dutifully followed the healer to the kitchen. She walked up to the shelves lining the kitchen walls, studying the herb-filled glass bottles on them.

"How are you feeling these days?" Edla glanced at her while opening a drawer and pulling out a few soft cloths.

Lillian fidgeted with the hem of her white tunic, picking at a thread that had come loose. "I feel great."

Edla's brown eyes bore into hers. "Please. Perhaps you can fool the boy in there, but I can sense your energy, you know. It seems weaker yet, Lillian."

When worry filled the healer's eyes, Lillian's chest tightened, and she blinked furiously at the tears that burned behind her eyes as she remembered standing in this very house five years ago, hiding behind the door to the kitchen, as Edla told her father she was dying.

Lillian slowly traced one of the wooden chairs with her finger. Her father had slumped down on one of them when Edla told him she couldn't explain what was causing her hair and eyes to pale or her energy to expend so quickly. And if she couldn't understand it, she couldn't heal it.

She winced at the jolt of pain that shot through her at the memory and cleared her throat. "I'm fine, Edla. I'm taking it day by day."

There was no point in telling Edla how exhausted she was after training these days or how much harder it was waking up in the morning. Edla couldn't help her, and Lillian had come to terms with her death.

At least on the good days.

Lillian pushed away the thoughts of the mornings she woke up with tears streaming down her face and dread coursing through her veins. She needed to be strong for her father and Eli, who were already in so much pain at her fate. But a tiny ember of dread lingered in her stomach. Her sickness progressed quicker now, and she wasn't sure how much more time she'd have.

"You've always been a stubborn girl." Edla reached out and touched her cheek. "Promise me, if you're in pain, you'll let me know? Even if I can't heal you, I can make it better. There is no need to suffer, Lillian."

"I promise." Lillian hugged the small woman, wiping her cheek as a stray tear escaped.

Chapter Three

After a lecture on not breaking each other's noses, Lillian and Eli walked through the small stone town, the soft light from fireplaces inside the homes casting the narrow cobblestone path in orange hues. She smiled at the gentle clangs of pots and pans as families finished evening meals, the muffled music from the taverns, and the soft rustle of stolen moments in the dark alley beside them. Lillian preferred it like this.

The veil of night made it easier to pretend that life in Echo was safe and comfortable. Like she imagined life would have been had King Alek not come into power, and the people of Orios didn't have to keep one eye peeled over their shoulders at all times.

She ground her teeth at the thought of the king and turned to Eli. "Will you talk to my father tonight? I can't wait any longer, Eli. I have such little time left."

"Lil..."

She gasped when Eli doubled over, clutching his stomach.

"Something is wrong," he got out, his breathing labored.

"Eli, what's happening?" Lillian frantically searched him for injuries, but there weren't any physical wounds. "Are you hurt?"

"Atli," he groaned.

Lillian went cold. It wasn't Eli who was hurt. He sensed her father's pain through their bond.

"Where, Eli?" She yelled at him, desperately scanning the dark alleys around them.

"House. Your house. Go." Eli fell to his knees.

Sprinting, she didn't allow herself to think about how she had just left Eli there; she only focused on getting to her father as fast as possible. Lillian ran past drunken townsfolk, ignoring the strange looks they shot her. Her chest burned, and every breath was a struggle, but she forced her body to continue running, cursing her sickness as she slowed with each step.

Lillian thanked the gods she didn't even believe in when she reached the beacon marking the edge of the town. It cast its eerie glow on her neighbors' dark homes, and she pushed herself further. But when she was almost there, voices stopped her in her tracks. Lillian couldn't make out what they were saying from the distance, but they were male, and there were several of them.

Her stomach dropped. She'd panicked and hadn't thought to ask Eli for another weapon. She only had the one dagger strapped to her thigh. It hadn't even crossed her mind that someone could purposely be hurting her father. She'd assumed that he might have fallen or, in the worst case, gotten into a drunken brawl. Not that she'd ever seen her father close to drunk.

She crept forward, taking cautious steps over the uneven cobblestone and keeping to the shadows of their neighbors' homes. The voices were clear now—there were four men. A chill snaked down her spine when she realized what it must mean, but she didn't allow herself to finish the thought. Lillian shook her head and told herself to be smart like her father taught her. He'd trained her for this. When she reached the last house before their own, she stopped. Holding her breath and praying that none of the men was a shifter with a heightened sense of smell, she peeked around the corner of her neighbor's home.

Her heart stopped.

Her father was on his knees in front of their house, two black-clad sentries holding his arms, while a third aimed a kick at his gut. It wasn't the first strike. Blood coated his brown hair, and by the way he curled his back, he was already in great pain.

"Tell us where the other rebels are, or we will kill you right here." The man who kicked him screamed into his face.

Lillian gritted her teeth as fear threatened to consume her. The men all had their backs to her—she could have killed them all within seconds if she'd had a bow. But four against one, with only a dagger and no magic? She had no chance.

Ice spread throughout her body when her father smiled, his teeth stained red. "There is nothing you can do to me to get me to tell you. You've already taken everything."

He laughed hollowly, specs of blood spraying onto the cobblestones and the sentries' black boots as the laugh became a coughing fit. "Just know, there will be retribution soon. And she who will exact your punishment will make you suffer more greatly than you can ever imagine."

Lillian frowned, but when the sentry struck him again, she clenched her fists until they were white. Her father could use his mind control to turn these sentries on each other in an instant. What was he waiting for? Dread coursed through her veins as she tried to will him to use his magic, but when her father did nothing, she sucked in a breath and stepped out from the shadows of the house. He would not die alone.

Only her father faced her way, and his head jerked as his brown eyes met hers. Lillian went to take another step when she was hit full force with the need to stop. A wave of shock washed over her when she realized her father was using his magic on *her*. She could not move. There was no way of evading it. Lillian pushed and pushed against his hold, but it didn't matter. Desperately, she met his eyes, tears streaming down her face.

Only one tear slowly made it down her father's cheek.

"This one won't speak. Just kill him and be done with it." A dark-haired sentry who stood to the side waved his hand impatiently before shifting into a large eagle—taking flight against the clear night sky.

Lillian screamed even though no sound came out, using everything in her to push back against her father's magic. One of the sentries lifted his sword.

No! Please, *please*! She begged every god she could think of for help, even Adeon. She'd do whatever they wanted to keep her father alive. *Please!* Her father didn't react to the sword raised above his head. He only continued staring into her eyes. Panic filled her, her eyes begging him to release his hold, but she couldn't even wipe at the tears that flowed freely down her face.

When the sword sliced through the air, her father mouthed, "I'm so sorry."

Lillian tried to shut her eyes, but her father's magic wouldn't allow it. She saw every moment leading the sword to its mark. Her father's head falling onto already bloody cobblestones. His magic released her instantly, and she fell to her knees.

Chapter Four

Lillian wasn't sure how much time had passed or how the sentries hadn't noticed her as she crawled to her father's still-warm body. She tried to put his head back, desperately mumbling, "It's going to be alright, it's going to be alright."

When a strong hand grasped her shoulder, relief filled her. The pain coursing through her would end—the sentries were back to finish her off as well.

But it was Eli's soft voice that broke through her grief. When he tilted her head up, the same heartbreak that filled her reflected in his blue eyes. She whimpered as Eli scooped her up into his arms.

"We need to get you away from here. We don't know if they are coming back or if they realize Atli had a daughter." Eli started walking, still carrying her in his arms.

"What about... what about his body? We need to bury him." Lillian's voice broke as she twisted to get him to set her down, starting toward her father's body once more.

"We've got him, Lillian. We'll take care of the body."

She hadn't noticed they weren't alone. Two enormous men, more wildlings than humans, stood behind Eli. She might have been afraid if she could feel anything other than grief.

"But...," she started.

"Lil, there is nothing you can do right now," Eli interrupted her.

"I swore to Atli that I'd always keep you safe, and I intend to keep that promise."

She shook her head but froze when her father's voice rang in her head. *You need to breathe, Lillian. You can't act on emotion alone.*

With a pang of pain, she realized that if she died tonight, she would not be able to avenge him. Drawing a shaky breath, Lillian told herself she would listen to him this one final time, even as every fiber in her body told her not to. So she let Eli lead her away from her father's body and from the home she'd known the past eighteen years.

Eli opened the door to his apartment, motioning for her to enter. Lillian glanced around the messy room, furnished only with a bed, a table, and a worn chair filled with Eli's clothes by the only window. Lillian hadn't spent much time here before—her father didn't believe that unmarried couples should be alone for long. A strangled sob escaped her when she realized her father would never caution her again.

Eli led her to the small table, set with two wobbly chairs. He opened one of the wooden cabinets, pulled out a dusty bottle filled with amber liquid, and poured two glasses.

"It will help with the shock."

She drained the whole glass in one go, the liquid burning her throat as it went down. While it didn't help with the pain in her chest, it did fuel the anger building inside her. She wiped her cheeks with her bloody sleeve, wincing at the coppery smell.

"Who would have betrayed him?" She stared at Eli, leaning against the wooden counter and waved her hand for him to refill her glass. As soon as he did, she drained it again.

"Take it easy, Lil. This is strong stuff." She narrowed her eyes, and Eli wisely swallowed the rest of his lecture.

Refilling her glass a third time, he shook his head slowly, his auburn hair falling into his eyes. "I don't know. We haven't heard any whispers that the King's Guard was on to us."

She took another big sip, wincing at the smell of the liquor. "He used his magic on *me*, Eli. I don't understand. Why didn't he use it on them?"

Eli walked up to sit down on the chair opposite her. "We don't know if the sentries had magic, Lillian." He reached out to grip her hand. "He spent every moment of your life protecting you. I'm guessing he wanted to do it to the end." Eli's eyes glistened in the candlelight, and Lillian's chest split open another inch.

Her father's death was hurting Eli as much as it did her. The breaking of a familiar bond was devastating—it could even kill the other shifter or magic wielder. Before King Alek, it was forbidden to kill a bonded shifter or human, regardless of the crime they committed.

Lillian stared into her drink, drops of tears joining the amber liquor. "When I find out who did this, I will kill them," she said quietly.

"We'll do it together," Eli promised.

Chapter Five

They finished their drinks in silence, both lost in their own grief. When they finally decided to try for a few hours of sleep, Eli pulled her into his arms, slowly stroking her back in the small bed. Lillian stared at the moon shining through the round window, not thinking she'd get any rest, but she almost immediately fell into a fitful sleep, dreaming of death calling to her.

It was her turn soon.

Lillian woke at the first rays of sunlight seeping into the room, sweat coating her body from nightmares but with a clear, made-up mind. She could spend what little time she had left searching for whoever had betrayed her father. Or she could do something about the one person who was really to blame.

The grief from last night had turned into ice-cold rage, and her movements were jerky when she pushed off the covers and got out of bed. She wanted to destroy something, kill someone. She'd never experienced rage like this before. Lillian had been angry at the world and her sickness, but this was different. It was as if there was no space for any other emotion within her, only cold, calculating rage.

Eli snored softly in the worn leather chair by the window, the sunlight reflecting in his messy hair. Her heart ached when a shadow crossed his sleeping face, and she took one of the blankets off the bed and gently covered him. After kissing his forehead, she slipped out the door.

It was early morning, just past dawn, but the summer sun already bathed the small stone town in a soft glow. The streets were empty, and the small windows in the homes lining the street dark, her neighbors not yet ready for the day.

Lillian walked with determined steps over the cobblestone toward her house. She was still in the same clothes from last night, covered in her father's blood. Shuddering, she ripped off her white tunic and threw it into an alley. A sob lodged in her throat—she needed to get out of them. Right now.

As Lillian reached the house, she prepared herself for the remains of her father's murder. But the ground was clean, seemingly entirely undisturbed. It made her even angrier. It was as if her father's death wasn't even significant enough to leave a mark.

She furiously stomped up to the house, slamming open the wooden door. When she walked inside, the familiar leathery smell of her father washed over her. She clasped at her chest—she was breaking, splitting right down the middle. With her hands on her knees, she forced air down her lungs. *Focus on the anger.* Anger would keep her moving.

"Clothes first," she mumbled. Lillian walked up the stairs and entered her bedroom, pausing for a moment to catch her breath after the walk and stairs. Tears burned behind her eyes as she leaned against the doorframe; it was becoming increasingly difficult to do even the smallest things.

She sniffed and glanced around the room. It looked exactly as she'd left it, her few belongings haphazardly strewn across her wooden desk and unmade bed. She quickly stepped out of her bloody vest and breeches and pulled on soft leather trousers, a simple black tunic, and her most comfortable boots.

Lillian braided her white hair to keep it out of her face, wiping her cheeks as more tears escaped. Finally, she grabbed a satchel and filled it with a few changes of clothes and a small pocket knife her father had gifted her. She didn't have much else of sentimental value.

When Lillian finished packing, she braced herself and walked downstairs to her father's study. A sword she'd never seen before leaned against his brown desk, the sun shining through the window reflecting in its clean blade and the single ebony stone embellishing its pommel. It was too small for her father to wield, but it was perfectly balanced for her when she weighed it in her hands. Frowning, she strapped it to her back together with her favored bow. She also grabbed a few daggers that she fastened at her thighs.

Her father's gray cloak hung over his chair. Lillian grabbed it and flung it over her shoulders, almost doubling over as his smell enveloped her. It was too big but easily concealed the weapons on her back. As she prepared to leave, she glanced at the few papers strewn across his messy desk. The first one was a flier for the King's Guard Trials. Anyone interested in participating was to report to the castle grounds in Echo in four days.

Another piece of paper must have been part of a letter. It was burned, like her father had tried to destroy it but had been interrupted. She could only make out the words 'progress' and 'she's ready.' But it was the last one that made her slump down on a chair —a note written in her father's sloppy handwriting. *Lillian, I'm sorry. I've left your mother's sword out. Take it. I know you will make me proud.*

A broken cry escaped her lips, and she tumbled to the floor, wrapping her arms tightly around herself. Lillian didn't want her dead mother's sword. She wanted her parents. She wanted her father to come and tell her it would be alright. *It will be alright. You just need to breathe.* She sobbed as his voice echoed in her head.

Chapter Six

Lillian lay on the floor for hours, her arms the only thing keeping her from shattering into a million pieces, until her tears finally dried. Shaking, she sat up and forced the broken pieces of herself together. It wasn't going to be alright; never again would her life be alright, but she could make sure these senseless killings stopped.

She used the scratched wooden table to drag herself upright and took a deep breath. When she'd seen the flier for the trials, an idea formed in her head; she would do everything she could to make her father proud while avenging his death. Lillian readied herself to walk out the door when it burst open. She quickly drew two daggers, letting one fly the moment the person entered.

At the last second, she shifted her aim when her eyes met familiar blue ones. The dagger just about nicked Eli's ear as it lodged in the wooden wall behind him.

"Do you need to practice your aim, or did you recognize it was me?" He tried to smile, but it ended up more of a grimace.

"Sorry," she murmured.

"Don't be. I'm glad you're protecting yourself. I was worried you would go into full martyr mode, planning something completely reckless."

Lillian bit her cheek, remaining quiet.

"You *are* planning something reckless then." Eli closed the distance between them and put a finger under her chin, lifting her eyes to his. "Lil, Atli would not want you to die for him. Please stop and think for a moment."

"I have been thinking my entire life, Eli. They will not stop. Not as long as Alek sits on the throne. Who will lose their parents next?" Her frustration brought fresh tears to her eyes, and she blinked frantically to get rid of them. She'd been so worried about leaving her father behind, had never considered he might be the one to die first.

"I have nothing left. I'm already dying. If I don't do something now, I never will."

"So what's the plan then? You're going to waltz into the castle and kill the king?"

Lillian laughed hollowly. "Something like that."

Eli reached out like he wanted to shake her but took a deep breath to calm himself. "Seriously, do you have a plan?"

Lillian held up the flier she'd picked off her father's desk. "I'm joining the King's Guard Trials."

It wasn't often she witnessed Eli stunned. She stared at the floor, studying the worn floorboards.

"I know it seems crazy, but think about it. If I can get a spot in the guard, I'll be close to the king. And I can take him out at the first opportunity."

"It's a suicide mission, Lil. Even if you succeeded, they'd kill you instantly. You know that's why we haven't tried it before." Eli impatiently brushed his untamed hair out of his face.

She shrugged. "It seems like a good enough way to go. Better than wasting away at home." She would die soon either way. Lillian was expendable, and if she succeeded, no more children would have to watch their parents get murdered and feel the excruciating pain coursing through her body.

When she met Eli's eyes again, she knew she'd won. She wrapped her arms around him and held him tight, her chest aching not just for her father's death but for Eli. He'd lose both her and her father this year. He hugged her back and whispered, "You still have *something* left. You still have me."

Lillian closed her eyes. It was for him she would do this.

Chapter Seven

They held each other for a long time. Eli slowly stroked her back, but no heat filled her at his touch. She was so cold that she thought she might never again feel warm.

When she finally pulled back, Eli cupped her face. "Let's work on a plan before you leave. I need to meet with Harald and Hjalmar to find out what happened."

When Lillian furrowed her brow, he continued. "They're the two men that helped us last night. They worked for Atli."

A wave of pain washed through her, but she tried to keep her voice steady. "I want to come with you. I know my father kept things from me so I wouldn't go off on my own mission."

Eli's face hardened, but when she raised an eyebrow, he blew out a breath. "Lillian. Everything Atli did was out of love. Always remember that. If you're going to do this, you need to be careful. He saved your life last night; don't let it be in vain."

Lillian's stomach churned. "I didn't mean it like that."

Eli nodded slowly. "I know. I'll find Harald and Hjalmar, and we'll meet you in the market. We have a safe house where we can talk."

He brushed his lips against hers, and then vibrating magic filled the room as he shifted into his fox, his clothes ripping as he turned. The red fox skipped out the front door with a sad glance at her.

Lillian walked through the small house she'd grown up in. She knew she would never see it again. The house held so many memories, and she had to brace herself against the wall as her mind replayed the last time she'd been here with her father.

Her father sat at the kitchen table, seemingly deep in thought. He looked up as she walked in, and she didn't miss the flash of sadness in his eyes.

"You look tired," he greeted her.

"Good morning to you, too," she responded, kissing his cheek.

Her father waved to the food on the table. "Anything to report from last night?"

Lillian grabbed a piece of cold chicken, shaking her head. "No. They were low-standing guards. They only wanted to get drunk and find a woman. It didn't seem they had a specific mission."

Her father nodded. "Good. I want you out tonight as well. There are more sentries around since the trials are coming up."

Lillian sighed. "Spying again? Isn't it time you used me for something more? I want to do something that actually will make a difference. Travel, find allies like you have Eli do."

His face hardened. "Lillian. You know your place is with me. And you will do as I say."

Glancing down at her feet, Lillian nodded.

"Your time will come, Lil." Her father offered her a small smile. "Now, head on out to train. You haven't been keeping up with your bow."

A dry sob left Lillian's throat at the memory, but she swallowed hard, squared her shoulders, and walked out the door without turning back.

Chapter Eight

Lillian slowly walked through the streets of their neighborhood. The summer sun beat down on her, sweat dripping down her spine even as her insides remained cold as ice. She braced herself against the stone wall of a home as a wave of dizziness overcame her, wincing as black spots danced in front of her eyes.

When she didn't feel as if she would faint, she started walking again, turning left toward the east market, the bustling center of this part of town. The sun hung directly over the small square, the worn stone buildings around it casting little shade on the many stands across it.

As she walked by the flower stand, Mr. Florian waved at her, and she offered him a slight nod in return. Lillian loved his stand. He used his magic to grow the most magnificent flowers in any color a buyer desired. Even some of the wealthier families in Echo would venture to the market to get their hands on Florian's flower crowns.

Her stomach growled, and while the thought of food repulsed her, Lillian told herself she needed the strength to keep going. The produce stand stood at the other end of the small square, and as Lillian began to make her way over, there was a commotion to her right. She froze with the rest of the people in the market when an agonizing scream echoed between the stone buildings. One of the king's sentries held a woman by her blonde hair while two other sentries gripped the arms of a young man, perhaps fifteen years old.

"Please! He's my only son," the woman cried.

The boy had tears in his eyes and pulled at the men to get free. Lillian gasped when a strong gust of wind filled the square, almost knocking over one of the sentries, but the sentry recovered quickly and swiftly clamped a metal cuff around the boy's wrist. The wind died down immediately.

"Enough," the sentry who had almost fallen commanded. "You know the rules. Anyone with magic is to report to the king for evaluation."

Heat spread across Lillian's neck, finally warming her icy insides. The king's 'evaluation' always favored those with defensive or offensive magic, like the boy's wind manipulation. And very rarely were those people ever seen again.

She glanced around but knew no one would dare help, the punishment for going against the king's men being immediate execution. Lillian clenched her fists, and without a second thought, she walked toward the sentries. Brushing her hands over her daggers, she opened her mouth to give them a piece of her mind, but before she could speak, a hand clamped down over her mouth and pulled her back into the crowd.

Hissing, she tried to spin around, pulling at the person's tight grip. She hadn't heard a whisper of whoever had sneaked up behind her.

"Hush! Be still," the man holding her breathed into her ear. A scream made her snap her head toward the boy again. A man pushed through the crowd and ran toward the sentries.

"Get your hands off my boy!" The man pulled the sword strapped to his back free, but when he came within fighting distance, his eyes glazed over, and the man stumbled as he stopped in his tracks. He turned his head from side to side, screaming at the sentries to give him his sight back. A shiver snaked down Lillian's spine when one of the sentries let out a cold laugh.

He released the boy and walked up to the blinded man. With no hesitation, the sentry swung his sword. Lillian screamed into the hand covering her mouth as the man's head fell to the ground. Panic ensued, and people ran in different directions to get away.

"Get out of here *now*," the man holding her ordered, finally releasing her.

She spun around but only caught a glimpse of green eyes under a black hood as the man turned and disappeared into the shade of the stone buildings. Lillian tried to follow, but with the chaos in the square, she lost sight of the stranger, and when she got to the street corner, he was nowhere to be seen.

"Lillian!" Eli ran up to where she leaned against a stone wall. "I've been looking for you everywhere. Did you hear they took the baker's boy?"

"I was there, Eli." Her eyes filled with tears. "They killed his father. Cut his head off right in the square. Like they did with..." Her voice broke as hot tears spilled down her cheeks. Eli pulled her into his arms, her tears soaking his brown leather tunic.

"Shh, shh, I know." Eli stroked her back.

She pulled out of his embrace. "I'm not upset, not in that way." She shook her head. "I am so done with all this death, Eli. I was going to stop it, but someone held me back."

"What do you mean you were going to stop it?" Eli raised his voice. "You know that's certain death, Lillian. They would have cut *your* head off. I know you're hurting because of Atli, but this is serious; you could have died!"

Lillian gritted her teeth. "I know, Eli. But how many more should die at their hands?" She covered her face with her hands. She knew it was his love for her speaking, but she couldn't breathe. "What is the point of my life if I don't do something before I go?"

When she met his eyes, the grief in them was unmistakable, and she hated the pity that also shone there. She knew how much pain it brought Eli when she mentioned her impending death, but it was happening whether they wanted to or not. She was tired of pretending.

Lillian went to walk off, but Eli grabbed her hand.

"I understand how you feel, Lil. I want to help, too. I hate that we can only do so much, save so few." His own anger burned bright in his eyes. "But you have a plan now, even if I disagree with it. Please, let's discuss it and hopefully end this once and for all."

When she nodded slowly, Eli squeezed her hand. "Come, I'll take you to the safe house."

Chapter Nine

Eli dragged her to a small apartment just a short distance from his own. Without knocking, he opened a door almost falling off its hinges, revealing a mostly empty, run-down room with boarded windows. Two cloaked men sat on a frayed couch, deep in conversation. Their heads snapped to the door when they entered, and both men rose, pulling off their hoods.

Lillian had to catch herself so she would not let her jaw drop. She'd been too deep in her grief yesterday to study them. They were huge. Both men pushed six foot five, with dark brown hair and wild eyes. They looked like they should be roaming the woods, killing animals with their bare hands. Lillian shuddered but kept her emotions off her face.

When Eli approached, one of the men pulled him into a hug, almost lifting him off his feet. "Hey, Red. How are you holding up?" The other one offered them both a small wave.

The hugger turned, towering over Lillian as he stalked closer. She backed up, the hair on the back of her neck rising as the man even smelled like a wild animal.

He grinned at her. "No need to be afraid. I'm sorry we're not meeting under better circumstances, Lillian. I've heard so much about you." Wagging his finger at Eli, he continued. "You didn't tell us she was such a pretty little thing, though."

She glared at him. He stood almost a foot taller than her, but she kept her chin high, holding his gaze.

The man laughed. "And tough as well. I can see why you like her."

"And you are?" Lillian ignored his comment.

"I'm Harald, and the quiet one is my younger brother Hjalmar. We're old friends of Eli and your father," he winked at her.

Her face crumbled at his words, and Lillian had to force air down her lungs to remain standing.

Harald put a massive hand on her shoulder. "I'm sorry, Lillian. I'm not the best in these situations." Hjalmar cleared his throat pointedly. "Well, in any delicate situation, really. But we buried your father in the woods, by the meadow. We'll take you there if you want."

Lillian nodded, not trusting her voice.

Harald gently guided her to the couch and immediately began telling the story of how he and Hjalmar met Eli. They'd been hunting in the woods when a large red fox challenged them for their game, cocky as hell. He'd been less cocky when they'd both shifted into their wolf form. She nodded, she wasn't surprised to hear that they both were wolf-shifters. They resembled wolves even in their human form.

Eli clasped his hands together. "Enough reminiscing. Lillian has decided to join the King's Guard Trials to kill the king, and we need to fill her in on our missions."

Hjalmar eyed her curiously from where he leaned against the crumbling wall but averted his gaze when she narrowed her eyes.

"Risky plan, but I like it. The trials are deadly. But from what I've heard about you from Atli, I'd expect you, if anyone, could get a spot. So, how much do you know about the king?" Harald asked.

Lillian shrugged. "I know what everyone in Orios knows, I think."

Eighteen years ago, King Alek and his forces stormed the castle in Echo and brutally murdered King Ivar and Queen Liv. Lillian's parents served the previous royals, and her mother died defending the queen that day. Lillian was barely six months old.

Her father had been out on a scouting mission, racing back as he heard of the attack, but arrived too late. The castle was already on fire, and everyone inside was dead. Lillian was lucky; her nursemaid had been able to sneak out during the chaos and found her father when he came rushing in.

Eli interrupted her. "And you remember the story of Queen Liv and King Ivar?"

She nodded. Of course, she did. Everyone in Echo knew the story of Liv, the beautiful leader of the Valkyries and Queen of Hindra, and Ivar, the most powerful magic wielder and King that Echo had ever seen. Hindra and Echo, the largest islands in Orios, had been at war for over a hundred years when Ivar and Liv ascended their thrones. In an attempt for peace, they met on neutral grounds, and somewhere during negotiations, they fell in love. The king and queen planned to unite Hindra and Echo to make both lands flourish. However, the old god of Orios, Adeon, did not bless their union.

Afraid that the two monarchs and any potential offspring would become more powerful than even the gods, he cursed the royal family. Their powers were taken, only to be given back if they broke the curse. No one in Echo knew how the curse could be broken. Even her father, who'd been King Ivar's right-hand man, hadn't known.

Apparently, the price of breaking it was so devastating that neither the king nor queen could bear it. Alek seized the opportunity, orchestrated an attack on the weakened royals, and took both thrones, crowning himself King of Orios. He then hunted the Valkyries, dragons, and other magical creatures he despised until the last few survivors fled to smaller, remote isles. Now, only humans and shifters remained on Echo and Hindra.

Eli nodded. "Some rebels are trying to seek out the Valkyries to convince them to stand against King Alek. That's what I did the past month. I went to some of the smaller isles in the Eastern Sea, but there wasn't a whisper of them."

Lillian frowned. She knew that her father purposely had the rebels focus on different missions, limiting the information he shared with each of them and keeping their identities a secret should they get betrayed. Still, it surprised her that he hadn't told her they were seeking out the Valkyries, but Harald interrupted before she could ask.

"And as you are well aware, some of us are trying to figure out where the king takes children like the baker's boy. We overheard the sentries from the market saying they would be out letting off some steam tonight. We should go, see if we can learn anything else."

Chapter Ten

Lillian waited in the dark alley by a shady tavern. Frowning, she studied the lowlifes that entered. As two drunkards dressed in tattered brown tunics and breeches strolled through the alley, she slipped into the shadows behind a few stacked wooden boxes, holding her breath as their stench made her eyes water.

When Eli finally neared the entrance, she stepped into the light of the dusty lanterns hanging above the tavern door. As his eyes found her, he stopped and drew a breath.

Lillian offered him a tight smile. Knowing most women inside would be courtesans, she'd dressed to blend in. She'd squeezed into a gray silk dress that fit her perfectly when she was perhaps twelve but that now hugged every curve on her body. After cutting into the neckline and removing some of the boning, she'd made space for her chest, although a small part of her worried it would spill out at one wrong move. Her hair was left unbound, but the contrast with the gray dress made her white hair sparkle in the moonlight.

Eli's blue eyes trailed over her body. "I don't know whether the men in there will fall at your feet or run away, Lillian. You are terrifyingly beautiful."

Lillian waited for the warmth his compliments usually evoked, but her insides were empty, a gaping hole where her heart should be. She used to love it when Eli looked at her like she was an ordinary girl—not the dying girl he needed to be careful with. But everything was different now.

She forced herself to joke. "If I knew it would have such an effect on you, I would have worn this old rag before."

"Oh, you should definitely wear this again. But perhaps not in public. I will have to fight off every man that comes within sight." Eli pulled her to him and brushed his lips against hers. "The men in there won't know what hit them."

Not even an ember of warmth. Lillian sighed but plastered a smile on her face when Eli glanced at her questioningly. For him, she would try to be strong.

When they turned to walk into the tavern, the sensation of being watched pricked her neck. She glanced over her shoulder, but the only thing in the dark streets was an owl perched on the roof opposite the tavern. Shaking her head, Lillian followed Eli through the door.

The smell of stale air from too many people packed into the small space immediately hit them. An unnecessary fire burned bright in the corner of the tavern, and beads of sweat rolled down the neck of the barmaid as she waved to them. Eli gripped Lillian's hand, walking confidently toward a wooden table in a dim corner where Harald and Hjalmar already sat.

"Any sign of our other friends?" Eli asked.

"They're gambling in one of the back rooms." Hjalmar spoke for the first time. His voice was quiet, completely opposite to his brother's obnoxious one. "We've tried to join, but the table is full."

Lillian scanned the room. The tavern was full tonight, people in a celebratory mood in the summer heat. Her chest tightened when a woman threw her head back and laughed at the next table, and Lillian wondered if she'd ever feel that light and carefree again.

Several courtesans worked the room, and a beautiful raven-haired woman was escorted into one of the back rooms by one of the two sentries standing guard outside.

Lillian cleared her throat. "I have an idea."

Eli followed her eyes and violently shook his head. "I know what you're thinking, and absolutely not."

"Come on, Eli, it'll be fine."

"Lillian, I know you're brave. You have nothing to prove by putting yourself in more danger than you're already planning."

Lillian ground her teeth but forced herself to remain calm. "Look how I see it; you three have no way of getting into that room. I, on the other hand, can. My father would have agreed."

He definitely wouldn't have, and Eli knew it. But when he opened his mouth to object again, Harald interrupted.

"I knew I liked you. Fearless and beautiful. What are you doing with Red, girl?" Harald winked at her. "Let the girl go, Eli. She's right, and you know we need any information we can get."

Eli's face was tight with disapproval, but finally, he nodded. "You're coming right out if something feels off."

Chapter Eleven

Lillian leaned against the bar, shaking her head when the barmaid questioningly pointed at a mug of ale. Out of the corner of her eye, she noticed a blonde, dirty-looking man walking toward her. He swayed slightly, and the reek of alcohol enveloped her as he sidled up next to her.

"Hi there, beautiful. How many silvers to take you for a spin tonight," he slurred.

She turned her head over her shoulder and gave him a once over, a smirk on her face. "Oh darling, you cannot afford me."

"Come on, you're just up here by yourself. You clearly aren't in high demand."

Color spread across his cheeks when Lillian only blinked at him and turned back to the bar.

"You look like a spirit, all pale." He grabbed her arm, and she winced at the hard grip. "I wonder if you have white hair between those legs as well."

Eli rose from his seat, but she shook her head imperceptibly.

"You alright there, miss?" The tall sentry she'd watched escort the raven-haired woman walked up to her side.

"This man may have had a bit too much ale." She smiled, glancing at him from under her eyelashes. "He seems to think he has a claim to me when I was promised to the brave king's men this evening."

The sentry studied her while brushing off some dust from his black uniform. "I didn't realize you were one of Madame Estrid's girls."

Lillian kept her eyes on him, willing her face to heat. "I'm new. I was trying to find the tavern and got lost. And when I got here, I wasn't sure where to go. I didn't see any of the other courtesans." She forced herself to babble, to seem like an inexperienced new courtesan.

"New, you say? The men will love a fresh girl." The sentry glared at the blonde man holding onto Lillian's arm. "What are you waiting for? Get your hands off the girl and get out of my way."

Lillian drew a silent breath of relief. The sentry led her to the door farthest on the left, where the raven-haired woman had entered.

"I'll see you later tonight when my shift is over." His wide-set eyes raked over her body as he opened the door, and Lillian had to stop herself from cringing. She really hoped not.

As she walked into the room, she subtly scanned it for exits, noting the people and any possible escape routes, as her father had taught her. She pushed the pain of his voice deep down; this wasn't the place to fall apart.

A small fire cast the room in hues of orange and red, its light flickering on the six uniformed men in the room. They all sat at a round table playing cards and, from the looks of the many cups littering the table, drinking large amounts of brown liquor. Good. If they're drunk, it would hopefully be easier to loosen their tongues.

Two courtesans were also in the room. The raven-haired girl sat on a large, red-haired sentry's lap, his meaty hands slowly caressing her thighs while she whispered something in his ear. The other courtesan, a curvy brunette in a red dress that shimmered in the fire-light, danced to the left of the table, her sensual movements hypno-tizing the two closest men.

"What do we have here?" One of the sentries fixed his dark eyes on Lillian while swirling a cup of liquor.

Lillian almost recoiled when she recognized him as one of the sentries from the square—the one who killed the baker. She didn't think she'd forget his face even after she moved on to the afterlife.

"You look like you're made of ice. Like my tongue would get stuck if I licked you." Her skin crawled under the man's gaze.

"What's your name, sweetheart?" A chubby sentry, no older than eighteen, stared at her as he folded the cards in his hand.

"I'm Ingrid," she said softly, plastering a smile on her face.

"Well, don't just stand there. There is a spot for you over here." The dark-eyed sentry waved her over and gestured toward his lap.

Lillian did her best to beam at him, swaying her hips as she walked over.

"What's your name, soldier," she purred into his ear, even as she thought she'd gag from the odor that reeked from him: sweat, alcohol, and something metallic. She prayed it wasn't blood from the baker.

"I don't think a common whore needs to know my name, do you, boys?"

All the men around the table laughed politely. Lillian winced inwardly and placed her hand against the back of his neck, squeezing softly.

"So tense, my lord. Did you have a rough day?"

She might be pushing too hard, too soon, but she needed to get out of here. Almost gagging from the murderous hands that rested on her thighs, Lillian thought Eli might have been right about this being a bad idea.

The sentry squeezed her leg hard, and Lillian held her breath. "Actually, I did have a rough day." He let go of her thigh but kept his hand resting on her knee, his rough uniform scratching her bare legs as she shifted. "Some kid tried to blow us away today. It was a valiant effort, but obviously no threat to us. My neck is slightly sore from it, though, so keep up with that massage."

Lillian let her fingers slowly drag down his neck, pressing down to soften the muscles. Another wave of nausea rolled through her, and she swallowed hard. He probably wouldn't tell her much if she vomited all over him.

"I'm sure few could ever best you, my lord. Let alone a child. Was he punished? Seems like death would be a lenience for moving against the king's men."

The raven-haired courtesan glanced at her from across the table, her eyes narrowing slightly, and Lillian's heart beat faster.

"He was not killed. The king has use for someone with his talents. But don't fret; his fate is much worse than death. As he'll see when he arrives at the castle."

The cold smile on the sentry's face made her skin prickle with goosebumps. Lillian hummed, continuing her slow massage, even as her heart nearly beat out of her chest.

The chubby sentry studied her, his face cocked to the side. "How did you know the child was a boy?"

Her body went cold, and Lillian almost wished she honored Adeon so she had someone to pray to.

"I...," she started, but something hit the window hard, causing the sentry to push her out of his lap and reach for his weapons.

"What was that?" He pointed out the window and ordered, "Everyone, outside now!"

Lillian tried to manage her breathing. She hadn't realized she'd held her breath since the chubby sentry had asked his question. When the men filed out of the room, she took the opportunity to sneak out, finding a back door out of the tavern into a small alleyway. She slipped into the shadows and stood with her hands on knees, breathing deep to avoid spewing her guts all over the cobblestones at the thought of the sentry's hands, when someone squeezed her shoulder. Lillian jumped three feet into the air.

"It's me. Eli."

She'd never been so relieved to hear his voice and flung her arms around his neck. When she pulled back, he laughed softly.

"You scared me," she punched his shoulder. "Thanks for saving me, though. I thought I was done for a moment. How in Orios did you know to throw something at the window right then?"

"What do you mean?" Eli stared at her, his eyebrows raised. "I saw the sentries run outside, so I took the back exit and hoped that's where you'd go. What happened in there?"

"You didn't throw something at the window? Who was it then?"

Eli shrugged, his forehead wrinkled. Lillian shook her head. She couldn't believe she'd just gotten lucky. Although, if it was luck, she hoped it would stick. She'd need it in the trials.

"I got the information, but we should get out of here before they see us."

Chapter Twelve

Back at the safehouse, Lillian told the men everything she'd learned in the room, and they speculated about the king's plans for the boy. Lillian shuddered as she recalled the sentry's cold smile when mentioning the fate of the children. After an hour, Lillian announced that she might very well drop dead tonight if she didn't wash off the feel of the sentry's hands on her. She still felt dirty when she went to sleep on the worn couch, listening to Eli and Harald's whispered conversation at the table behind her.

When she woke the next day, waves of nausea rolled through her. She'd rarely left their small town. Her father hadn't wanted her to travel and had only brought her to the capital twice when she was younger, and she'd cried until she lost her voice at the thought of staying back. But today, she would leave. And never come back.

Silver lined Eli's eyes when she hugged him goodbye, and her heart ached as she gently kissed his brow. Even when she promised him she'd be careful, not even risk a nightly walk, did the corners of his mouth lift. It made sense; the trials were known to be deadly, and many who joined had magic or were unusually large brutes like Harald and Hjalmar. Lillian would have to rely on speed, wits, and cunning to make it through. And even then, it was unlikely. But she had to try.

Harald hugged her, nearly lifting her off her feet, and promised to see her in the capital. He and Eli would come to the capital once Eli settled some of her father's affairs. Eli had tried to convince her to let him join her in the trials, but she'd refused—Eli was to take over her father's place as rebel leader, and she wouldn't risk his life. The people of Orios would need Eli should she succeed.

Hjalmar offered her a sad smile. "He is on the left side of the meadow. We left a raven feather on his grave."

Lillian nodded, tears spilling down her cheeks as she hoarsely responded. "Thank you."

It was quiet when she reached the meadow, the grass still wet from morning dew, even as the sun broke through the tall pine trees surrounding the clearing. The dew soaked through her leathers when she kneeled before her father's grave.

Lillian breathed in the fresh smell of sap. They'd laid him to rest under a tall silver fir. The one her father usually had her practice her bow against, and she smiled through her tears as she remembered the many times they'd been here together. She quietly told her father about her plans, how much she loved him, and that she would see him soon. Then she fell silent, a warm breeze blowing through her unbound hair as she picked at a few flowers around his resting place.

After a while, the heat became unbearable, sweat pooling under her tunic, and Lillian made to rise when something black glistened in front of her. She whipped her head up and stared right into large icy-blue eyes. Lillian's eyes widened as she took in the massive black creature. Almost as tall as the trees, its frame cast half the meadow in shade as it glared at her. Shimmering black scales covered its entire body, and inch-long spikes lined its long back. She froze as it unfurled its wings.

The dragon's warm breath blew her white hair around her face. Despite the heat radiating from its large mouth, a chill snaked down her spine, and she stumbled back when the dragon let out a loud huff.

Shaking, she lifted her hands. "I'm sorry, I'll go. Please don't kill me."

It tilted its head when she backed up further, and her stomach dropped when the dragon stepped forward. Shit. This was it. Lillian closed her eyes.

When nothing happened, she cautiously peeked under her eyelashes. The dragon had bent one of its front legs, its head lowered. But it was still watching her intently, a low rumble vibrating in its throat when they locked eyes again. Slowly, with her eyes fixed on its icy-blue ones, Lillian backed into the tree line and turned to run for her life.

Chapter Thirteen

Her heart beat out of her chest, but she didn't stop running until she was sure the dragon was far behind. And despite the next part of Lillian's journey being uneventful, her heart rate didn't lower. She glanced between the trees, squinting against the sunlight filtering through the leaves, expecting to see the dragon open its large mouth and burn her alive.

Sighing, she wondered if she had gone mad. Dragons hadn't been seen since King Alek drove them from the island. And even before then, they'd been a rare sight. The dragons kept to themselves —they didn't particularly care for humans—only tolerated the Valkyries. And from the stories she'd been told, even the mighty Valkyries couldn't control them.

Focusing on the sunlit path ahead, Lillian decided she'd try to walk as far as she could today. Not just to get away from the dragon but to arrive in the capital with time to spare. The summer sun was high in the sky, and she was grateful for the shade the pines and silver firs provided as each step through the dense forest drew more of her energy.

They were fortunate to be living in the eastern territory of Echo, her father used to say. He'd traveled to all four parts of Echo, and Lillian loved to listen to his stories of the different lands. The flatlands in the south, where rough winds blew year-round, and Echo's large harbor was located. The mountains in the north, where few lived due to the harsh conditions and wild beasts. The archipelago in the west, where people *lived* on the water. She'd wanted to visit them all, but apparently, the capital was where she'd live out her life.

As darkness fell, the woods came alive with the sounds of the night. Leaves rustled softly as the evening wind whistled through the forest, and Lillian's soft steps were joined by the scurrying and chirping of animals and insects that awoke to the moonlight streaming through the trees. Lillian closed her eyes and took a deep breath, letting the darkness embrace her and infuse her with new energy. When a high-pitched hoot from an owl nearby jerked her out of her trance, she stumbled, almost falling over a branch on the forest floor.

Glancing around to gather her bearings, Lillian realized she'd walked further than she planned. Through the thinning tree line ahead, lights from lanterns lining the capital's outer ring flickered, and the crumbling stone wall told her she was close to the slums. Eli had warned her that these towns were even poorer than their own, its people desperate enough to kill and steal to survive. Lillian planned to walk around them, not cutting into the capital of Echo until she was a few hours' walk from the castle.

While her mind was clear, her body was sluggish. Her muscles ached, and the flu-like symptoms she'd gotten used to in the past years made her head pound. She needed to take a few hours to eat and rest.

Scanning the dark forest around her, Lillian made sure no one was around, including the terrifying creature she'd encountered that morning, before finding a large tree to use as cover. Sitting down at its base, she drank from her water skin and ate some dried meat she'd brought. The throbbing in her head eased slightly, and with her hands on her daggers, she closed her eyes, drifting off into a light, dreamless sleep.

Lillian jolted awake, gripping her daggers tightly. She peered into the darkness, jerking as the trees' shadows rippled across the forest floor, but couldn't make out any immediate threats. Something woke her, though. Shuddering, she prayed the dragon hadn't caught up with her. Closing her eyes and willing her pounding heart to calm, she listened to the night around her.

A branch snapped softly to her right. Lillian opened her eyes and silently grabbed her satchel, rising to slip away from whatever was roaming the woods beside her.

She had only taken a step when a man spoke. "There's someone over there."

Lillian stiffened, but as another voice responded, further away this time, she realized she wasn't the only one who'd chosen to rest in these parts of the woods.

"Yes, I see the fire. Let's go."

She shook her head. It was a warm summer night, and anyone with even a little knowledge of the nearby dwellers would know not to draw any attention to yourself out here. She hoped for their sake they were prepared to fight.

Lillian quickly took off in the opposite direction, wanting to avoid running into whoever was out there, especially in the dark. But she slowed her strides when a scream broke through the trees.

Lillian shifted her weight from foot to foot. She shouldn't get involved. But when the scream rang again, she started running between the tall trees, grateful that the soft ground masked her steps. *Here you go, being impulsive again.* She winced as her father's voice echoed in her mind.

When she drew closer to the fire, Lillian slowed and cautiously surveyed the scene from behind a tree. The fire flickered on the trees surrounding the small clearing, and next to it, a bearded man held a red-haired woman by her neck while another rummaged through her things. The men weren't wearing the telling black uniforms of the King's Guard; they wore tattered tunics that had seen better days. The woman, dressed in a simple cotton dress, sobbed, begging the man to release his hold. He only laughed and kicked her in the side.

Lillian gritted her teeth as she remembered how the sentry kicked her father before he killed him. She removed her cloak, set it beside her on the ground, and reached for her bow. Taking an arrow from her quiver, she blew out a soft breath and aimed. Lillian knew the arrow would hit true before she released it, rage keeping her hand steady. It pierced the bearded man's thigh. Before he could open his mouth to scream, she nocked another arrow, sending it through the other man's calf. Lillian strode into the small clearing, shaking her head.

"Tsk, tsk. Two against one. Pretty cowardly if you ask me."

The woman had gotten free and was scrambling to her feet, casting scared looks in Lillian's direction. Both men were on the ground, trying to stop the bleeding from her arrows.

As Lillian approached, the man she'd hit in the calf rose and unsheathed his sword. He was tall, but it looked like it'd been a while since he'd been properly fed, and his skinny arm shook as he pointed a rusty sword at her. "Who are you?"

"No one of importance. And please, put that sword away. If you just let me and my friend here leave, I won't hurt you. Anymore, that is."

Lillian waved impatiently for the red-haired woman to grab her things. The woman's eyes widened, but she started to pick up her strewn-out belongings.

"I don't think so." The man lashed out with his sword, and Lillian quickly drew hers to meet his blow.

But before the clash of steel could echo through the night, the red-haired woman smacked the hilt of a dagger—a dagger Lillian hadn't even noticed—into the back of his head. He fell unconscious to the ground.

"I think I must have underestimated you." Lillian smiled tightly. "Now, let's get the hell out of here."

The woman searched her eyes, her flaming red hair shimmering in the firelight. "Can I trust you won't hurt me?"

Lillian met her stare. "Yes. Let's go."

The woman nodded, picked up her strewn things, and hoisted her satchel onto her shoulder. The bearded man was still on the ground, bleeding heavily. Her stomach churned at the amount of blood that pooled beneath him, staining the grassy ground red.

Lillian paused for a second and then dug through her bag for a strip of fabric. She threw it to the man.

"You better stop that blood flow quickly."

Spinning around, she left the clearing, motioning for the other woman to follow her.

Chapter Fourteen

They walked quietly, keeping a steady pace to get away from the clearing lest the noise drew attention from others wandering the woods. When the gray morning light seeped through the forest, the red-haired woman finally broke the silence.

"Why did you give him the tourniquet?"

Lillian studied her for a moment. "Because I know what hunger can drive a person to do."

She also felt that while she technically was on a death mission, she needn't leave a trail of bodies in her wake, especially if those bodies acted as a result of the king's neglect, not because they were ultimately bad men.

"What's your name? And what the hell were you thinking, lighting a fire back there?"

The woman winced. "My name is Astrid. And the darkness got to me. I kept hearing animals crawling about, and I thought the fire could help keep them away."

Lillian shook her head.

"I'm Lillian," she said. "And I guess you've learned your lesson. There are worse things than animals out at night." Although, she'd almost wet her pants at the sight of a certain animal. If a dragon could even be called an animal.

She examined the woman's face. As the sun peeked through the trees around them, she realized Astrid was younger than Lillian had initially thought. Maybe only a few years older than herself. She had a soft, round face with huge blue eyes that contrasted against her red hair. She was beautiful.

"Where are you headed?" Lillian asked.

"To the castle. I'm joining the King's Guard Trials."

Lillian huffed a shocked laugh. "You're joining the trials?"

"What?" Astrid stared at her defiantly, her red hair glowing in the sunlight streaming through the trees. "My family needs the money. My mother can't work, and my little sisters are too young. I refuse to become a courtesan, so this is the only option left."

Lillian knew that money was why so many joined the trials every year. But so few made it to guard ranks. And people died during the trials—a lot of people.

"Do you know how to fight?"

Astrid nodded. "My father taught me to defend myself before he died. He couldn't teach me everything, but I know basic sword-work and hand-to-hand combat."

Lillian winced at the sharp pain piercing her chest at the reminder of her own father's death. She quickly changed the subject. "Do you have any magic?"

"I can tell when someone lies." Astrid gave her a shy smile. "That's why I followed you. I knew you told me the truth when you said you wouldn't hurt me."

Lillian nodded; being able to tell lies from the truth was helpful, but it probably wouldn't help Astrid in the trials.

She'd never met a truth-teller before. One of the boys she'd grown up with had been able to read emotions but not outright know if you lied. Magic was so finicky. It manifested differently in everyone.

Most people fell into two categories: those manipulating physical elements like fire and water and those with mental powers like mind control and telepathy. The shifters have their second forms but no other magic. That's why King Alek allowed the shifters to stay when he hunted the rest of the magical creatures on Echo and Hindra—with no magic they posed little threat to him. Shifters could typically access some of the benefits of their animal form as humans, though, like heightened hearing, sense of smell, and strength.

And then there were people like Lillian. With not even an ember of magic. She sighed; she'd held a small kernel of hope when she turned twelve—when powers typically manifest, but nothing sparkled within her that day.

"I'd suggest keeping that to yourself next time. I'm sure there are ways to evade it if people know what you can do." Lillian smiled to take the edge off her words. "Well, I guess this is where I leave you."

"Wait. Where are you headed?" Astrid's hands trembled, and she kept shooting glances behind them like the men could pop up at any second.

"I'm also headed to the trials." There was no point in skirting the question; if Astrid made it, she'd see Lillian there.

"Let's go together. Please. I promise I won't slow you down." Astrid stared at her with wide eyes.

Was this how Lillian looked when she tried to convince Eli and her father of things? She shook her head; no wonder they never fell for it.

Lillian debated with herself for a moment. What was the harm in bringing her along? While Lillian didn't plan on making any friends, she could just leave Astrid once they got to the trials.

"Alright. But no more fires." Lillian winked at her.

They walked silently for the next few hours, following the line of trees and keeping far away from the slums. Thankfully, they didn't run into anyone or anything else, but Lillian still watched the forest around them in case the men were out for revenge. When the sun was at its highest in the sky, Lillian suggested they take a break.

Astrid hadn't complained at her pace, but beads of sweat trickled down the redhead's forehead. They found a small creek lined with pine trees that cast the trickling water in blissful shade. Lillian splashed water on her face and neck, sighing happily at its cooling effects.

Astrid took out some bread from her leather satchel and offered Lillian a piece. Astrid's father had been a baker and taught her how to make the best chocolate bread in Echo. When Lillian popped it into her mouth, she groaned. She'd never tasted anything like it.

While they ate, Astrid peppered Lillian with questions. Where she was from, how old she was, what her parents did. Apparently, 'east, eighteen, and orphan' weren't satisfactory answers. Even if they were true.

Lillian finally interrupted her. "Let's keep moving. If we reach the northwest outpost before midnight, I will teach you how to use a bow."

It would be about half a day's walk from the outpost until they reached the castle grounds. Then, they'd have a full day before they needed to report to the trials. Lillian planned to find the closest inn and sleep the whole time. Astrid quickly stopped her interrogation, and they continued the walk in silence.

As they neared the end of the tree line that signaled they were close to the outpost, Lillian suggested they stop for the night. If they wanted to catch some sleep, it was better to stay under the cover of the trees.

"Looks like we made it before midnight." Astrid stared at her expectantly.

Lillian groaned quietly. Her body hurt, and she desperately wanted to sit down. But she couldn't afford Astrid asking any questions that would make her suspicious. There was no way she'd be allowed into the guard if they knew she was sick.

She nodded. "I'm just going to make sure we're alone."

Lillian did a quick sweep of the area. The woods around them were quiet, and the tall trees provided good cover. She unfastened her bow and waved Astrid over to a small clearing where the moonlight broke through the leaves, casting the grassy ground in silvery light.

Lillian spent a few minutes showing Astrid how to hold the bow and use breathing to stabilize her aim. When Astrid understood the basics, Lillian had her practice aiming at a large tree. Astrid laughed delightedly when she finally pierced the bark with an arrow.

"Can you show me how you saved me earlier? You shot those

two arrows with only seconds in between." Astrid mimicked releasing two arrows, giggling as her pale blue dress got stuck in a low-hanging branch from the movement.

Lillian nodded. She searched the dark forest floor, picking up a few large pinecones that would suit the purpose.

"Throw these as hard as you can, in different directions."

She gripped the bow. When Astrid threw the first cone, Lillian let everything else fade away, only focusing on the tip of her arrows and the pinecones.

Chapter Fifteen

"I can't believe you hit that last one. You had your back against it until the last second." Astrid grinned as she patted Lillian on the back.

Lillian's face heated—she'd maybe shown off a little bit. It was nice being the teacher for once.

"If you continue practicing, you will be able to do it in no time, too." She strapped the bow to her back. "I'm starving. Let's eat something and then try to get some rest."

When Lillian started walking back to where they'd left their things, a wave of dizziness washed over her, and she couldn't stop herself from falling to her knees, wincing as sharp needles from the pine trees pierced her hands.

"Are you okay?" Astrid rushed to her side. "What happened?"

A knot formed in her stomach—she knew bringing the truth-teller along would come back to bite her.

"I'm tired." She gave Astrid a tight smile. At least she hoped it was the right Astrid as she appeared to have grown two more heads.

"I haven't had much sleep the past nights. Someone needed rescuing, remember?" Lillian forced herself to rise. "I just need a few hours, and I'll have my energy back."

Astrid furrowed her brow, but Lillian hadn't lied. She *was* tired, and she always felt better after some sleep.

"Can you take the first watch?" Lillian sank down against a tree. She didn't hear Astrid's response before her eyes closed, and she drifted off to sleep.

Astrid woke her after what felt like five minutes. "It's almost dawn. Do you mind if I sleep for an hour, and then we can get going?"

Lillian jerked upright. Being on the road must have taken a bigger toll on her body than she'd thought—and made her lose her mind. She'd been at the complete mercy of this stranger. Even if Astrid seemed kind, she didn't know her. She shuddered; her father always told her that the only ones she could trust were himself and Eli.

"Of course. I'll get everything ready to go."

Lillian packed her things and sat down to wait for the sun to rise above the horizon. The forest woke up to a new day, birds chirping as they left their nests. In a tree above her, a large owl cleaned its feathers. She sighed as she met its amber eyes; she hoped she could find somewhere to clean up before tomorrow.

When the first rays of sun peeked through the leaves, painting the forest in beautiful hues of yellow and green, she gently woke Astrid, and they began the final trek to the castle. Being out of the woods made Lillian anxious, and she kept her hands hovering above her daggers. They had to walk through the slums and into the heart of Echo before they reached the castle grounds.

When her father brought her as a child, she mainly hid behind his legs, overwhelmed by the sheer number of people. She'd never understood why anyone would willingly live in such cramped conditions.

"Where are you planning on staying?" She tried to distract herself by getting Astrid to talk again.

When Astrid raised her eyebrows, Lillian winced. She guessed she hadn't been the most talkative companion on this trip.

"My aunt married a guard. He is retired now, but they still live close to the castle."

Lillian whistled softly. The neighborhoods close to the castle were the most expensive in Echo. If Astrid's uncle still lived there when he retired, the guard must pay very well. No wonder people risked their lives to join.

"Where will you be staying?"

"I'm planning on finding an inn on the way." Lillian could not afford anything close to the castle. She'd have to settle for something further out, hopefully avoiding the slums. The silver she'd brought would have to last for the whole time the trials ran.

Chapter Sixteen

When they reached the slums, the streets filled as its people woke up. Street vendors unpacked their goods, and half-dressed children chased each other between the worn-down stone buildings. The slums were eerily similar to the town she'd grown up in, the small homes twins to her own. The gray stone buildings favored in all of Echo helped keep the heat in winter and out in summer. Although, the houses here seemed like they did neither. Time had taken its toll on the slums; stone walls were crumbling, and windows were boarded up.

Lillian and Astrid kept their heads down, their eyes fixed on the cobblestones on the narrow path, even as people cast curious glances their way. As they approached the castle, the path broadened, and the gray stone houses grew larger and better kept. Lillian's eyes widened when they passed homes with little gardens surrounded by white fences and actual glass windows. The smell of food wafted through the streets from the taverns lining their path, and she marked a few inns that she'd check out later.

The people were different, too. Women in colorful dresses strolled in pairs, fanning themselves in the morning heat. Sentries paraded in fours, their black uniform jackets and slim trousers stark against the stone buildings, while their embellished swords gleamed in the sunshine.

"There's the castle," Astrid whispered in awe.

Lillian trailed her eyes up. The street in front of them snaked up a steepening hill, the houses lining it seemingly carved into its side. The path grew steeper as the street curved closer to the massive black castle on top, towering over the slanted stone city, with only clear sky behind it. She understood why Astrid had whispered. The dark castle walls loomed over them, casting the hillside in shade and squeezing the air out of her lungs.

"Well, I plan to avoid scaling that hill as much as I can. I'm going to find somewhere to stay. Are you good from here?" Lillian tried to keep the unease the castle instilled in her out of her voice.

Astrid nodded. "Thank you for helping me yesterday. I won't forget it."

Lillian offered her a small smile. "Good luck tomorrow." They would both need it, she thought.

Lillian headed back down the path they'd come from, aiming for one of the inns she'd seen on the way. The streets were busy now, and she jumped out of the way of several horse-drawn carriages making their way through the narrow cobblestone roads. She stopped outside a building with a crooked sign stating 'Hill's Tavern.'

A wave of greasy, sweaty heat washed over her as she stepped inside the tavern full of people enjoying a midday meal. Mostly men sat at the wooden tables, probably here for the same reason she was, based on the number of weapons resting by the walls and the leather tunics they wore. A few of them turned their heads as she walked by. Used to the stares her unusual looks brought, Lillian ignored them.

The innkeeper greeted her, claiming she was lucky. There was only one room left. For ten silvers per week, she would get full lodging and boarding. When she tried to bargain, he told her almost all inns nearby were full. This was the best deal she'd get.

Lillian furrowed her brow. She didn't even have enough coins for one week. Leaning over the innkeeper's table, she cocked her head to the side and asked him sweetly if she could pay at the end of each week. After fluttering her eyelashes and a few subtle touches to his arm, he agreed, his face reddening as he shook her hand. She released a breath. That would give her some time to make up for the missing coin.

The innkeeper showed her to a room on the third floor, and after promising to send up a meal, Lillian was finally alone. She walked into the small bathing chamber, where a bath was already drawn, the water glittering in the sunlight that sifted through the open window. It wasn't as hot as she preferred, but Lillian still took her time to scrub every inch of her body and thoroughly wash her hair. She hated the feeling of grime being on the road left on her.

After she'd eaten the meal that the innkeeper brought up, some type of meat and potatoes, she laid down on the small bed, staring at the wooden beams lining the stone ceiling and the dust swirling within the rays of sun streaming in through the small window above the bed. She should rest before tomorrow. Lillian didn't expect the following weeks to be easy, and after her near-fainting spell yesterday, she would have to conserve her energy carefully.

But when she closed her eyes, thoughts of her father and Eli kept her awake. She missed their company, feeling utterly alone in her small room. Eli would have found a way to cheer her up and brought her out on an adventure in the capital, becoming unlikely friends with whoever he encountered. Tears welled in her eyes, but Lillian clenched her fists, furiously blinking them away.

After a few hours, unable to settle down, Lillian finally gave up and decided to head downstairs. Maybe she could learn more about the trials. Or where the children were kept. There had been a few sentries drinking in the tavern. She pulled on her leathers and a thin tunic, glancing at her father's cloak that she'd folded on the small chair in the room, but shook her head upon remembering how warm it had been downstairs.

Chapter Seventeen

Even more people filled the tavern than when she'd first arrived, but Lillian found a small table by an open window that offered a welcome breeze. She motioned for the blonde barmaid rushing by her table and ordered a mug of chilled wine. Glancing at the strangers surrounding her, a wave of wistfulness washed over her. She'd loved to frequent the taverns by her home, but she'd known all the patrons. Lillian blew out a soft breath; at least Eli was coming soon. She would have a little piece of home.

At the table next to her, three men in black fighting leathers discussed the upcoming trials and what they could expect. A man with long dark hair claimed that last year's contestants had to fight giant spiders the size of horses, equipped with vicious claws that could cut a full-grown man in half. Lillian shook her head and smiled into her cup.

"A girl who smiles at the thought of giant spiders, now that's my type of person."

A man slipped into the chair opposite her, and as she looked up from her drink and met his eyes, her whole body tingled, goose-bumps rippling across every inch of her skin. He was beautiful. It was as if he had been dipped in pure gold with his tan skin, light blonde hair, and amber eyes. He was also huge; his muscular arms resting on the table left little room for anything else. Lillian blinked.

It wasn't his beauty that made her react like this. She'd never felt someone's presence in this way before.

"Who are you?"

"The better question is, what am I?" the man grinned at her with perfect white teeth.

He had a slight accent that Lillian couldn't place, and she narrowed her eyes.

His smile widened. "You're a suspicious one."

Lillian held his gaze, impatiently clicking her tongue.

"Ah. You win. My name is Finley, Finn to my friends. You may call me Finn." He winked at her.

"Hello, Finley. Why are you sitting there." She prayed he'd take the hint and get up.

"Well, Lillian, I saw you through the window and thought it was time we said hello."

"How do you know my name?" Waves of warmth filled Lillian, her body tugging at her to lean forward. She gripped the table to steady herself. "And what *are* you?" It was the better question, she admitted to herself grudgingly.

Finn waved to the barmaid to bring them two more of what Lillian had ordered. He leaned back in his chair and studied her.

"You really don't know? I thought you were smart, Lillian." That stupid grin still graced his face.

Lillian examined him. The tug was stronger now, and her hand embarrassingly twitched toward him. She had to sit on both hands to not do something rash.

"Look, golden boy, I have no idea who you are. But I am very busy, so I suggest you skip along now."

Finn threw his head back and laughed so loud that several of the other patrons glanced their way. "Golden boy. I love it."

Lillian gritted her teeth and made to get up, but before she could rise Finn grabbed her arm. A jolt went through her as his hand touched her skin, and she slowly lifted her eyes from his hand to his face. She shook her head. There was no way.

"I'd finish that thought if I were you."

Lillian glared at him. "Let go of my arm, or I will maim that pretty little face of yours."

Finn laughed again, but he did let go of her arm. "I think you just called me pretty. That's progress, right?"

She pinched her nose, blowing out a soft breath. "Tell me what you are right now, or I won't just mess with your face. You might lose other body parts you value."

"So feisty," he threw her a wicked grin. "We're going to make a formidable pair, you and I."

When Lillian shot him a warning look, he lifted his large hands. "Sorry. I thought you'd catch on by now. You don't feel the bond?"

She knitted her brows. Was he saying what she was thinking he was saying?

"The *familiar* bond, yes," he nodded enthusiastically.

"Are you reading my mind?" Bile rose in her throat.

"No."

She blew out a breath of relief.

"Not yet." He winked.

She nodded slowly. The familiar bond had to be accepted before they could speak within each other's minds. And even then, he should only be able to hear what she wanted him to hear. That's how it had been between Eli and her father, at least. It would have been quite awkward otherwise. Lillian shuddered at the thought.

"Your emotions are written all over your face. It was quite easy to deduce what you were thinking." He patted her arm.

Lillian tried to school her features back to neutral, but given how flustered she was, it was proving hard. She had prepared for so many different scenarios and challenges she might face coming here. Finding her familiar was not one. She didn't have any magic. It didn't make sense.

Humans without magic did not have familiars. Dying humans without magic definitely did not have familiars. But here she was. She could feel the bond humming between them now that she acknowledged it. Lillian realized that Finn still patted her arm, staring at her with a worried, albeit slightly amused, expression.

She quickly pulled it away. "I should get going."

She needed some time to figure this out. She obviously needed to reject the bond, but she would have to come up with a good reason. As rare as it was to have a familiar, rejecting a familiar bond was almost unheard of. Accepting the bond made both partners stronger, and most familiars could share their powers, lending either magic or the shifter's abilities through the bond.

"Please stay. I realize I overwhelmed you, but let's talk about this." Finn reached out for her again. When Lillian flinched and pulled away, his smile finally fell, an expression of hurt instead taking over his features.

"Did you think we'd sit here and tell each other our life stories?" Lillian clenched her fists. She knew her words were harsh, but she needed to leave before she did something that would risk everything she had planned. She needed to focus on avenging her father, not making friends or bonding familiars. "I'm heading into the trials tomorrow. I need to focus."

Finn shook his head. "So am I. We'll be stronger together, Lillian. Even if you don't want to accept the bond today, we can at least help each other."

"I've only just met you. You haven't told me how you know my name or how you knew where to find me. I think I'll take my chances." Lillian stormed off before he could argue further.

But she swore she heard him mumble, "I guess it's too early to call you silver girl, then."

Chapter Eighteen

Lillian cursed. She hadn't thought it through when she stormed out of the inn instead of up to her rooms. She couldn't just walk back in. What if he was still there? Wandering the narrow streets aimlessly as darkness fell, she replayed the conversation in her head, trying to make sense of what had just happened. A twinge of guilt settled in her stomach. Finn had probably meant well.

She wished she could tell him why it was for the better. Explain how she wouldn't live to see the following year—very much not a suitable familiar. But there was no way she could do that without him questioning why she would partake in the trials. He might even try to stop her if he was anything like Eli and her father. No, she needed to come up with another explanation for why she'd reject their bond.

Distracted, she almost walked right into a group of drunk sentries. Only at the last second did the loud singing bring her back to her senses, giving her just enough time to slip into a narrow alleyway to avoid them. Lillian waited in the shadows until their voices were muffled, barely audible in the distance. As she was about to walk back out, she noticed something out of the corner of her eye. Turning slowly, she realized it was a ladder.

Glancing around to ensure there weren't any stragglers from the group, she inspected it. The ladder was dusty, as if no one had used it in a long time. Lillian shook her head; she shouldn't. Eli's warning to be careful rang in her mind. But curiosity got the better of her.

She started scaling the ladder, slowly making her way up, taking care to inspect each step for rot. The ladder led up to the roof of the building, and when she peered over the ledge, there was more dust. She scaled all the way, cautiously pulling herself onto the roof. Lillian got to her feet, used her hands to brush off the dust from her clothes, and looked around.

She sucked in a breath. The full moon hung suspended above her, so big it seemed close enough for her to reach out a hand and touch it, and its silvery glow bathed the slanted city in a soft light. The stone castle was at her back, not as haunting anymore but beautiful in the moonlight.

The same sensation she would get from her nightly walks filled her, a sense of calm and vibrant energy coursing through her veins. She smiled at the moon watching over her. It dulled the pain in her chest, and she drew the first full breath since her father's death. Sitting down with her back against the ledge, she watched the moon travel across the sky.

When the moon began its descent, Lillian pushed herself up. She would need some sleep before the trials. As she carefully descended the ladder, hushed voices rose from the street outside the alleyway. Making no sound as her feet touched the ground, she kept close to the building wall and tiptoed toward them.

"Did you hear the Crown Prince left Hindra?" She couldn't see the person from where she was lurking, but she thought it was a man.

"Is he coming here?" A woman's voice, and something about it was familiar, but she couldn't put her finger on it.

Lillian strained to see, but a cloak hid the woman's face. They didn't seem like sentries, though, keeping to the shadows and in clothing meant to blend into the night.

"No one knows. It seems the king gave him orders, but where hasn't been revealed."

"We need to inform Red. If the Crown Prince is coming here, it could interfere with his mission."

Lillian frowned and pressed closer to the exit.

"He'll be here soon enough. You just have to stay close to the girl."

When Lillian shifted, a small piece of rubble fell from the wall she was pushing against and landed on the ground with a soft thud. She winced, silently cursing her clumsiness.

"What was that?" The woman turned her head toward where Lillian was standing.

Lillian held her breath, backing further into the shadows of the alley.

"It's probably these old buildings. They're falling apart. But let's go; it's almost morning."

Lillian didn't dare move, barely breathing, as she listened to them walk away. When she was sure they were far gone, she hurried back to the inn, marking her path so she would remember how to get back to the rooftop. As Lillian lay down in the small bed, she thought of how Eli had not mentioned a mission before she'd left. He had some explaining to do, she thought, as she drifted off into a fitful sleep.

Chapter Nineteen

The sun hung high in the sky when Lillian woke. She quickly dressed in her leathers, groaning as she glanced at herself in the mirror. Dark circles lined her gray eyes, like purple bruises on her pale skin.

Not that her appearance mattered today, but she prayed her body would be up for the challenges she was sure to face. She brushed her hair, pulled it up into a high ponytail, and tied a leather band over her brow to keep any stray strands out of her face.

Finally, she strapped her weapons to her back and walked out the door without stopping to think about everything she'd learned yesterday. As she followed the winding path up to the castle, others joined her, also fitted in fighting gear, heading the same way. Thankfully, Finn wasn't among them. Maybe she'd scared him away yesterday.

Lillian was winded when she finally arrived at the castle grounds. Glancing over her shoulder, it was as if she'd climbed a mountain, the stone town small and far away. She forced herself to take controlled breaths when she walked through the metal gates in the stone wall that surrounded the courtyard. Even if she felt like dying already, she didn't need everyone to know it.

The pebbled courtyard bustled with activity. Guards marched in and out of the massive wooden doors to the castle, and a dozen or so stood in attention by the castle's shining walls. Their black uniforms were stark against the lush ivy that snaked up the castle behind them. When she trailed her eyes up, the ivy weaved all the way to the many towers looming over the castle grounds. Several training rings and a large archery field stood to her right, and to her left, a line formed in the shade of a large balcony.

Lillian walked to the end of it, positioning herself behind one of the largest men she'd ever seen. He must have been almost a foot and a half taller than her and three times as wide, his scruffy leather tunic straining over his barrel-thick arms. Lillian swallowed; hopefully, standing next to him wouldn't make her seem smaller than she already was.

The man turned around when Lillian approached, giving her a not-so-subtle once over. It was everything she could do to keep a cringe off her face as he flashed her a leering grin, baring a mouth full of rotten teeth in his fleshy face.

"You're way too pretty to be here, little girl. I'd pay good coin for you as a lady of the night."

"So would I," another man in line shouted.

Several men around them snickered as they took her in. She narrowed her eyes, staring each of them down, marking who had laughed.

"I think she's a mute, boys. The perfect woman, all play no mouth."

Lillian bit her cheek. She needed to make them understand that they couldn't mess with her, or the following weeks would be unbearable. Lillian took a step toward the massive man.

"Hear now, you mongrel..."

Before she could finish her sentence, someone wrapped their arms around her waist and snatched her up, carrying her out of the line.

"Let me go right now," she snarled, kicking her legs to get free.

As the person carried her away like a child, the other men's booming laugh made her see red. She forced her body to go limp, angled her head, and bit down hard on the arm of the person holding her.

"Shit!"

Wrangling free, Lillian spun on her heel, crouching low in a fighting stance. Finn stood before her, cradling his arm, sporting the same grin he'd worn yesterday. Like he found this funny.

"I didn't need saving," she hissed.

Finn's grin widened. "I know. I was trying to save those poor men. How would there be any decent trials if you took out half the men on day one?"

Lillian forced herself to take a shaky breath. She didn't need to kill Finn. It probably wasn't a good look to kill someone before she even entered the trials.

She blew out a deep breath.

"Since I apparently only amuse you using violence and since you refuse to stay away from me, how about a truce?"

Lillian reached out a hand. As he approached to take it, she pulled it back. "No more rescuing me from anyone or rescuing anyone from me. And definitely no more lifting me. Understood?"

Finn nodded.

Lillian took his hand and shook it, the bond between them humming with pleasure.

"Yes, silver girl. We're a team."

Sighing, she shot him a dark glare. He only chuckled and led the way back to the line.

Chapter Twenty

As they waited for their turn to sign up, Finn took it upon himself to tell her his life story. He was born and raised on Hindra. She nodded; it explained the melodic accent Lillian hadn't been able to place. Finn was the oldest of three brothers, and his father was a blacksmith who'd once forged a sword for the king's hand. While they weren't starving, it was tough to support three children, so Finn decided to join the guard to help his parents and give them one less mouth to feed.

Lillian tried pretending not to be interested, but she'd never met anyone from Hindra, and she couldn't stop herself from asking what life was like there.

Finn shrugged and said it was probably a lot like life on Echo, although it did seem like Echo had more slums. Few on Hindra were starving in the way he'd seen on his travels through Echo from the coast. Lillian frowned. To her knowledge, Hindra and Echo were similar in climate and relied on the same resources.

Finn quieted when they reached the front of the line, and they remained silent until it was their turn. Two guards sat behind a small wooden table that looked out of place in the large cobblestone courtyard. With bored expressions, they waved them forward.

"Name, age." The guard before her didn't even meet her eyes as he held a pen, ready to note down her responses.

"Lillian Deimhal, eighteen"

"Parents?"

"Orphan." She winced as she said it, and Finn shot her a look.

"Any magic?" She tensed, glancing at Finn to see if he was still listening. He raised an eyebrow as he met her eyes.

"No," she said quietly, staring at her dusty leather boots.

She didn't know why she cared; it wasn't like she would accept the bond anyway. Still, a lump formed in her throat, and she swallowed hard.

"Alright. Head on over there where everyone else is standing. The commanders will be out shortly to tell you what's next."

Not waiting for Finn, she walked toward the group the guard pointed out.

"Wait. Lillian." Finn jogged up next to her. "What you said back there..."

"I know, I know. I don't have magic. I'm sorry to ruin your vision of us as a *perfect pair*. Now you can move on." Lillian stared intently at the castle beside them, watching the many dark windows lining the impossibly high walls.

Finn furrowed his brow. "I wasn't talking about your magic. I don't care about that. You seem pretty lethal without it. I meant the orphan part. I thought you had a father?"

White-hot pain sliced through her chest, and Lillian's face fell before she had time to manage her features. As she scrambled to gather herself, Finn placed a large hand on her shoulder.

"Did something happen," he asked quietly.

"He died," she got out.

She couldn't bear coming up with a story, praying Finn wouldn't press. He didn't; he only squeezed her shoulder and kept on walking. Lillian blew out a soft breath.

By the time they reached the other participants, Lillian had gotten a hold of herself, schooling her features back to neutral. They stood slightly apart from the group as they waited for more orders, and when she could finally breathe again, Lillian nudged Finn with her elbow.

"How do you know so much about me?"

Finn threw an arm over her shoulder, only grinning when she glared at him. "Well, as soon as I stepped off the boat, I felt something pulling me toward your parts of Echo. My mother always tells me to follow my gut, and I had a few days before I needed to be here anyway, so I followed it. It brought me to you."

Lillian narrowed her eyes. "So why didn't you introduce yourself then? Why wait until we got here?"

"Well, when I finally drew up the courage, I found you locking lips with a handsome auburn-haired man. In quite the scandalous outfit, I must say. I wasn't sure that it was the right moment. No judgment, of course." Finn winked at her.

Lillian ransacked her brain—it must have been the night she'd pretended to be a courtesan. "It's not what you think. That was Eli. He is my friend."

"If that's what I'll get as your friend, I'm excited for what's to come." Finn wiggled his eyebrows at her, and she punched him in the shoulder.

"No, he's..." Lillian's face heated. She and Eli had been friends for so long—she wasn't really sure how to introduce him now that they were more than that.

Finn snickered. "Don't worry, I'm just messing with you."

Lillian scowled at him, quickly changing the subject. "Were you the one who threw something at the window then?"

A wrinkle appeared between Finn's eyebrows, but when he opened his mouth to respond, he was cut off by three men exiting the large wooden doors of the castle and stalking up to the group. Everyone quieted, the authority rolling off the men layering over the group like a thick blanket.

The guard in the middle stepped forward.

"You can call me Commander Atlas. This is Commander Jon and Commander Eirik. From the moment you signed the papers, we became your superiors. As of this moment, you will do as we tell you. If we tell you to run, you run. If we tell you to fight, you fight. Understood?"

No one spoke, a few men fidgeting as the commander glared at them.

Commander Atlas repeated himself. "Understood?"

"Yes," they all responded in unison.

Lillian didn't hear what the commander said next. When he turned to stare them all down, she got a clear view of his face for the first time. If Finn was sunshine and gold, this man was the embodiment of night. He had midnight black hair almost down to his shoulders, tan skin, and dark green eyes that seemed almost iridescent in the sun. His face was striking, with a strong jawline and a straight nose, both accentuated by the dark stubble covering his face. With its fitted jacket and pants, the black guard uniform she hated emphasized the hard muscles playing beneath.

Finn elbowed her and whispered, "Stop drooling."

Lillian huffed and shot Finn a venomous look. She was *not* drooling. Then she realized it had gone quiet. Lillian's stomach churned as she slowly lifted her eyes and met the commander's green ones.

His eyes widened, although she wasn't sure if she imagined it, when the bored expression instantly returned. Lillian prepared herself for a scolding, but the commander just glared at someone else in the group and continued.

"From now on, you are all novices. We will address you as such. You have no name, and until you've been selected to join the guard, you are nothing."

He glared at them again, the green in his eyes burning like two flickering fires. "You will not talk back, or you're out. You will not fight among yourselves, or you're out. The next five days, you will train. We will split you into three groups, each led by one of us commanders. The first trial will take place on the sixth day, and after that, you will have a trial every three days. You will be evaluated on your performance in both training and trials. The first trial will test your skills working as a group; the last two are individual. There are thirty of you here today. Only five will be selected to join the guard."

Commander Atlas stalked back to join the other two men. They had a quick exchange, and then Commander Jon stepped up.

"You will now be divided into groups. We will each select one novice at a time until everyone has been chosen."

Lillian gritted her teeth. She understood the underlying message; being picked first meant that the commanders saw something in you. Being picked last, not so much. She studied the other novices. There were a couple of bulky men, not as massive as the one she'd almost punched in the face, but large enough to intimidate most people. Finn was in this group.

She was surprised to find the majority weren't as impressive—quite a few were skin and bones, their tattered tunics hanging off their skinny shoulders. But she knew better than to assume them weak. They could be magic wielders or, like her, be good fighters regardless of their size.

The sun reflected in bright red hair. Astrid had made it after all. She stood alone on the opposite side, nervously fidgeting with her black tunic, her face a little green.

Only two other women were in the group. A dark-haired, muscular woman stood to Lillian's right. Lillian shuddered as she met her eyes—they were completely dead, like black pits. The last woman was Lillian's size, a beautiful blonde with the most exquisite leather tunic. The intricate silver and gold embroidery adorning it sparkled in the sunlight. She gave Lillian a lazy smile as they locked eyes.

Commander Jon spoke. "You." He pointed at the monster of a man Lillian had almost fought.

She rolled her eyes. Even if the man seemed dumb as a sheep, he did look like he could eat a man alive. Commander Eirik waved forward another of the bulky men with tan skin and black hair almost as long as Lillian's.

Lillian fingered her white hair, slightly envious of how the sun made his hair shine like ebony. Shifting her weight, she sighed quietly. She expected to be among the last selected; how long would she have to stand up here and endure hearing name after name called?

Commander Atlas took his time, a sneer on his face as he surveyed the group of novices like no one here was good enough for

72

him. Lillian's eyes drifted to Astrid again. Even if she weren't planning on making friends, it might be good to keep the girl close. She worried Astrid wouldn't fare so well if the men approached her in the same way they did Lillian. And it would be nice to have a female around. She'd never had any female friends; her father and Eli were the only ones she'd been close to growing up.

A surge of longing washed over her at the thought of Eli. She could see him here, rolling his blue eyes at the grumpy commanders and whispering something that would make her laugh—getting them both in trouble. Although he'd definitely be picked first, he was almost as tall as that mongrel, and his years as a rebel had made his body into pure muscle. Not that she complained.

Finn cleared his throat loudly, and she narrowed her eyes.

"What?"

Finn looked pointedly ahead.

"If you can come forward any time today, I'm sure we'd all appreciate it."

It almost seemed as if Commander Atlas was looking at her.

"Yes, *you*, ice princess." His words dripped with mockery, and Lillian's face heated. "Do you need someone to escort you?"

The other novices snickered, and Finn nudged her. "Go," he whispered.

Lillian lifted her chin and forced herself to walk excruciatingly slowly to the commander. When she finally took up a spot beside him, she smiled innocently.

"I was just enjoying the view."

His green eyes gleamed, the intensity pricking the back of her neck, and Lillian quickly averted her eyes.

As the commanders selected more novices, Lillian wondered if it had been so smart to piss off her commander on the first day. Lillian assumed he would have a say in whether she joined the guard or not. Maybe she'd acted a little bit rash, but the way he'd called her *princess*. She clenched her fists so hard she was surprised her nails didn't draw blood.

Commander Jon picked Finn, and soon, only the three women remained. As Commander Eirik picked the tall, dead-eyed woman,

Lillian found herself hoping Astrid would join her group. She caught the redhead's eye and gave her an encouraging smile when Commander Atlas waved her forward.

Astrid walked up to her side. "Hi," she whispered. "I'm glad we're in the same group. Some of these men scare me to death."

Lillian leaned in. "You just have to scare them more."

"Like you with the commander?" Astrid winked at her.

Lillian winced. She wasn't sure she'd scared him as much as infuriated him.

Chapter Twenty-One

Commander Atlas gathered the group in a corner of the square courtyard. In front of them stood a raised platform, no fence around it, but red lines defined its borders.

"Over the next few days, we'll evaluate your skills in swordplay, archery, hand-to-hand combat, and knife throwing. Today, we'll start with hand-to-hand combat. Rules are simple. Stay within the red line. Once you're outside of it, you're out. If you lose consciousness, you're out. No weapons. Magic is okay. No shifting today."

The commander glared at Lillian. "You. And you."

She sighed when he pointed at one of the bulkier men Lillian noticed before. He towered over her, his arms the size of Lillian's torso. As they approached the platform, the man stepped forward and offered Lillian his hand. His blonde hair hung in his face, but he flicked his head, offering Lillian a genuine smile.

"I'm Sam," the man said. "I saw you hissing like a wild cat when Finn stopped you from kicking that man's ass. I will not be underestimating you."

Sam was older than her, maybe in his midtwenties. He wasn't conventionally attractive, his features slightly too big for his face, but his eyes were kind when they met hers. Something in them reminded her of her father—as if his soul went beyond his years. Lillian hesitantly smiled back. It was nice to have someone give her credit for something other than her appearance, for once. Although she felt like she'd lost the element of surprise that would have helped take him down.

Lillian and Sam turned to face each other. They glanced at the commander for a sign to begin, and as soon as he mouthed start, Lillian took off before Sam could turn back toward her entirely. Keeping low to the ground, she went straight for Sam's kneecap, throwing a punch that threw him off balance. She spun around and aimed a kick at his chest that made him fly back, landing right on the edge of the red line. Sprinting forward, she planned to end it, but Sam was too fast. He got to his feet quickly and landed a hit to her chest that knocked the breath out of her.

Lillian backed up, trying to force air down her lungs, while Sam circled her.

She smiled at him and wheezed, "Don't go easy on me."

Sam winked and charged her. Lillian ducked under his outstretched arm, but he'd planned for it, landing a hard blow to the back of her head. Stars danced in front of her eyes, and the world spun, but she flipped around and darted out of the way of his next jab. Her father's voice rang in her head. *Fight dirty, Lillian. You don't have the luxury of playing the hero.*

She backed up close to the line, shifting her weight from foot to foot as Sam approached. When he charged forward again, she veered to the left, crouching down low. As he spun to follow, she straightened, throwing out both hands to connect with his chest, using his own momentum to push him right outside the red line. Sam glanced down; both his feet were now on the wrong side of the markings.

He shrugged and smiled at her, "I guess you win."

Astrid clapped her hands, beaming at Lillian. Lillian bowed slightly to the group before jumping off the platform onto the dusty courtyard.

"No points for style, but a technical win." Commander Atlas yawned.

Lillian hissed; while it might not have been the prettiest performance, she'd still won against someone twice her size. She opened her mouth to respond.

Commander Atlas narrowed his eyes. "Remember the rule of no talkbacks?"

She quickly closed it. These three weeks would be very long if she couldn't defend herself against Commander Atlas. Commander Dick was a more fitting name, she thought. Lillian settled for giving him a murderous glare.

She bit back a snarl when his mouth twitched. The commander turned his back on her and gestured at two other novices. The next few fights were uneventful, the men mainly using brute force to push their opponent out of the ring or knock them out.

One of the men had magic, though. Every time his opponent charged him, the ground beneath him shook, throwing off the man's balance and allowing the magic wielder to hit jab after jab to his face until he passed out. When the man slammed into the ground, Lillian was grateful Sam hadn't seemed to hold any power that would have given him the upper hand.

Then, it was Astrid's turn. Commander Atlas paired her up with a cruel-looking man. He wasn't of any great height or build, but there was a nasty look in his dark eyes as he stepped onto the platform. When they circled each other, Lillian instinctively inched closer, holding her breath. Astrid's face was tight as she prepared herself, and as soon as Commander Atlas gave the order to start, Astrid darted forward and landed a blow to the man's face. Lillian smiled encouragingly when she caught Astrid's blue gaze.

When Astrid prepared to strike again, the man grabbed her arm. Astrid's body went rigid, her eyes wide, before she fell backward, and her head hit the ground with a sickening thud. She didn't move again. Lillian rushed into the ring and dropped down to feel for her pulse, releasing a breath when she found a steady heartbeat.

Spinning around, she stalked up to the man. "What in the hell was that?"

He wiggled his fingers. "Want to try it out?"

Absolutely not. She glared at him until he turned around and walked off the platform.

That was some magic, Lillian thought. She glanced at the commander, but he only declared the man the winner and turned his back on them. As she knelt by Astrid's side, gently tapping her cheek to get her to wake up, she wondered how this man had slipped through the king's claws.

Astrid finally stirred, opening her eyes. "I'm guessing I didn't win."

Lillian shook her head, wincing. "Sorry."

She helped Astrid to her feet, and they joined the others. Commander Atlas began telling them the schedule for the following day when he was interrupted by a group of men approaching them. The commander immediately stood in attention.

With the sun in her eyes, Lillian squinted to see who it was. A man flanked by several guards strolled toward the group. As they drew closer, the sun reflected in the adornments the man in front wore over his black uniform. A thick gold chain rested diagonally over his chest, and several medals hung over his heart.

Lillian sucked in a breath. This was the King of Orios.

"*Bow*," Commander Atlas hissed.

Bile burned in her throat when she bowed with the rest of the novices.

"At ease."

The king's voice was more shrill than Lillian expected. Straightening, she studied the man she'd come to kill. He looked so average. Nothing like the monster she'd imagined in her dreams. He had light brown hair, was of average height, and sported a belly from excessive food and wine.

King Alek turned to Commander Atlas. "How are the recruits faring?"

"Inexperienced, Your Highness. But we'll get them there."

Lillian ground her teeth. The commander had seen them fight for five minutes. She was *not* inexperienced. The king turned to examine the group, and Lillian glanced at the people around her. Most were covered in dust, some bloody and beaten. She winced— none of them seemed too impressive right now. The king's raised eyebrows confirmed that he was of the same opinion.

A chill ran down her spine when the king's eyes fell on Lillian. While he might look average, his green eyes seemed to peer into her soul. As he stared at her, she scrambled to remember what she knew of the king. He was a powerful fire wielder—that's how he killed Queen Liv and King Ivar. He'd burned them alive together with most of their guards, including her mother.

"You're an unusual one."

The king's eyes curiously surveyed her, and Lillian bowed her head, praying he'd move on from her quickly. She fought a smirk when Commander Atlas stiffened beside her, turning toward Lillian as if readying himself to stop her if she did something inappropriate.

"Raise your head, girl."

Lifting her eyes, Lillian met the king's gaze. Her whole body went cold under his stare, fear pricking her scalp. He narrowed his eyes, examining her face closely.

Lillian forced herself to continue meeting the king's eyes. She might have to bow to him, but she would not be the first one to look away.

Finally, the king broke his stare and waved lazily. "Carry on."

As soon as the king left, Atlas dismissed them and ordered them to report at dawn.

Chapter Twenty-Two

"What was that?" Astrid slipped up next to her as they walked out of the metal gates. "He looked like he was about to eat you."

Lillian shook her head. "I have no idea."

Lillian didn't think of herself as paranoid, but the meeting had unsettled her. Before she could get lost in replaying what had just happened, a now familiar sensation brushed her neck.

Sure enough, a strong arm wrapped around her shoulders moments later.

"I heard you kicked some ass back there." Finn grinned at her. "Sam knew you'd be good, but beating him in less than two minutes? It's going to take a while for his ego to recover."

Lillian couldn't help herself; the corners of her mouth twitched as she met Finn's glittering eyes. "He was too much of a gentleman. He should have knocked me out when he got a hit in."

"He won't make the same mistake again. Come on, we're grabbing drinks to celebrate we survived the first day. You're coming."

Before she could respond, Finn was off down the hill, waving for her to follow.

Astrid elbowed her. "And who was that?"

Lillian jerked; she'd almost forgotten about Astrid.

"Just someone I ran into yesterday. Come on, if I have to go for drinks, you're joining too."

Finn led them to a packed tavern, where the red-faced barmaid sighed as they entered and told them they were on their own. Luckily, a small table opened up, and Lillian gratefully slid onto a chair. Even if she'd only been fighting for a few minutes, exhaustion spread through her body, and her head pounded.

Sam, who'd also joined them, braved a trip to the bar, returning to the table with four of the biggest cups of ale Lillian had ever seen.

"I'm not planning on going back," he warned them as he handed them each one of the cups.

They toasted to the first day, and Lillian took a big gulp of ale, enjoying the warmth filling her stomach.

Finn and Sam, who was also from Hindra, entertained them with stories of their home, each one getting increasingly more bizarre as they tried to outdo each other. An ember of warmth filled her chest when listening to the boys bicker and watching Astrid bend over from laughter helped distract her from thoughts of her father, Eli, and what had happened earlier with the king.

But when a small voice inside her mind reminded her that she wasn't there to make friends but to avenge her father, her insides chilled again. She stayed quiet, observing until Sam and Finn began discussing rumors of how supposedly long-gone magical creatures had been seen on Hindra.

"What type of creatures?" Lillian leaned forward, her heart beating hard.

"People are saying that they've been hearing the echo of wings at night," Finn lowered his voice. "There are rumors that the Valkyries are stirring, their ravens traveling the lands."

Lillian furrowed her brow. The ravens were said to be the messengers of the Valkyries. They traveled the lands at night, collecting information for their mistresses. In the stories her father told her as a child, the ravens were also protectors, fighting alongside the Valkyries and the dragons. Queen Liv had two ravens who died protecting her from King Alek.

"Why would the Valkyries be stirring now? I thought they hadn't been seen for eighteen years?" Lillian glanced around the busy tavern to ensure no one was listening. Collaborating with the outlawed Valkyries was treason, and mentioning them, even if it was only rumors, could result in severe punishment.

"I've heard there has been an increase in rebel movements lately. Maybe they have heard the same thing and are looking for allies." Astrid offered.

"Or they're searching for their long-lost heir." Finn winked. "My parents told me stories of how the Valkyries would steal children at night, hoping to find her."

Sam threw his head back and laughed. "That story was just made up to scare us from going out at night."

Eyes twinkling, Finn began telling other children's tales he'd been told to instill fear and obedience. But Lillian couldn't stop thinking about what he'd said about the Valkyries. It couldn't be a coincidence she'd encountered a dragon, and whispers of Valkyries were rising on Hindra.

Lillian's head spun from the information and tiredness, and she rested it in her hands while letting her eyes drift across the packed tavern. Several other novices stood in a corner, their faces red from the heat while greedily drinking from cups of ale.

"Lillian!" Finn smacked her shoulder.

"What?" She glared at him.

"I said your name a hundred times. You're so pale. Are you okay?" He scanned her face worriedly.

Her eyes widened, and she quickly straightened her back. "I'm fine. This is just my coloring, Finley. Not everyone is blessed with your golden tan."

Finn tilted his head. "Are you sure?" She nodded, and thankfully, Sam jumped in to say he was calling it a night.

Astrid and Lillian walked back from the tavern together as Sam and Finn shared an apartment in a different part of town. Lillian debated whether to ask Astrid more about the rebel movements she had heard of, but wariness of Astrid becoming too inquisitive made her hesitate. She didn't want to risk having to lie.

"I hadn't heard the Valkyrie children's tale they talked about back there."

An uneven cobblestone almost sent Lillian sprawling when

Astrid's question ripped her from her thoughts, but thankfully, she caught herself at the last moment.

"Neither had I. Maybe it's only a story told on Hindra?"

"Maybe," Astrid mused. "My aunt has a huge library. I was planning to see if she had any books on them tomorrow. Maybe it could give us an edge knowing more about our enemy in the trials. Would you like to come?"

Lillian didn't really see how knowing more about the Valkyries would help them in the trials, but it would provide her with an opportunity to see what Astrid knew of the rebels, away from prying eyes on the streets, so she shrugged.

"Sure."

Chapter Twenty-Three

The next day, Lillian joined the rest of the novices in the courtyard just as the sun peeked over the horizon, bathing the pebbled courtyard in its soft glow. Finn waved to her from the fighting ring, his usual wide grin reflecting the first rays of sunshine.

She offered him a small smile in return, feeling lighter than she had in days. It was the first morning she hadn't woken up from pain constricting her chest, her father's last moments the first thought in her waking mind. Although anger and grief still brewed inside her, her mission not forgotten; hope fluttered in her stomach this morning.

Her father and Eli always spoke as if everyone in the capital was as evil as the king, his guards likened to demons. Always told her not to trust anyone. But after last night, Lillian realized there were good people here too, like Finn and Astrid, both determined to become her friends even as she pushed them away.

They weren't joining the guard because they were evil. They were trying to support their families. She hoped they would help Eli rebuild Orios if she succeeded in killing the king. The world would need people like them to recover from the horrors of King Alek.

Her smile fell as Commander Atlas appeared. The sun's rays danced over his black uniform as he stalked up to the group, and she bit back a smirk at how hot the trousers and jacket must be. Even if it was early morning, sweat pooled under her light tunic.

Commander Atlas studied the group with a frown on his face. The frown turned into a sneer when his gaze settled on her, and she lifted her chin, holding his stare. He narrowed his eyes as he continued to look into hers. They might have stood there all day if Commander Jon hadn't tapped his shoulder and the green fire finally settled on someone else.

Lillian couldn't hide the sly smile that spread across her face when the commander explained that they would practice archery today. She would show him just how *inexperienced* she was. They lined up one by one to practice on the targets in front of them, the furthest perhaps seventy feet away. Lillian had practiced these distances when she was just a child, but some of the other novices weren't as experienced with a bow. Wincing, she watched several of them fail to hit even the closest target.

"Ice princess."

She whipped her head around when the commander beckoned to her. Leaving the line, she grudgingly walked over.

"Why are you here?" Commander Atlas trailed his blazing eyes over her face.

"You told us to show up at dawn." Lillian smiled sweetly.

"Why are you in the *trials*?" His murderous glare returned.

She rolled her eyes. No sense of humor then. Not that it was much of a surprise.

"I'm an orphan from the outskirts of Echo. I didn't have many prospects. And since I know how to fight, I believe I would be useful in the guard, serving the king."

Commander Atlas raised an eyebrow. It seemed he was about to say something else, but then he spun on his heel and stalked off without another word. Lillian glared at his broad back and the stupidly decorated sword strapped to it. He was the rudest person she'd ever met. He didn't even have the courtesy of dismissing her.

She used the anger the commander evoked in every arrow she shot that day, hitting the target's inner circle without exception.

The commander didn't even notice. After their conversation, he completely ignored her; he didn't even spare her a glance as she far outperformed the other novices. It made her blood boil.

Chapter Twenty-Four

When Atlas finally dismissed them, Lillian was hot, dusty, and in a foul mood. She'd forgotten all about her promise to join Astrid at her aunt's house when the girl looped her arm through hers, chattering away about the novices' varying performances.

Lillian sighed; she'd kill for a bath and a nap right now. But she forced herself to smile and share a few pointers to improve Astrid's archery skills. If she would try to get information about the rebels out of Astrid, she'd need to indulge in small talk first.

Thankfully, Astrid's aunt's house was closer to the castle than Lillian's inn. They didn't have to walk for long before they arrived at a large stone house surrounded by a metal fence, although Lillian wasn't sure if 'house' was the correct term.

A mansion seemed like a better description. The cream home even had a small rounded tower attached, and vines weaved their way up the tall walls. Astrid explained that her aunt and uncle weren't home as they walked down the pebbled walkway to the house. They were visiting one of their friends in another neighborhood.

A servant opened the double doors for them, politely ignoring their dirty state. Lillian frowned; if Astrid's aunt and uncle were well enough off that they had serving staff, why didn't they help Astrid's family? For Astrid to be desperate enough to join the trials, despite her limited training, her family had to be struggling. She shook her head. It wasn't any of her business.

Astrid suggested they eat before beginning their research, and Lillian did not object, already tired of the meat and potatoes the inn served every day. She'd only been able to afford the one meal per day included in her stay. Lillian needed to find a way to make more coins soon. Otherwise, she'd both be homeless and starving before the second trial.

Lillian's mouth watered from the aromas that filled the room when they entered the large kitchen. Newly baked bread lay on the wooden counter, and something that smelled like vegetable soup brewed on the stove in the back. Remembering the bread Astrid had shared in the forest made her stomach growl loud enough for Astrid to giggle.

The white-clad servant gestured toward the large wooden table in the middle of the room, and Lillian's eyes widened when she walked over the white marble floor to reach it. The kitchen was bigger than the house she'd grown up in.

Lillian barely slipped onto one of the high wooden chairs before exhaustion swept through her, and she had to brace herself against the table.

When Astrid raised her eyebrows, Lillian quickly straightened, her stomach churning as Astrid studied her face. Thankfully, the servant placed two steaming bowls of soup in front of them at that moment, and Lillian promptly stuffed her mouth full of food before Astrid could ask any questions. They were quiet as they ate, the servant refilling Lillian's bowl twice before she leaned back in her chair, declaring that there was no way she could eat another bite without being sick.

As they thanked him for the food and rose to head to the library, the servant promised dessert and wine for them to enjoy when they were hungry again. Rubbing her full stomach, Lillian offered him a small smile, grateful that she hadn't found an excuse to get out of joining Astrid today. She could get used to this, she thought wistfully.

Astrid led them down a marble stairway lined with large,

colorful paintings and into an arched hallway illuminated by torches fastened to the walls. The hallway was lined with a plush gray carpet, making their steps entirely silent as they passed several wooden doors. Astrid stopped in front of one with a painting of a bird. A raven, Lillian realized.

She turned to Lillian. "Can I trust you?"

Lillian furrowed her brows. "What do you mean?"

"In his work for the king, my uncle procured many forbidden items, including books, that the king gave him for safekeeping." Astrid eyed her in the dim light. "I'm not supposed to know about this place, but I stumbled upon it when I did a little exploring."

"When you were snooping you mean?" Lillian smiled at her.

Astrid grinned back. "Yes, yes, when I was snooping. But I need you to promise me that I can trust you. If anyone found out that we were in here, my uncle would have me killed for treason."

Lillian tilted her head and studied the red-haired girl before her but finally held out her hand. "You have my word. I will not betray you."

As they shook hands, Lillian prayed she was right.

The library was huge. It was oval and spanned half the cellar floor. Bookshelves lined every inch of the curved walls, with glass lanterns above them and rows and rows of books of all colors and shapes. Astrid and Lillian started on opposite ends of the room, walking along the shelves, searching for books that might reference the Valkyries. Lillian picked up a book titled 'History of Orios' and a few others on the land's origin and brought them over to the glass table in the middle of the room. Astrid also carried over a large pile of books, stumbling as she tried to peer over the stack to join Lillian.

They quietly skimmed the books for a while, and Lillian read the familiar story of how the gods had created Orios. How Adeon personally formed Hindra and Echo to be the homes of his favored children: the Valkyries and the humans.

The original Valkyries were direct descendants of the offspring between Adeon and the angel Eir. Being demi-gods and demi-angels, the Valkyries were considered bringers of both light and dark, beauty and evil—all beautifully vicious females. Adeon gifted them wings and superior strength to be his warriors, to defend him against rival gods. Eir gave them beauty and fierce loyalty so that they would also protect each other.

Adeon created humans as more of an experiment. With the Valkyries all being female, he needed males for them to breed. Adeon thus created humans and gave some of them the power to wield magic to ensure powerful offspring. When Adeon realized that the humans interbred more easily and their population grew faster, he bestowed the Valkyries with one final gift.

A fated soulmate who would rival them in strength and beauty to ensure the Valkyries would all do their duty in continuing the Valkyrie bloodline. All females of such a joining were born with the Valkyrie wings and strength and the magic from their paternal line.

Lillian hadn't heard about this part of their history before and was just about to point it out when Astrid gasped.

"There is a story like the one Finn told here."

Astrid held up a children's book with drawings of Valkyries flying across the lands, human children in their arms.

"Well, it is a children's book, just like Sam pointed out. It's probably just some old tale." Lillian continued flipping through the book she'd picked up.

"But all these stories are based on some truth. Look, this one talks about how you must run if you hear singing over the water. Everyone knows that sirens occupied the north cliffs on Hindra before they were driven from the island." Astrid handed Lillian the book. "Just read."

Lillian flipped back to the story of the Valkyries. The book spoke of the echo of wings in the night, of a long-lost heir born out of the truest of love, that the warrior women would stop at nothing to find.

"Let's say you're right, and there is a Valkyrie heir. Wouldn't the king have had her killed a long time ago? He hunted the Valkyries almost to extinction."

"Not if he hasn't found her either." Astrid stared at her with wide eyes, and a chill snaked down Lillian's spine.

Her father had talked of a 'she' that would exact punishment on the guards in his last moments. And the king was capturing children to have them examined when they manifested magic. Could he be looking for a Valkyrie heir? Lillian shook her head. He was also taking males, like the baker's son. And if her father were referring to the Valkyrie heir, he would have told her. Eli hadn't mentioned it either. Although from the rebel conversation she'd overheard, there were a few things he was not telling her.

A pang of pain hit her chest at the thought of Eli. It had only been a few days, but she ached to have him by her side. He always knew what to do, and Lillian's head spun. She forced herself to laugh, even if it sounded hollow even to her own ears.

"I think this basement is messing with our heads." Lillian closed the books in front of her. "I should be getting back."

Too late she noticed Astrid's narrowed eyes, but Astrid eventually just shrugged and helped Lillian put the books back where they belonged.

Chapter Twenty-Five

When Lillian showed up for training the following day, she frowned at the tension that lay heavy over the courtyard. Despite the midday sun beating down on her, a chill spread in her body as sentries ran in and out of the castle, and the novices nervously whispered in smaller groups in the shade of the large castle balcony.

Finn and Sam stood right inside the metal gates, and Lillian rushed her steps to join them.

"Do you know what's going on?"

"Rebels broke into the castle." For the first time since she'd met him, Finn wasn't smiling. "The night guard caught one of them, and he is to be executed by dusk."

Lillian's blood ran cold, but she released a soft breath when she realized there was no way Eli would have made it here already, not without seeking her out first. She forced her voice to remain steady. "Do we know what they were after?"

Finn shook his head, fidgeting with his black leather tunic. "No, it didn't seem like they took anything. The guards found the one they caught in one of the guest chambers, supposedly where prestigious guests of the king stay. No one was in the room, though."

Lillian frowned, studying two guards who urgently whispered orders to each other as they passed through the gates on their way to the castle.

None of the commanders were around, and most of the novices used the time to rest, leaning against the stonewall surrounding the courtyard and enjoying the sunshine, but Lillian was too anxious to sit down for long. After a few hours, she, Astrid, Finn, and Sam decided to practice swordplay, taking turns to face each other.

Neither Astrid nor Sam were very skilled with a sword and posed little challenge to her. Finn, on the other hand, was an excellent fighter. They danced around each other for what felt like an eternity until he eventually bested her, his sword pointed to her heart. By the time they finally put their swords down, Lillian was out of breath, every limb hurting, but they'd each won one round. A small crowd gathered around them, a few novices clapping their hands as they stepped out of the ring.

"What's going on here." Commander Atlas strolled up to them, glaring at a group of novices who quickly scattered.

"We were just practicing our swordplay, Commander." Finn pointed to Lillian. "Lillian here just kicked my ass."

"Did she now." The commander didn't spare her a glance. "Commander Jon's group is on archery today. I suggest you head over there now, Finn. Jon is known to make people run laps if they're late."

Finn grinned at the commander and waved as he jogged back over to his group.

Lillian studied Commander Atlas, who impatiently flicked his thick black hair out of his face as he ordered any lingering novices to return to their groups. He called Finn by name; was he perhaps warming up to them?

The commander turned to her. "What are you waiting for. In the ring."

She rolled her eyes and walked back into the ring with heavy steps. Lillian assumed that the commander would select one of the other novices for her to fight, so when Commander Atlas himself stepped into the ring, she raised her eyebrows.

"Scared, princess?" He smirked while unsheathing the embellished sword from his back.

Heat rose on her neck, and Lillian couldn't help herself; she bared her teeth at him. Once again, his mouth twitched, his green eyes glittering. Oh, she'd wipe that off his face quick enough. Lillian raised her mother's sword.

The commander was good. Better than good. But the smile he'd held back set something off in her, and she slid into the ice-cold rage she'd become so familiar with lately.

I'll show you, *ice princess*, she thought as she charged him again. The metallic clangs of their swords clashing were the only sound filling Lillian's ears. She parried each blow he dealt her, pushing forward to deal her own. They were equally skilled, each taking turns going on the offensive. Lillian would have enjoyed it if it were someone other than the commander she was sparring with.

They drew back, circling each other. When Commander Atlas charged again, Lillian saw an opportunity. He left his left side open, and she spun to tap her sword at his side. But as she rushed forward, she found herself in the air, landing hard on her back, and her breath knocked out of her. Her ears rang when the commander's sword pricked the thin skin of her throat.

Lillian growled as she tried to catch her breath, and the commander laughed softly.

"Did I hurt your feelings?"

She ignored his outstretched hand and scrambled to her feet. "Again."

"You're bleeding, princess. Go take care of that, and we'll see about another round." Commander Atlas searched her face, his brow furrowing slightly before he spun on his heel and walked off.

Lillian anxiously surveyed her body. When she turned her head, a few drops of blood landed on the pebbled ground, and she went cold as she lifted her hand to face. Her nose was bleeding, and Lillian wiped at it as best she could with the sleeve of her tunic, but before she could demand another round, the sound of drums beat through the courtyard. She winced as they accelerated the ache building inside her head.

Lillian whipped her head around when the drumming grew louder. The sound came from inside the castle, and soon, two lines of sentries, headed by four drummers, exited the castle doors. Two sentries hauled a hooded man between them, his feet dragging in the dirt. Her stomach dropped; yet again, she would stand by and watch the King's Guard kill an innocent man. Waves of cold guilt crashed through her body—she hadn't even tried to save this man.

Astrid walked up to stand beside her, but Lillian didn't dare look at her, fearing her mask of neutrality would break at a friendly face. They were quiet as the sentries placed the man on his knees in the middle of the courtyard, the dark castle walls behind him casting long shadows on the courtyard as the sun descended.

When one of the sentries pulled back his hood, Lillian bit back a gasp. It was Harald. The rebel wolf-shifter who convinced Eli to give her a chance to prove herself, who took care of her father's body as she'd broken apart. They must have beaten him; Harald's face was bloodied and bruised as he glared at the guards.

The drums silenced, and a familiar wave of panic rose within her as the image of her father on his knees flashed in front of her eyes. Harald didn't cower either; he kept his chin high, glaring at everyone in the courtyard. His brown eyes found hers as his gaze slid across the group, and Harald's eyes widened slightly. But he quickly locked down any expression of recognition and moved on.

Lillian struggled to breathe, trying to come up with any type of diversion that could stop what was happening. She flexed her hands, her whole body tensing, when a small hand slipped into hers. As she glanced to her side, Astrid shook her head imperceptibly.

Astrid squeezed her hand, and Lillian faced forward again. A sword glistened over Harald's neck, and the courtyard quieted. Harald met her gaze again when the sentry let the sword whistle through the air. The world shattered around her when he gave her a small smile. Tears clouded her vision, but she forced herself to continue looking into Harald's brown eyes even as the sword fell, even as his head rolled onto the dirt. Biting her cheek until it bled, Lillian promised herself that she would never look away again.

Chapter Twenty-Six

Lillian sprinted through the narrow cobblestone streets. As soon as Harald's head fell onto the ground, she let go of Astrid's hand. Mumbling an excuse that she needed to tend to her nose, she walked as quickly as she dared out of the courtyard. As soon as she was out of sight, she broke into a run.

Her heart pounded, blinding pain stabbing at her chest with every step she took. Never again would Harald boast his obnoxious laugh. Never again would his brother tease him. Lillian wanted to scream. But she just continued running as fast as she could, darting out of the way of people and carriages on the narrow road.

Gasping from the run and the pain from Harald's death, she finally slowed. She was close to the rooftop she'd found the other day. Slipping into the dark alley, Lillian quickly scaled the ladder. When she reached the roof, she stilled. There were footprints in the dust covering the black roof.

In too much pain to be careful, Lillian still dragged herself onto the rooftop. Sitting down and wrapping her arms around her legs, she rocked back and forth until the moon hung high in the sky.

A coughing fit interrupted her silent mourning. Her lungs were on fire, and she coughed into her arm to not alert anyone of her position. When it finally subsided, she straightened, and her heart stopped as her eyes snagged on her sleeve. It was full of blood.

Lillian shakily touched her mouth, her fingers coming back covered in red. Fresh tears burned behind her eyes as she realized her sickness must have moved on to the next stage. Perhaps the final stage.

Drawing a trembling breath, Lillian prayed she'd be able to hold on for as long as it would take her to kill the king. Dread filled her, making her whole body shiver as she tried to push it away. She told herself that she would not be scared. Like her father and Harald, she'd greet death with her chin held high.

When she no longer thought she would break apart if she let go of her body, Lillian rose and walked up to the ledge, angling her face to the moon. She would see her father and the others soon enough. For now, she'd watch the moon and try to find the calm the night usually brought her. Lillian watched the sky for a long time, but the thought of everyone she'd lost, and everyone she would lose when she died, wouldn't leave her mind. One hour of self-pity, she told herself. She'd allow one hour.

"I didn't realize this roof was already occupied."

Lillian spun around, her daggers ready in her hands, at the sound of the voice.

A cloaked man pulled himself onto the roof, holding up his hands. "No need for those."

"Remove your hood. And I'll make that decision, thank you very much," Lillian ordered, keeping the daggers ready to fly.

The man moved deliberately, slowly pulling back the hood covering his face. Green eyes met Lillian's gray ones.

"Commander?"

Her stomach dropped, and she did not lower her daggers. No way. She was not going down without a fight.

"Threatening your commander. I'd say that's definitely in the 'you're out' category," Commander Atlas mused. "But I'll let it go if you put them down immediately."

Shaking her head, Lillian gripped the hilts tighter.

"Why are you here?" She mockingly mimicked the commander's question yesterday. Apparently, she'd lost her mind.

"I used to come all the time before I was stationed on Hindra. I didn't realize someone else had found their way up here."

She was surprised he even bothered answering, but not enough to lower her weapons.

"Are you okay?" The commander studied her face, his posture relaxed.

"What do you mean?"

He gestured to her face. "It looks like you've been crying."

Lillian used the back of her hand to feel her cheeks, wincing when she found them wet.

"I'm fine. It must be the moonlight. My eyes are sensitive."

She didn't even convince herself with the lie and planted her feet firmly, ready if he charged her.

But the commander didn't approach her. He only strolled up to the railing surrounding the rooftop and turned his face to the moon.

"It is a big moon tonight."

Lillian followed his movements closely.

"Keep the daggers if it makes you feel better. But I'm not going to hurt you." Commander Atlas turned to her again. "I find being under the night sky helps after a tough day, don't you? It gives me hope that someone looking at the same moon might have had a better one. That there is something better out there."

Lillian narrowed her eyes as she continued to study him.

"So angry," he said quietly.

Commander Atlas turned back to face the moon, swinging his legs over to sit on the railing, his back to her. When he didn't speak again, Lillian slowly lowered her daggers. She backed up to the ladder, her eyes fixed on his back.

The commander didn't move when she quietly climbed down, but she heard him whisper halfway down. "Goodnight, ice princess."

Shaking her head, she slipped through the shadows back to her room.

Chapter Twenty-Seven

Lillian glared at the tall castle as she ran around it, sweat coating her body and dust sticking to her skin. She'd overslept, and apparently, Commander Jon wasn't the only one who favored running as a punishment for being late. Commander Atlas hadn't acknowledged their late-night run-in when she came sprinting into the courtyard, gasping for breath. He only pointed and told her to run thirty laps, one for every minute she'd been late.

When Lillian finished the final lap, she wasn't sure how she'd survive the rest of the day, her body already on the verge of burnout as she stumbled to a stop. But she made herself walk up to the others with steady steps, swallowing hard and praying another coughing fit wasn't coming on. Commander Atlas had them practicing throwing knives today, and she frowned when he winked as she stepped up to the targets.

Thankfully, the training ended early as the commanders were called away to respond to rumors of more rebel movements. Lillian tried to overhear what they were saying, but the three men spoke too softly as they walked into the castle. Astrid and Finn invited her for drinks, but she declined. She needed to rest and find a way to make more coins.

After a lifesaving nap, she woke to darkness casting long shadows in her small room. Lillian dressed quickly, putting on her father's cloak and pulling up the hood to cover her face. She quietly asked the innkeeper where she might find a gambling room, and he directed her to a shady-looking tavern on the border of the slums. There was no sign outside the crumbling stone building, but she followed the smell of smoke and ale to a partly rotting door and slipped inside.

The tavern was half full, with many patrons cloaked to hide their identities as they huddled by the bar or sat at the sticky wooden tables, murmuring to each other.

While gambling wasn't technically illegal, this place seemed like a rendezvous spot for small-time criminals, and a whisper of unease brushed her skin as a few hooded figures studied her closely when she entered.

Lillian quickly made her way to the back of the room, where several round tables stood. The room was dim, with only a small fire burning in the fireplace in the back and a single window, too dusty to allow the moonlight to break through.

"One silver to buy in." A man at the closest table glanced at her. "And no cloak. We'll need to see that face of yours."

Lillian shrugged; it wasn't like she had a choice. She needed to win some silver tonight if she wanted to have a roof over her head for the next few weeks. Pulling back her hood, Lillian took a seat at the table.

Four men sat down as the dealer began shuffling a deck of cards, preparing to deal. Lillian threw a silver on the worn wooden table and studied the men around her. The blonde man to her right leered at her, staring at her face while he licked his cracked lips. She sighed; this was going to be a long night.

Lillian purposely folded the first few rounds, reading the other men's signals. One tapped his leg if he sported a poor hand, and another's eye twitched. She won back what she had lost so far in the fourth round. Lillian folded the fifth one, even though she was pretty sure she would have won. She didn't want to draw too much attention to herself—she'd still have to walk back to the inn with her winnings. By the eighth round, she'd managed to pocket twenty silvers and announced that she was calling it a night.

Walking back under the dark sky, listening to an owl's soft coo, Lillian blew out a breath of relief. That was easier than she had thought. She would have to return, but for now, she had enough for two more weeks at the inn. Eli would have been proud of her. She'd paced herself, not walked away with every silver the men had in their pockets. Just enough to keep her afloat.

She smiled as she remembered Eli's face when he believed he'd taught her how to play; but she'd already studied the men at their neighborhood tavern for years and took every silver he had.

It was the first time he kissed her. When she shivered on the walk home from the tavern, he pulled her close and whispered how proud he was of her. As she glanced up at him, snow fell, and he leaned in to kiss a snowflake off her cheek. When she didn't pull back, he searched her face and finally kissed her. Lost in thoughts of Eli, she didn't hear the footsteps behind her until it was too late.

A man leaped out of the shadows, his fist connecting with the side of her face. The sudden blow caught Lillian off guard, her head slamming into the stone wall beside her. Black spots danced in front of her eyes as she put up her arms in front of her face to deflect his next strike. But he wasn't alone, and another hand snagged in her hair, yanking her head back as he swept her legs out from under her. She hit the pebbled ground hard, her breath knocked out of her.

Lillian crawled over the cobblestones, her heart pounding as she desperately tried to get a few feet away. She only needed a moment to get her vision back. And get hold of her daggers. A hard kick in her stomach thwarted her efforts, her body involuntarily curling at the pain. The cold blade of a knife slid against her throat, and she froze.

"Stupid girl. Did you really think we'd let you walk away with all that silver?" The raspy voice belonged to the leering man from the card game. "You joined the wrong table tonight."

His fleshy hands searched her cloak, lingering when he grazed her chest. When she twisted to get away, the knife pressed harder against her throat, and warm blood trickled down her neck.

"I will kill you." Lillian's voice was hoarse, and she tried to squash the panic threatening to bubble up as the man pressed the knife further into her neck.

The man searching her cloak laughed coldly. "I think I'd like to have some fun with you before *we* kill *you*. Ah. Here it is."

He pulled out the small pouch filled with her remaining coins. She clenched her fists. How could she have been dumb enough to bring every coin she had tonight? She deserved to get her ass kicked.

Lillian reacted instinctively, flinging up her arm to shift the knife away from her throat. Rolling into a crouch, she prepared to draw her daggers, but before she could, one of the men slammed the hilt of his dagger against her temple.

The world went dark.

Chapter Twenty-Eight

The world swayed, and for a moment, Lillian wondered if she was on a ship. She blinked, trying to get back to consciousness. When she opened her eyes, rooftops and the clear night sky looked back at her. Not on a ship, then. Someone carried her.

She cursed silently and remained limp until she was confident the man carrying her believed she was still unconscious. Then she struck, sending her elbow hard into his throat. The man lost his grip, and she stumbled back when her feet met the ground, lifting her arms to meet his returning blow.

Her eyes met amber ones, and she stilled. "Finn?"

Too dazed to feel their bond, she hadn't realized it was her friend. Finn massaged his throat, wincing as he tried to catch his breath.

"I'm sorry. Someone attacked me. I thought you were one of them."

"Clearly." Finn winked at her. "I'm glad you're back to your usual, vicious self. I was worried there for a while. You were totally out of it."

Lillian did not feel like she was back to her usual self. When she relaxed, knowing Finn was there, her head spun. As black spots danced in front of her eyes, she took a shaky step toward him before darkness consumed her once more.

The next time she woke, she was lying down, nestled into a comfortable couch. She stretched her hands over the velvety fabric.

"Are you back with me?"

Lillian turned her head. Finn sat at a small table to her left. She made to sit up but fell back onto the couch as her head pounded.

Lying down, Lillian took in the room. She was sprawled on a couch in what looked like a combined sitting room and kitchen, a little outdated with paint chipping off the wooden shelves lining the walls but cozy. She sniffed; the room smelled of leather, but there was also a hint of the familiar scent of woods at night, and a sense of calm settled over her.

"Where am I?"

"You're in our apartment." Finn walked over to sit beside her on the couch, the moonlight streaming through the window behind it reflecting in his golden hair. "I think you might have a concussion. You've been in and out for over an hour."

Flashbacks of the men's attack flooded her mind, and she groaned when she realized they had gotten away with all of her silver. Lillian started to ask Finn if he'd seen where the men had run off to but was interrupted when the door to the apartment flung open.

Sam and Commander Atlas walked in, deep in conversation. They both froze when they noticed Lillian, and she forced her body upright, ignoring the pain searing through her head.

"What is he doing here?" she hissed.

Finn put a hand on her shoulder, squeezing gently. "This is Atlas's apartment. Sam and I were looking for a place to stay, and Atlas was looking to rent out his other bedrooms. And here we are."

So *that's why* they were on a first-name basis. Lillian frowned as she tried to make sense of the information she had gathered about the commander. He was like a puzzle of pieces that didn't quite fit together. He was rude and grumpy, but he had also been gentle when they ran into each other on the roof last night. And he lived with two novices, far below him in rank.

The commander recovered his ability to move. Atlas's eyes narrowed as they scanned her body and face while he stalked toward the couch. A wave of goosebumps rippled across her skin when she accidentally met his gaze. Lillian quickly averted her eyes and started to rise to escape the thick tension in the room.

"Who did this to you?" he said quietly, a muscle popping in his jaw.

A knot formed in her gut, and Lillian stared intently at the worn velvet couch.

"Lillian." Atlas placed a finger under her chin with surprising gentleness and lifted her face to look at him. "Tell me who did this to you."

The knot in her stomach grew at his cold voice, but concern filled his eyes when she met them. She blinked, realizing it was the first time he'd used her actual name.

Lillian found it hard to keep his gaze, a lump forming in her throat. She clenched her fists—she'd already cried in front of this man once. She wasn't about to have an encore in less than twenty-four hours.

Clearing her throat, she said quietly, "I went to the gambling room, and apparently, the men at my table didn't take it too well when I won."

Her voice sounded smaller than she liked, but she blew out a breath of relief when no tears threatened to fall.

Atlas glared at her, and she braced herself for a lecture, but he simply leaned in and tucked a stray strand of hair behind her ear. Then he spun on his heel and stalked out of the apartment, slamming the door behind him. Lillian gaped at the closed door.

"What just happened?" Finn's mouth also hung open.

Lillian shook her head. "I have no idea."

She didn't know if it was the adrenaline or the shock, but the shocked expression on Finn's face sent her into a fit of hysteric giggles. Finn and Sam frowned, which only made Lillian giggle harder. Once she finally calmed down, Finn shook his head and suggested she use their washroom to clean up.

Upon seeing her reflection in the dusty mirror, Lillian recoiled. She looked like death. Dried blood coated her hair and face, and a large bruise was forming on the side of her face. When she lifted her tunic, her ribs hadn't fared much better, black and blue bruises blooming on her pale skin. She cleaned up as best she could, using cold water to scrub her face and a bucket to rinse her hair. When she exited the washroom, Finn and Sam sat at the small table in the kitchen, plates of meat and fruit in front of them.

"We thought you might be hungry," Finn waved her over.

Lillian slipped onto a free chair. She wasn't about to say no to a free meal. Since she would likely be kicked out of the inn tomorrow, she didn't know when her next one would be. She made quick work of the food before her while listening to Finn and Sam talk about the upcoming trial. They only had tomorrow left before the first one would take place.

Once she pushed her plate away, her stomach full, Finn leaned forward. "Are you going to tell us why you were gambling in the first place? You don't strike me as someone who gambles for fun."

"I will if you tell me how you found me."

Lillian was stalling, but she also wanted to know how he kept finding her without her noticing him. Finn grinned and rose from the table. Then, he began removing his tunic and breeches.

Her face heated. "What are you doing? I asked how you found me, not to see you naked." Although, she could appreciate the muscular, golden-tan body he revealed. What was he eating to pack on that much muscle?

As if he could read her mind, Finn's grin widened. "I'm showing you."

Sam chuckled, covering his mouth with his hand when Lillian glared at him. Thankfully, Finn kept his undergarments on, and the room filled with the vibrations of magic. An owl perched on the back of the chair in Finn's place. It cocked its head, its amber eyes set on Lillian, and then spread its wings and flew to her. She extended her arm, and the owl placed itself on it, cooing softly in her ear.

"So you're the owl I've been seeing?" She couldn't believe she hadn't realized it before. Finn let out a hoot in confirmation and flew off, shifting in mid-air and landing back on his feet. Stark naked.

"Show off," Lillian muttered, averting her eyes. She knew shifters quickly got comfortable with nudity, but Eli, the only shifter she'd been close to, had rarely shifted in her presence. At least not back into his human form.

Her cheeks were still faintly red when Finn pulled on his trousers and sat back down at the table leaving his tunic on the floor. Lillian had a feeling he did it on purpose.

"I think you owe me an answer now." Finn stared at her expectantly.

Lillian took a deep breath and quietly told them how she didn't have enough silver for her stay and how she'd decided to acquire more by gambling. How careless she'd been walking back to the inn. When she finished, Lillian couldn't look either of the men in the eye, not wishing to see the pity she was sure she'd find there.

"Well, it's settled then." Finn grinned at her. "You'll stay here. There is too much male energy in this apartment anyway, and there's a free room."

Lillian scanned his face for sympathy, but there wasn't any. Only excitement glinted in his eyes.

"Why would you help me?"

Finn's grin widened. "I am your familiar, you know. Even if you won't acknowledge the bond." There was an unspoken *yet* in his tone, and she narrowed her eyes. "But mostly, you're quite entertaining to have around. I've never met anyone quite as wicked before. I like it."

Sam nodded in agreement. "As soon as you kicked my ass the first day, I knew you'd be an excellent addition to our crew."

"Your crew?" Lillian bit her cheek to keep herself from smiling.

These two were really something else.

"The most beautiful, smart, and talented guards there ever were, of course." Finn winked at her.

Lillian laughed as warmth spread in her stomach. She couldn't remember when she had laughed last and couldn't help but think that her father and Eli had been wrong when they'd told her all men who weren't rebels were evil. Finn and Sam's eyes widened.

"What?" She frowned. "What did I do?"

"I don't think we've ever seen you smile before," Finn said gently.

Another wave of warmth washed over Lillian. She tipped her head forward, her white hair covering her face, to avoid them seeing the pink that threatened to creep up her neck.

"If you made Atlas react like that when you looked like a bloody mess, I can't wait to see what he does when he sees you smile for the first time."

Lillian swatted at Finn, shaking her head. She didn't know why the commander had reacted like he did, but it was not because he had some kind of warm, fuzzy feelings for her.

They stayed at the table talking for a long time. Lillian, to her surprise, grilled Finn on his shapeshifting abilities. When he'd learned he was a shifter and what abilities his owl granted him. Thoras, the shifter goddess, apparently gifted him excellent vision, both day and night and very sensitive hearing.

"Quite useful skills for a soldier," Finn winked at her.

Lillian nodded; the superior senses were one of the reasons shifters made up a big part of King Alek's army. And they were easy to control if they were bonded. Her father and Eli had hidden their bond so the sentries couldn't use them against each other. But Eli had told her the king didn't hesitate to capture and torture either the human or the shifter if one of them didn't fall in line.

Finn went on to entertain them with stories of how he learned to fly, and Lillian found herself doubling over from laughter at how he'd fallen down so many trees and rooftops that his mother threatened to lock him up.

"Doesn't this look cozy."

Atlas leaned against the door frame. None of them had noticed him return, too captivated by Finn's stories. When they stared at Atlas's serious face and then back at each other, they all burst into laughter again.

Lillian hid her face in her hands, gasping for air and unable to fully comprehend what was so funny, but every time she glanced at Finn or Sam, they howled with laughter again. Atlas patiently waited for them to finish, the corners of his mouth curling slightly.

When they finally settled down, Lillian found herself wondering why he didn't allow himself to smile.

At last, they fell silent, catching their breath. Lillian braced herself against the table as the lack of oxygen made her head spin, and she swallowed hard as a cough rattled in her chest. When Finn cocked his head to the side and studied her, Lillian forced herself to take deep breaths, shakily squashing the coughing fit.

Atlas stepped away from the door, reached into his black jacket, and pulled out a pouch. Lillian's pouch. He dropped it onto the table.

"Here you go."

Sucking in a breath, she realized his hands were covered in blood. She narrowed her eyes, suddenly not feeling like laughing at all.

"Where did you get this?"

"I know where those lowlifes hang out, so I thought I'd get it back." Atlas shrugged. "Don't worry, they won't bother you again."

Lillian's nostrils flared, heat creeping up her neck. "I don't need a hero to save me." She clenched her jaw, stopping herself before she added, *especially not you.*

Atlas glowered at her, his eyes darkening. "I can promise you, I am no hero."

"Well, don't do me any more favors then, *Commander.*"

Glaring back at him, she pocketed the pouch before doing something stupid. Like, throw it in his face.

"Don't worry, *ice princess*. I didn't do it for you. I am one of the king's commanders, and my responsibilities include keeping criminals in check. The king would expect me to take care of it."

Lillian doubted the king would give one shit that she lost her pouch, but before she could retort with another snarky response, Atlas stalked into what she assumed was his bedroom and slammed the door. Her cheeks burned, and she wasn't sure if it was from anger or the tiniest bit of guilt that settled in her stomach. Pinching her nose, she blew out a deep breath. That man really got under her skin.

Finn cleared his throat. "Well, wasn't that entertaining? I knew this was a great decision."

He elbowed her in the side. "Let's go. We should get your room set up."

Realizing they hadn't even asked Atlas if he was amenable to her staying there, she shook her head. "I'm guessing Atlas won't be too happy to find me here in the morning. I have my silver again. I should just head back to the inn."

Pointing to the door, Finn said gently, "It looks like he had the same idea we did."

Lillian glanced toward where Finn indicated, and her eyes widened when she found her satchel by the door. A knot formed in her chest when she quietly followed Finn into the room they intended for her to stay in, wondering why the commander bothered to help her. And what it was about him that made her so furious.

Chapter Twenty-Nine

Lillian did not sleep well. After tossing and turning for most of the night, she finally gave up when the gray morning light shone through the small window above the bed. She quickly used the washroom connected to the room and got ready. The bruise on her face had spread, stretching from her temple to her chin. Lillian grimaced as she pressed a finger to it. She'd be sore for a few days.

When dressed, Lillian paced back and forth in her room, wondering if it was too early to knock on Atlas's door. She couldn't shake the feeling that she'd been unfair to him yesterday. Atlas going after those men and getting her pouch back would save her the headache of making coins some other way. And he was her commander. She should probably, *definitely*, apologize.

Making up her mind, Lillian walked out of the room and approached his door before she could talk herself out of it. She knocked softly, calling his name. No response. When she knocked a bit harder the door slipped open. Lillian peered in through the small crack. Atlas's bed was made, and he was nowhere to be seen. With a glance behind her, she slipped into his room.

It was tidy. A few books lay on a wooden desk, and his black uniform was neatly folded on a chair by the bed. Lillian took another hesitant step. Maybe she could find something to under-stand the grumpy commander. She picked at the books; she recognized a few of the titles from the books her father had kept in his study.

A small piece of paper protruded from a book on the gods. She shouldn't, but she inclined her head to try to read what was scribbled on it. When Lillian finally made out the words, she sucked in a breath. *The rebel leader was found and eliminated—no sign of her.*

The note was addressed to the king.

A strangled noise escaped her throat. Any guilt she'd felt faded in an instant, and she clenched her fists until they were white. She'd make him pay for this.

When a door opened in the apartment, Lillian quickly slipped out of Atlas's room, closing the door softly. Finn waved to her with a sleepy smile, and she forced herself to return it. But in her mind, there was only one word replaying: murderer, murderer, murderer.

Lillian was quiet as they made their way to the castle grounds, praying Finn and Sam would attribute it to the trial that would take place tomorrow.

Chapter Thirty

Astrid gasped when Lillian entered the courtyard.

"I'm deducing from your expression that I don't look ravishing this morning?" Lillian gave her a tight smile.

Astrid inspected her face and winced. "What happened?"

Lillian thought of trying to find a way to avoid the truth, but an ember of warmth filled her chest when she met Astrid's friendly blue eyes. Lillian had enough enemies, and the red-haired girl had somehow clawed herself into her broken heart. In a hushed voice, Lillian told Astrid a short version of the events of last night, including how she'd come to stay with Finn and the others.

"So you're living with the sex-on-legs soldiers?"

Lillian choked. "Sex-on-legs soldiers?"

"That's what the ladies around here call the three of them." Astrid pointed to a group of women in beautiful dresses standing, fanning themselves, and gossiping outside the metal gates. "They have their own fan club."

At that moment, Finn joined them, one eyebrow raised as he studied their faces. The women outside the courtyard turned and smoothly inched closer, trying to get into Finn's line of view.

Lillian and Astrid exchanged a glance and erupted in hushed giggles.

"If the princess and her court are done with their gossip session, perhaps we can begin the last day of training before the trial tomorrow." Atlas glared at them from a few feet away before turning his back.

Lillian narrowed her eyes. But she held back the retort on her tongue, instead opting to stare daggers into his back.

As if he felt her eyes on him, Atlas flipped around, and his green eyes fixed on her. He eyed the bruise on her face, the muscle in his jaw flexing. Lillian refused to break his stare, keeping her chin high. When Atlas raised an eyebrow, Lillian bit her cheek to stop herself from snarling at him. If he had anything to do with her father's death, she'd kill him. Slowly. Atlas stared at her for a moment longer before returning to his conversation with Commander Jon.

All novices were free to spend the day practicing what they wished, and given Lillian's sore ribs, she'd settle for the bow. Dragging Astrid along, she headed for the practice range.

When Lillian unfastened the bow, a screech echoed through the courtyard. All the novices stopped what they were doing and whirled around. Lillian followed their gaze, and her stomach flipped. King Alek held court at the far end of the courtyard, close to the castle entrance. But it wasn't the king that made her heart stop.

Beside the king stood a gilded cage, glowing softly in the midday sun. And inside it, a dragon, smaller than the one she'd encountered in the woods, sat, its icy-blue eyes fixed on her. While smaller, it didn't look any less vicious than the black monster that had been seconds from turning her into a pile of ash. This dragon was pure silver, as if it had been spun from the moon itself, and black razor-sharp spikes covered its entire back. The dragon's long tail whipped the floor of the golden cage, making the whole thing shake.

Lillian's blood ran cold when she felt the dragon's eyes track her as she took a step back. She cautiously lifted her gaze to meet the dragon's, and a sharp pain pierced her chest when they locked eyes.

There was so much sorrow in them. Lillian sucked in a breath as the ache spread through her body, clasping at her chest, trying to force air down her lungs. Tears filled her eyes, mirroring the silver lining the dragon's icy-blue ones.

"The king keeps her as a reminder of his power."

Lillian jumped at Atlas's voice but didn't break the dragon's stare. The ache inside her spread, every single one of her joints hurting.

She drew a shaky breath. "What do you mean?"

"He keeps her for entertainment and security so the dragons won't rise against him." Atlas's voice was edged, and Lillian finally tore her eyes from the dragon.

His jaw popped, his eyes locked on the dragon. When he sensed her stare, Atlas turned his head, and she flinched at the green fire burning in his eyes.

Another screech rang across the courtyard, and Lillian turned her head as several sentries carried the cage into the castle. She swallowed as she met the dragon's gaze again, another wave of sorrow crashing through her body.

I will get you out, she promised quietly.

The dragon inclined its head.

Lillian stared after it, her mouth hanging open, until it disappeared inside the castle.

To her relief, Atlas was gone when she glanced to her side. The novices were gathered and instructed to show up at midday for the trial in fighting gear and with their preferred weapons. The only other information they received was what they had been told before; tomorrow was a trial in groups. They would have to collaborate to win.

Lillian frowned. There were only three people she could imagine herself collaborating with, and it was unlikely they'd all be in the same group.

Chapter Thirty-One

Finn convinced Lillian to walk back with him, claiming he needed her to join him in procuring a specific liquor. Apparently, they needed a glass of it to relax before tomorrow.

When Lillian questioned why he couldn't purchase it himself, Finn mumbled something about maybe having flirted with the saleswoman and never followed through. Despite herself, Lillian grinned.

Finn really knew how to cheer someone up. Lillian wheezed from laughter when they left the small liquor store. She refused to enter without Finn, and the woman had done just about everything but physically throw herself at Finn—to Lillian's immense joy.

Lillian took a long time to study the dusty bottles lining the walls, reading the text on them, to stretch the moment out as long as possible. It wasn't until Finn pinched her leg—quite hard—that she took pity on him, and they finally left.

Lillian's laughter turned into a coughing fit as she tried to regain her composure, coming on so quickly that she didn't have time to quench it.

Panic surged within her, both from the lack of air and fear, and she tried to pull away from Finn. But he held on to her elbow, worriedly scanning her face as she struggled to force air into her lungs.

When she met his wide eyes, a chill snaked down her back, and she knew she'd been coughing blood. The warmth on her face and Finn's horrified expression told her enough, even without looking at her arm, which she winced to find drenched in red. Lillian removed her white tunic, grateful that she'd worn a vest beneath, and used it to wipe her face. She quickly disposed of it in an alley beside them. Drawing a deep breath to brace herself, she faced Finn.

He gripped her hand. "Lillian. What just happened? And please, don't lie to me."

His expression was so pained that she struggled to breathe yet again. It reminded her so much of the one her father bore during his last months. Lillian didn't know what to say. Couldn't find the words to explain what was happening to her or why she was in the trials despite it.

"Lillian, *please.*"

Hearing his voice so far from the happy, upbeat tone he usually favored broke her heart.

"I'm dying." The words left her mouth before she could think about another, gentler way to break it to him.

Finn was quiet, his eyes begging her to explain. She sighed; maybe it was time she trusted someone other than Eli and her father.

So she did.

Dragging Finn far into an alleyway and with a hushed voice, Lillian told him how they'd found out a few years ago that her body was shutting down, her very essence fading away. She told him of her father's murder, of the rebels, of her mission.

When finished, Lillian took a deep breath and steeled herself for his reaction. She might have signed her death sentence, but her gut told her that she could trust Finn. She wasn't disappointed.

Finn simply looked at her and said, "Count me in." And that was that.

Lillian promised to tell him more about her plans, what she'd learned about the missing children and anything else he wanted to know when they were back home, where they didn't risk someone overhearing. Finn kept his hold on her hand as they walked back, but Lillian didn't mind. He needed to anchor himself, and she was happy to be strong for him tonight. Like she'd been for her father and Eli the past years.

Finn hesitated when they stood outside the stone steps up to the apartment, then turned to her and asked, "Are you scared?"

A lump formed in her throat, and Lillian fixed her eyes on the weathered exterior of the building, worn smooth by rain and wind. No one had ever asked her if she was scared before. Her father was so focused on his own pain, and Eli mostly pretended as if she wasn't sick.

She cleared her throat. "No one is promised tomorrow, Finn. I'm grateful for every day I have, even if they might be numbered in this world. But yes, I am scared of dying. But mostly, I'm scared of what it will do to the people I leave behind."

The golden flecks in his eyes burned like molten amber as Finn bore them into hers. "You don't have to go through this alone, Lillian. And you're allowed to be scared. Hell, I'm scared, and I am not the one dying."

She nodded, not trusting her voice. Finn offered her a small smile, gripped her hand again, and led her up to the apartment.

Chapter Thirty-Two

Lillian and Finn downed their third glass of liquor when Sam and Atlas walked through the door. Lillian fought a smile, watching Finn wobble as he stood up to bring over two more glasses from the kitchen. But when she met Atlas's eyes, her smile instantly turned into a scowl.

"Perfect. Commander Dick is here. No more fun for us."

Finn choked and almost dropped the glasses he carried. Wincing, Lillian picked at the wooden table; she hadn't meant to say that out loud.

"You both know that you have a trial tomorrow, right." Atlas ignored her comment and sat down at the table, accepting the glass Finn offered him.

"It's not until midday." Lillian rolled her eyes. "We'll have time to sleep it off."

Atlas stared at her for a moment and then downed his glass in one go. "You're right."

Finn refilled it for him, and Lillian raised her eyebrows. She wasn't sure what she was most surprised about, that Atlas had told her she was right or that he was drinking to catch up.

Leaning back in her chair, she watched the boys propose toasts to the stupidest things, like the chair they sat on and their bread. Lillian made herself take small sips from her glass. While she would never admit it, there was no way she could keep up with them. When Finn fell off his chair after trying to reach the bottle, his bewildered face sticking up just above the table, the corners of her mouth twitched.

A sense of belonging, of being home, slowly crept up on Lillian. She was comfortable here, with the sex-on-legs soldiers as Astrid had called them. Lillian snorted; Finn's head would probably swell to twice its size if he ever heard that nickname.

If only Atlas would leave, she might actually enjoy herself.

Ice-cold guilt swept over her at the thought, leaving a bitter taste in her mouth. Here she was—comfortably sitting at a table with someone who might have had a hand in her father's murder. Atlas threw her a questioning look when a strangled noise escaped her throat.

"I'm done."

Lillian rose so quickly that her chair fell over, and the three men stared at her with wide eyes as she fled into her room. Inside, she sank down against the door, the weight of the world on her shoulders.

Her father would have been ashamed if he'd seen her tonight. And she didn't even want to think about what Eli would say. Lillian pulled out her father's note from her tunic, and a tear fell down her cheek and dripped onto the wrinkled paper.

After re-reading the note a few times, her heart aching as she thought of her father, she steeled herself and wiped her cheeks. Tears wouldn't make him proud. He'd given her her mother's sword for a reason, and it was time she did something with it. She grabbed the sword, strapped it to her back, sheathed her daggers at her thighs, and flung the door open.

None of the men sat at the table anymore, so Lillian stalked to Atlas's room. The door was open, and Atlas sat on the bed, still in his black uniform trousers and jacket, cleaning one of his daggers. The moonlight streaming through his open window shimmered in his inky black hair and cast the room in a soft, silvery light. She gripped her own daggers tightly and stormed in.

"Are we back to weapons, ice princess?" His green eyes danced with amusement as he studied her, casually flicking his hair out of his face.

"Did you kill my father?" Lillian hissed.

Atlas's playful expression turned cold. He rose from the bed, stalking toward her, and she quickly threw one of the daggers. It lodged in the wall behind him, but not before grazing his ear.

Atlas didn't flinch; he only continued closing the distance between them, and she went cold under his narrowed gaze. For all her talk, she'd never killed anyone before. Lillian readied the second dagger, her other hand twitching toward her sword.

Atlas stopped an inch away, close enough to envelop her with his rich, foresty smell. Gritting her teeth, she tightened her grip on the dagger. But as she thought he would come for her, he side-stepped and closed the door behind her. Glancing at her hand, white from gripping the hilt of her dagger, Atlas rolled his eyes.

"Why would you ask me that?" He bridged the space between them again, towering over her, and bore his green eyes into hers.

She lifted her chin and willed her hands to stop shaking. "I saw the note. About the rebel leader."

Atlas tilted his head. "Did you go through my things, ice princess?"

Lillian glared at him. "Don't try to change the subject. I swear I will kill you." His mouth twitched, and she snarled. "Don't test me, *Commander.*"

Atlas laughed softly. "You won't hurt me, *Lillian.*"

She lifted the dagger, but Atlas only leaned in further, his face close enough that his warm breath caressed her cheek. Her breath hitched in her throat.

"*Ice princess.*" His voice was quiet, soft as velvet, and she didn't have time to react before Atlas disarmed her. "See? I told you you wouldn't hurt me."

Lillian reached for her sword, cursing herself, but Atlas caught her hand. Pulling her flush to him, he shook his head. "Tsk tsk, let's not do that."

She struggled against his hold, but he only gripped her tighter, holding her firmly against his hard body. Lillian growled, her face heating.

"So angry," he mused. "Now that we are not at risk of bloodshed, will you sit down?"

Lillian shook her head, hissing, "I won't sit down with a killer. Let go of my hand."

Atlas laughed under his breath. "I don't think so. We'll do this standing then. I might be a killer, but I did not kill Atli."

Lillian narrowed her eyes. "Did you order him killed?"

She tried to ignore the usual stab at her chest at the reminder her father was dead, biting her bottom lip to stop it from quivering. Atlas's gaze shifted to her mouth, his eyes darkening.

"No, Lillian." A shadow crossed his face. "Believe it or not, but not all non-rebels are evil."

She glared at him. Debatable—Eli and her father had told her enough to prove him wrong. But a small voice inside her reminded her that Finn and Sam weren't rebels. And they were good people.

Atlas pinched his nose, his other hand softening its grip on her arm. "I came too late. The order was to capture him, but some guards are difficult to control."

"Difficult to control?" Lillian raised her voice, her cheeks burning. "They killed him! Cut his head off right in front of me." Her voice broke, and Atlas reached out to touch her face, but she slapped his hand away. "Don't touch me."

Atlas's face hardened into that impenetrable mask he favored. "I didn't know you were there, Lillian. I'm sorry."

A strangled sob escaped her, and she pushed at his chest. Atlas finally released his hold on her arm but stood firm when she pushed him again.

Taking a step back, she cleared her throat. "Did you know who I was when you saw me in the courtyard?"

Atlas nodded slowly. "I did. But I won't turn you in."

She narrowed her eyes, waving her hand for him to continue.

"There is much you don't know, Lillian. But it's not my place to tell you. You should ask your *friend* when he arrives." Atlas's lip curled at the mention of Eli.

A tear fell down her cheek, and before she could slap his hand away again, Atlas reached out and gently wiped it off with his thumb. She stared at his hand as it moved to play with a strand of her white hair.

"I'm so sorry, Lillian," he mumbled.

When she looked up, he stood close enough that she could see the dark green swirls in his eyes. She took another step back.

"If you won't tell me anything else, I think we're done here."

When Lillian turned to leave, Atlas grabbed her hand again. As she met his green gaze, a memory flashed in her mind.

She gasped, "You're the one who stopped me at the market."

Atlas offered her a half-smile. "Couldn't have you getting yourself killed, could I, ice princess."

Shaking her head, she whirled around and left his room.

Chapter Thirty-Three

Her mind spun, and there was no way she could sleep, so instead of returning to her room, Lillian slipped out the front door. She mindlessly walked the dark cobblestone streets, wondering what Atlas had meant with her knowing so little and debating whether she trusted him when he said he wouldn't turn her in. Lillian ached for Eli to get here, if only so she could yell at him for keeping her in the dark.

After a while, she found herself scaling the winding roads up to the castle. The courtyard was dark when she reached it, not a single lantern lighting the stone wall surrounding it. A few guards stood outside the closed metal gates, and she slipped into the shadows of a home outside the wall when they opened, and two guards, with broad swords strapped to their backs, exited the courtyard.

"The king wants us to check on the beast," one muttered.

Holding her breath, Lillian inched closer, following them as they rounded a corner, walking to the back of the castle. She stayed in the shadows, making her steps silent as she kept close to the stone homes lining the road opposite the castle.

The silver dragon glittered in the moonlight when she peeked around the corner. It was still in the gilded cage, mounted to the side of the dark castle, and its nostrils flared as she inched closer.

When it whipped its head toward her, Lillian's eyes widened, and she pressed a finger to her lips as she met its icy-blue eyes.

The dragon blinked and turned to study the two guards approaching the cage while it let out a screech that made Lillian want to cover her ears. The two guards stopped a few feet away, discussing something Lillian couldn't make out and gesturing to each other. The silver dragon screeched again, the sound of its desperation slicing into her heart like a knife. Apparently, the guards had enough of it, as they quickly spun on their heels to return to where they came from.

Lillian hovered in the shadows outside the wall surrounding the back of the castle until she was sure the guards were long gone. Slowly, she stepped out of the darkness and cautiously walked up to the cage. A few lanterns fastened to the castle walls cast their orange light over the grounds, and she prayed no one was standing in the many dark windows of the castle facing it.

As she neared, the dragon opened its mouth, and Lillian quickly raised her hands and whispered, "I will help you, but you can't let anyone know I'm here."

She blew out a breath when the dragon closed its mouth again, eyeing her curiously as she closed the distance between them.

"Hi dragon, I'm Lillian," she whispered when she reached the golden cage, its bars shimmering in the fire from the lanterns. "I'm sorry they're keeping you in here. I promise I will try to get you out." The dragon huffed, its warm breath blowing through her clothes.

Lillian examined the cage, sensing the vibrations of magic that reverberated between the bars. Some kind of magic was definitely subduing it, but there was a lock on the door.

"Can they open this with a key?"

When the dragon inclined its head, Lillian almost laughed.

"Did one of the guards just here have a key?"

The dragon inclined its head again.

Lillian nodded. "I will steal it when I can and let you out. Can you fly?"

She swore the dragon rolled its eyes. "Well, I had to check, didn't

I?" The dragon huffed again, whipping her hair around her face. "I should get going before they find me here. But I will be back. I promise."

When she started to turn, the dragon bent its front knee and lowered its head. Lillian frowned; the black dragon in the meadow had done the same thing. Shaking her head, she slipped into the shadows. When she glanced back, the dragon winked at her before lying down in the gilded cage.

Chapter Thirty-Four

When Lillian entered the kitchen in the morning, a half-asleep Finn greeted her before resting his head on his arms at the table, his golden hair spilling out on the dark wood like the liquor he'd spilled onto it last night. Atlas was gone when the rest of them woke up, leading the preparations for the trial.

"Shouldn't a benefit from living with a commander be getting some clues as to what we can expect today?" Sam greeted them both, his hair tousled but otherwise fresh-faced.

Finn only groaned and threw his head back on the table, but Lillian's stomach began to flutter with nerves. She forced herself to straighten. She would get through the trial today and then think about everything that happened last night.

They were quiet as they walked the winding path to the castle grounds. The sun hung high in the sky, and sweat already pooled inside Lillian's jacket.

She had dressed for war. Black fighting leathers, soft so they were easy to move around in, black boots, her hair in a tight braid falling down her back. Lillian finished by tying a black band over her brow to ensure her hair wouldn't get in the way if it fell loose from the braid. Her mother's sword and bow were strapped to her back, and her daggers were sheathed by her thighs. Atlas had thankfully left the one she'd lodged in his wall on the kitchen table.

She caught Atlas's green stare as soon as they entered the courtyard. His eyes darkened when he took her in, and Lillian quickly averted her eyes, her face heating thinking of their intense exchange yesterday.

Together with Finn and Sam, she joined the other novices. Most were fidgeting, casting nervous glances at the commanders where they stood below the fighting ring. Sweat dripped down the novices' necks, most dressed in similar leathers to Lillian's—good for fighting but unforgiving in the sun.

An ache spread in her chest as she nervously glanced at the group, and for a moment, she wished she'd let Eli join her in the trials. His presence would have soothed the cold dread that slithered up her neck as she studied the table with cups behind Atlas. Lillian sniffed the air, trying to detect the pungent smell of magic. Nothing.

Her stomach churned. She hadn't given the nature of the trials much thought, believing they would mainly focus on physical skills. Swallowing, she squared her shoulders. Too late to turn back now. Keeping her chin high and her gaze ahead, Lillian waited quietly until the last novices walked up and took their places.

"Form a line. Everyone, take a cup and drink. All of it." Commander Jon pointed to the table. Lillian drew a shaky breath and joined the line with Finn and Sam behind her.

When she passed Atlas, he whispered, "Good luck, ice princess," under his breath.

Turning her head over her shoulder, she glared at him. Then she downed the cup in her hand.

She woke up on the ground. Lillian's hands sank into soft dirt as she pushed herself up. Realizing she was blindfolded, she quickly pulled at the cloth and glanced around to orient herself. On the ground beside her were four other novices, who, like Lillian, were just getting to their feet and removing their blindfolds.

The ground was reddish brown, almost clay-like, and smooth, curved walls surrounded them. When Lillian reached out to touch the wall, her hand skimmed effortlessly over its soft surface. She traced her eyes up—far, far up, a glimpse of the clear sky shone through a rounded opening. The sun's rays didn't reach the circular enclosure, the space murky and cold, and Lillian shuddered as she realized the earthy smell must mean they were far underground.

A hand squeezed her shoulder, and she bit down a startled cry before spinning around. Sam's kind eyes met hers, and Lillian threw her arms around him without thinking.

"I, too, am glad we're in this together," he laughed in her ear. She pulled back sheepishly.

"What do you all think this is," another novice asked.

Lillian thought his name could be Olaf, a tall, lankish boy she'd seen slam down opponents in the fighting ring. She'd guessed he was some type of shifter whose animal form lent him increased strength.

"It looks like we've been trapped in here. The only way out appears to be up." Sam pointed to the sliver of sky Lillian had glimpsed before. "I'm guessing we're to face something they won't let us run from." When Sam pointed, something reflected on his arm.

"What is that?" Lillian looked down at her own arm, finding an identical iron bracelet encasing it. A quick check confirmed that they were all wearing them.

"Magic repellent bracelets." The blonde woman she spotted the first day confirmed the suspicion beginning to form in Lillian's mind. The bracelets were identical to the one the sentries placed the baker's son in at the market.

"I guess we're only supposed to use strength then." Sam winced as he inspected the bracelet. "It feels strange, like I've lost a limb."

Lillian hadn't realized he was a magic wielder and was just about to ask about his abilities when a loud crack rang on the other side of the circle. They stood frozen as the reddish ground split in two, opening a dark passage into the space.

"What is that smell?" Lillian wrinkled her nose as she stepped closer to peer into the hole. A faint thumping rose from the darkness.

"Someone, or something, is coming." Lillian backed up as the hair on the back of her neck rose, unstrapped her bow, and pulled an arrow from her quiver. "From the smell, I'm guessing it's not human."

"Everyone spread out in a line. Backs to the wall. If there are several of these things, we don't want them to surround us. Let's keep them in front of us at all times," Sam ordered.

Lillian stared at him; she'd mostly found him quiet so far, but perhaps out of Finn's shadow or in battle was where he thrived. All novices listened and fell into line around Lillian and Sam. Olaf and the blonde woman were to Lillian's right, with Sam and a bald man Lillian didn't know the name of to her left. The bald man was one of the men who laughed that first day. She instantly decided that she did not trust him.

The thumping was louder now, almost in rhythm with Lillian's pounding heart. When the first flicker of movement appeared at the bottom of the black pit, Lillian steeled herself and willed her mind to fall into the cold rage that would help her aim.

She'd been wrong in assuming that whatever was coming was not human. When the first creature emerged from the darkness, it bore human features and gripped a sword in its hand. But there was something off about them.

"They're dead," she gasped.

Sam nodded solemnly in agreement.

The king must have a necromancer. And a strong one, considering the amount of undead pouring out from the pit. Lillian shuddered but didn't have time to contemplate further as the undead descended upon the group of novices. Lillian fired arrow after arrow to hold them off but with little effect.

Disregarding her bow, she unsheathed her mother's sword and began slashing. But no matter how many she tore down, more climbed out of the hole, replacing them. And the ones that went down rose again.

"Their *heads*! *Get their heads!*" Sam barked at them.

Lillian allowed herself a quick glance to her left, wincing as Sam beheaded a particularly gruesome man. He did not rise. She changed her tactic, wishing she'd opted for two swords, and sliced at the undeads' throats.

The assault was never-ending, with more and more bodies crowding the circular space. Lillian stared at the others by her side. They were overwhelmed, gasping for breath in the small moments of reprieve before the area filled yet again.

Lillian growled as yet another undead charged her. There must be something we're missing. Between trying to behead as many undead as possible, Lillian cast desperate glances around the space.

There was no way they could escape through the hole; it was full of undead. The only way out was up. Lillian was already close to the wall but backed up further, using her left hand to feel the wall's outline, her right hand wielding the sword to hold off attackers.

The reddish surface was smooth, with nothing that could be used for traction. Lillian shifted slightly to the left while her arm shook as she deflected a blow from an attacker.

There! There was a small indent on the wall. Lillian pressed her hand against it, and a step extended above her head. When she removed her hand to reach for the step, it retracted again. Remembering what Atlas had said about collaborating, she realized they would have to work together to get up.

"*Over here*," Lillian screamed as loud as she could to get the other's attention, the sound of swords clashing drowning all noise.

Sam glanced her way, and she pointed to the wall, showing him how the step extended and retracted.

"Move to the middle! Form a circle!"

Sam's voice carried better over the chaos, and the novices began fighting their way toward Lillian. Sam reached her first. Standing shoulder to shoulder, they hacked and slashed against the undead that threatened to crush them against the wall.

"I was wondering..." Sam kicked an undead that dove for Lillian. "If they were planning to see who would die from exhaustion first." Sam grinned at her, his face covered in grime and whatever else was leaking from the dead bodies.

Lillian grinned back. "I could go all day."

Sucking in a breath, she ducked under a sword. "I'm surprised they didn't give us an actual challenge."

Sam huffed out a laugh as he beheaded a woman who came a bit too close for Lillian's liking. She shuddered; it was time to get out of here. The undead might be uncoordinated, but their sheer number would overrun them.

"Tell me you have a plan. I'm..." The blonde woman reached them, panting as she tried to hold off two undead who charged her. "I'm losing my mind." She was drenched in grime, and the undead had gotten a few slashes in, blood trickling down her temple.

Lillian nodded, but a particularly eager one charged her before she had time to respond. She spun and kicked him in the chest to get some distance between them. Lillian gripped her sword tight when he charged again, and his head rolled onto the ground.

What was it with the king and beheadings? Unease cascaded through Lillian; she couldn't help but be reminded of her father and Harald.

Finally, all five stood shoulder to shoulder in a half circle, with their backs against the wall.

"What are your names," Lillian demanded. If they were doing this together, they would need to direct each other, and she had a feeling she might be left behind if she referred to the ones she didn't know as 'blondie' and 'baldie.'

Struggling to speak, their voices hoarse as they fought to keep attackers from breaking the circle; they eventually identified themselves one by one. Ketil and Thyra were the novices she hadn't known.

"Cover me."

Lillian stared at Sam, the only one she truly trusted in this group. Backing up to the wall, she showed the others what she'd learned, pausing when a new onslaught had them flip around.

When she'd finally been able to show them, Lillian spoke again. "We'll need to work together." She drew a deep breath, exhaustion laying heavy on her limbs now that she had a moment of reprieve. "Someone has to get up on the step and search for the next one."

Sam met her eyes in understanding while slashing at an undead coming for him. They had to be intentional about the order in which they scaled the wall. It probably wasn't beneath any of the others to leave someone behind.

"Please, let me go first!" Thyra desperately cried.

She was the least skilled of the group, and Lillian doubted she'd be much help anyway once there were fewer of them on the ground.

With a glance at Sam for confirmation, she nodded. "Get on, I will keep pushing. The rest of you will have to continue to cover us."

Ketil opened his mouth, but he shut it quickly after a murderous glance from Lillian.

Thyra backed up, taking cover behind the men, and pulled herself onto the step with surprising strength. Once Thyra was up, the pressure from the indent softened. It appeared to stay in without Lillian pressing it. She relaxed her hold for a second to test out her theory. Thankfully, Thyra didn't come crashing down onto the ground.

"The step stays out as long as someone is on it." Lillian showed her hands. "We'll need to go two and two and pull the last person up. Thyra, let us know when you've found the next one."

Lillian stepped back up to the men, continuing the merciless slashing to keep the bodies away from the wall.

"Take your time up there; it's not like we're in a rush or anything," Ketil spat out.

They all ignored him, too busy with the fresh wave of undead storming them.

"I've found it." Thyra stood on her toes, pressing another indent. "I can't reach the step, though." She reached up with her hand and missed the step by several inches.

"We'll need to get one of you guys up there," Lillian growled as one of the monsters pushed her into Sam's chest. "I won't be able to reach it either."

"Olaf, you go ahead. You're the tallest."

There was no way she was letting Ketil go first; he'd probably reach the top and 'accidentally' leave the rest of them to fall to their death.

Olaf didn't spare them a glance before he backed up and hoisted himself onto the step, joining Thyra. There was barely enough space for the two of them, but somehow Thyra shifted against the wall, allowing Olaf to haul himself onto the next step. Once he was up, Thyra released the pressure on the indent, and Lillian breathed in relief as the second step also stayed out.

Without Olaf, it was becoming increasingly challenging to stew off the undead. Lillian panted as she lifted her sword again and again. She wiped at her forehead with her arm, trying to stop the grime from getting into her eyes.

"Sam." Lillian's voice cracked as she struggled to catch her breath. "You should go next."

Sam turned to her, ready to disagree. Lillian lowered her voice, praying Ketil wouldn't hear.

"I won't be able to reach the second step without someone pulling me up." Kicking another undead back, she continued. "And I am not strong enough to lift you or Ketil if there is a higher step further up. I will have to go last, and I don't trust Ketil to go before you."

Realization flashed across Sam's face.

"We'll have to move fast." In a small moment of reprieve, Sam stared at Lillian and Ketil. "Once I am on the step, don't bother with their heads; just keep them away with whatever means possible." He glanced at Thyra and Olaf. "Olaf, as soon as I'm up, grab her."

They both nodded grimly.

Lillian smirked, "Let's win this stupid challenge. I want a bath."

She tried not to dwell on the fact that she would be alone with these disgusting creatures for as long as it would take Sam to get to the next step. She'd figure it out.

"Ready?" Sam reached out with the hand not holding his sword and touched her cheek.

She winked at him. "I was born ready."

Sam lashed out once more, pushing back as many undead as he could from the new assault, and then turned, swiftly throwing himself onto the step. Lillian stepped closer to Ketil, their backs nearly touching the wall.

"Ketil, go!"

Lillian didn't dare look above her as Ketil left her side, bodies now coming at her from all directions.

Something cold grazed her arm, and sacrificing a few precious seconds, Lillian glanced down. Blood trickled down her shoulder, courtesy of the sword of an undead. She gritted her teeth and continued kicking and pushing as much as slashing with her sword to keep them off her.

"Lillian!"

Lillian searched deep inside her for an extra burst of energy, and with a growl, she cut down the bodies closest to her, spun on her heel, and ran for the step. Her arm burned as she scrambled to pull herself up.

"Go, go, go," she grunted to Ketil as bodies slammed against the wall.

As Sam heaved Ketil onto the second step, Lillian peered down.

"Guys?" *Shit.* "Guys!" The undead piled onto themselves, the first already reaching the step Lillian stood on.

Sam's eyes widened. "Hold on."

He made it to the next step, freeing up space for Lillian. She used her sword to cut down an undead that made it onto the step, then sheathed it and lifted her arms.

"Ketil, pull me up *now*."

When he glanced down, his eyes narrowed, and Ketil hesitated. Willing herself not to panic, Lillian met his eyes.

"I will kill you if you leave me here," she promised through gritted teeth as she kicked another undead snatching for her legs.

Finally, Ketil reached down and gripped her arm. She grabbed him tight, her other hand reaching for the step.

When she was safely on the step, she hissed, "Don't *ever* hesitate again."

Sam's furious face hovered above her. "Come on, they're still coming."

As Ketil reached the next step, Sam grabbed his leather tunic, dragging Ketil's face close to his. "What is wrong with you? She was the one who figured it out. She saved your life!"

Ketil's face turned crimson. "You two think you're so special.

The rest of us see how you suck up to the commander, you know. She's probably sleeping with him to get a spot." He laughed hollowly. "Better rid of you now."

Lillian saw what would happen before it did, screaming Sam's name in warning as Ketil pushed him. Sam's eyes widened before he stumbled backward and fell over the step. Lillian made her decision in a split second.

"Grab my hand!" Her uninjured arm shot out to grab Sam's as he plummeted toward her, her voice cracking as she screamed at him. Lillian's fingers locked onto his sleeve at the same time as his hand wrapped around her arm. Clenching her jaw, she tightened her grip.

"Don't you dare let go," she growled.

The sickening crack of her shoulder dislocating echoed in her ears when her arm stopped his fall. Lillian couldn't hold back a scream, pain shooting through her body at the impact. But thankfully, Sam didn't let go. Panting, she reached out with her other hand to ensure he had a good grip on the step. Once he swung his legs over, Lillian leaned back against the wall, cradling her arm.

Sam rose, his face tight with worry.

"I did ask for a challenge," Lillian got out, trying for a smile. It turned into a grimace with another pulse of pain.

"I'm so sorry, Lillian, but we need to keep going." A glance up confirmed that the others had left, already several steps ahead. And below, the undead still threatened to reach them.

"Can you press the indent?" Sam scanned her arms, both now injured.

Lillian nodded slowly. "It's not like we have another choice."

Sam would have to go first, pulling her up the rest of the steps. There was no way she'd be able to hoist herself up.

Lillian reached out with the arm she could move, gritting her teeth as blood dripped onto her face from the earlier wound, but got the step to extend. Sam quickly scurried up, reaching out a hand to lift her. The pain was almost unbearable, but Lillian kept telling herself that this, *this* was not how she would die. She'd prefer not to be eaten alive or whatever else those creatures would do to her.

They slowly made their way up, one step at a time, and Lillian kept her mind off the pain by imagining ways she would kill Ketil. Below, the undead kept creeping up, but as they neared the opening, they slowed, fewer and fewer reaching the next step. Lillian blew out a breath of relief.

When Sam pulled her onto the final step, Lillian wanted to cry from happiness, wishing for nothing but solid ground under her feet. But she paused, quietly asking Sam to wait.

"You need to relocate my shoulder before we ascend. We don't know what waits beyond this wall. It could be another part of the trial. Or Ketil could be waiting to finish what he started."

While plotting Ketil's death, she realized that Atlas's instructions not to hurt each other hadn't been extended to the trials. And she really needed to be able to use her arm in case she was right, however painful it may be.

Sam furrowed his brow. "We should wait. If I can get this stupid bracelet off, I can help you."

Lillian wondered if he meant that he was a healer. That would be wonderful. But she shook her head. "We can't risk it."

She began explaining how to relocate her shoulder, but Sam interrupted her. "I have a brother. And we got hurt a lot when we were younger, so I've done this a time or two."

Nodding, she turned so he would have better access.

"Ready?"

Lillian met his eyes, but Sam pulled her arm into place with a loud crunch before she could confirm. She cursed violently, calling Sam a few unwarranted names.

"Sorry, sorry. I thought it might be easier if you weren't prepared."

Lillian flexed her fingers, painful, but she had movement back. "Alright, let's get out of this hellhole."

Chapter Thirty-Five

Light blinded her as they crawled over the ledge. Lillian blinked against the sun, keeping a hand on her weapons as her eyes adjusted.

"You made it."

Lillian drew her daggers at the voice, stepping in front of Sam. Commander Jon stood a few feet from the edge, his black uniform forming a dark silhouette against the clear sky surrounding them. They were on solid ground, the commander the only other person there. Lillian slowly lowered the daggers but kept them ready in her hands.

Other openings lined the barren ground around them, and faint screaming rose from some of them. Her chest tightened at the thought of Finn and Astrid still down there. Lillian prayed that they had already ascended.

"Step forward, novices."

Lillian tensed, but Commander Jon only motioned for them to reach out their arms, using some type of key to remove the iron bracelets. Sam sighed at whatever release the absence provided. Lillian felt nothing.

Commander Jon directed them to a stone staircase carved into the steep grass-less hill they stood upon. At the bottom, the rest of the novices who had passed waited. They stood huddled in a small meadow surrounded by tall trees, and Lillian and Sam were to join them. Lillian started toward the staircase, eager to escape the smell of death and decay still filling her nostrils.

"Wait," Sam gently touched her arm, careful of her injuries. "Since I caused some of these, can I help you?" He pointed to her arms.

"You didn't do this. It was all that damn Ketil's fault."

"Regardless, I can help."

Lillian nodded, offering Sam a small smile.

"I need to touch you for this to work." Sam glanced at her for permission.

Lillian shrugged, then winced as another jolt of pain seared through her shoulder.

"Please."

When her father still believed someone could cure her, she met a new healer almost every month, and most of them also required a physical connection. Edla had, she remembered, a pang of a different sort of pain hitting her chest. That night when Edla healed Eli seemed so long ago—when her only concern had been getting a better mission.

She'd been so naive.

Sam lifted his hands and placed them on each one of her arms. His magic tickled like a soft vibration across her skin, and Lillian moaned as the pain dulled into a light ache, no worse than after a tough day of training. Glancing down, she found her skin healed and no bruising around her shoulder.

Lillian rolled her shoulders, offering Sam a broad grin. "Thank you. I feel brand new. And ready to kill Ketil."

Sam chuckled. "You'll still be sore for a while."

Lillian scanned the group for their friends as they descended the stairs. But only a handful of novices stood in the clearing or sat against the large trees to get shade from the sun beating down on them. She was surprised that so few had finished. It felt like they had been in that hellhole forever.

To the right, the three novices that had left them behind stood, and Lillian bared her teeth when she caught Ketil's gaze. His eyes widened for a moment before he turned his back on her.

As she made to stalk over to him, the smell of trees and night filled her nostrils, and Atlas spoke behind her.

"You took your time. The rest of your group has been here for a while."

Lillian was about to snarkily respond that they had nearly died when Atlas stepped in front of her. He was disheveled, his black hair tangled around his face, and his green eyes were feral as he raked them over her body.

"It's good to see you too, commander." She winked at him, and the corners of his mouth lifted slightly before he stalked off to speak to Commander Jon, who had followed them down the stairs.

Sam shot her a strange look, but Lillian just shrugged.

Strong arms wrapped around her waist and spun her around. "We made it, silver girl!"

Once Finn let go, Lillian turned and wrapped her arms around him, hugging him tight. She wasn't sure if it was the adrenaline, but her heart beat faster, knowing he was in one piece.

"Look at that; she shows affection," Finn laughed. "You must have had a near-death experience down there."

Sam shook his head and mumbled, "You have no idea."

Lillian elbowed him. "It wasn't that bad. We didn't end up as dinner."

Wincing, Sam elbowed her back. "Yes, it was."

They stood huddled together under a tall tree to get shade from the relentless sun as they waited for the rest of the novices to finish. Lillian nervously scanned the stone stairs above them for red hair while Sam asked about Finn's experience.

It had been similar to theirs, albeit no one was left behind. However, the undead overran one of the novices, and they couldn't save him before they stumbled upon the hidden steps.

Finn's voice shook as he recounted the terror they'd been through, and Lillian reached out to grip his hand. He shot her a grateful smile and squeezed hers quickly.

A commotion atop the stairs interrupted their hushed conversation, and they whipped their heads up. Commander Eirik held Astrid by her arms while the redhead fought his grip and screamed at the mongrel Lillian encountered the first day. They were the only ones returning from their group.

When they reached the bottom, Lillian ran up to them.

"Let her go." Lillian tried to keep her voice calm as she glared at the commander, but worry made it sharp.

"Gladly. As long as she behaves. If she hurts him, she is out." Commander Eirik gave her a blank stare.

"Him?" Lillian pointed to the enormous man. "How do you expect *her* to hurt *him*?"

The commander shrugged and let Astrid go. She ran straight into Lillian's arms.

"Hush, it's okay," Lillian spoke softly into her ear as Astrid began crying.

"He killed them, Lillian. We were almost at the top, and he pushed them all down." Astrid hiccupped. "He would have killed me too if I hadn't managed to cut him and pull myself up."

Lillian held her friend tighter, stroking her flaming red hair. She silently vowed to take down that monster and Ketil with the king. Lillian stayed with Astrid, separated from the rest, as they waited for the final group to emerge. Astrid eventually stopped crying but wouldn't answer any questions, her eyes cast down.

Lillian tried to distract her by telling her stories of how it was to live with the 'sex-on-legs soldiers.' When Lillian told her that Sam was scared of the dark because of a particularly gruesome story his father told him as a child, Astrid finally raised her eyes.

"I've done more digging since we looked into the Valkyries."

Lillian hushed her, casting a nervous glance at the rest of the group. Thankfully, most were tending to injuries or recounting the events, sitting down on the grassy ground beneath the trees surrounding the meadow.

"We can't talk about this here, Astrid; it's not safe."

Astrid glared at her defiantly. "Then we need to talk soon. I am tired of all this death, Lillian. I want to do something."

Narrowing her eyes, Lillian studied her friend. Astrid had almost word-for-word echoed what she had told Eli a week ago. But, since this wasn't the place to ask her what she suspected, which would get them both instantly killed if overheard, she only nodded.

"I promise."

When the last group emerged, thankfully all five in one piece, Commander Jon informed them that they had all passed the trial and would move on to the second stage. There would be no more formal training between trials, but they were welcome to use the equipment in the courtyard if they wanted.

Lillian quickly estimated how many were left as they began a somber trek back to the city. Twenty-one novices walked quietly through the dense forest. Nine of them had died today.

Even if she hadn't known them personally, a twinge of sadness filled Lillian—such a waste of nine young lives.

Chapter Thirty-Six

Finn convinced them they needed to let off some steam when they finally entered the city walls. He knew of a tavern where there would be live music, and they allowed anyone who wanted to take the stage. Surprisingly, several of the novices decided to join, including Atlas and Commander Jon.

When Ketil and the other monster also made to join, Lillian hissed that they'd not see the sunrise if they stepped one foot within the tavern.

Thankfully, they listened. Her cutting off their private parts was probably not what Finn had meant by letting off steam.

Sam offered Astrid his arm, making it his mission to make the red-haired girl smile, and kept them entertained with wild stories from his and his brother's adventures growing up as they walked through the bustling city while the sun set behind the castle and cast flickering shadows on the stone homes lining the pebbled road.

Despite Sam's smile, his brown eyes darkened when someone asked about his parents. He mumbled that they had passed when he was a child, that it was only him and his brother now. Lillian locked eyes with him, the sorrow inside her mirrored in his kind eyes.

Finn, affectionate as always, took Lillian's hand and was content walking beside her quietly, listening to Sam's stories. Her scalp tingled, and Lillian glanced over her shoulder, catching Atlas studying them, frowning.

When Finn snorted, Lillian narrowed her eyes. "What?"

Finn grinned at her, then released her hand. "Just wanted to see if I was right."

Lillian glared at him. "What do you mean?"

"Nothing." Finn laughed softly. "What was that I heard about researching Valkyries earlier?"

Lillian froze, scanning the novices walking beside them.

"Don't worry, I think everyone else was preoccupied. And it doesn't seem like many of us have my super hearing," Finn winked.

Lillian shook her head. "I'll tell you later."

"You better." Finn grabbed her hand again.

The dim tavern was nearly empty when they arrived, and Lillian was relieved when no fire burned in the back of it; instead, all windows were open, allowing the cool evening breeze to blow through the tavern. The group spread out across different tables. Sam, Finn, Astrid, and Lillian snagged their own.

"May I join you?" They all raised their eyebrows when Atlas pointed to the empty chair.

Finn pulled it out. "Of course, Atlas. But the first drinks are on you."

Atlas smiled at him and nodded, then walked back to the bar.

"Did he just smile, or am I actually losing it?" Astrid stared at the commander's back.

Lillian blew out a breath. It was good to see Astrid speak again. "I think it might have been a tic," she joked.

When Atlas returned with the drinks, some type of golden liquor, the group shared stories from their childhoods. Sam and Finn were in their prime, making the rest of them cry from laughter at their stories. When Finn told an unlikely tale about sneaking aboard a pirate ship, Lillian rolled her eyes, and Finn stuck out his tongue at her.

"So Atlas, how did you grow up to become the big bad commander?" Astrid's words slurred slightly, and Lillian discreetly switched her cup of liquor to water.

Atlas, having been mostly quiet so far, paused.

"It's a family tradition," he finally responded.

"So your father was also a commander?" Sam asked.

Lillian was silently glad for the questioning, curious to learn more about the mysterious Atlas.

"Yes, something like that."

Astrid narrowed her eyes. Leaning close to Lillian, she whispered, "He's lying."

Lillian studied Atlas, but before she could ask a follow-up question, a small stage formed in the tavern's center, people moving the wooden tables so they faced the circular space, and the singing began. Anyone who wanted was welcome to come up and entertain the crowd with a song.

As the night went on, the crowd became braver, liquid courage coursing through their veins. The songs changed from the family-friendly ones they sang at holidays to more daring ones. Most of the latter songs were new to Lillian, and a particularly crude one threatened a blush to creep up her neck. She fixed her gaze intently on her drink, avoiding eye contact at all costs.

"Lillian, you should go up there." Finn gestured toward the stage.

She shook her head violently. "No, thank you."

"Aw, come on." Sam jumped in. "I have a feeling you're a great singer."

Lillian was quite a good singer if she could say so herself, but she would not go up there. She had no idea what she would sing anyway.

"I'll only do it if Atlas does a song first," she winked at them.

"Sure."

She whipped her head around. Atlas stared back at her, a challenge in his eyes.

"What do you mean?"

Atlas offered her a lazy smile. "I said sure, I'll do it."

Lillian couldn't believe her eyes when he confidently approached the stage.

"He got you there." Finn grinned at her, the rest snickering as Lillian stared after Atlas, her mouth open in disbelief.

Atlas sang an old song about a man meeting the love of his life in a forest. It was an upbeat tune, and Atlas's deep voice was perfect for the lyrics. The whole tavern clapped when Atlas walked through the crowd, serenading some of the women.

Lillian couldn't stop the corners of her mouth from turning up as Atlas enjoyed himself. His shoulders relaxed, and a playful smile graced his face as he tapped the tables in tune with the music. There was no sign of the troubled commander she was used to.

Atlas turned to their table, and Astrid howled with laughter as he approached Lillian to sing the chorus, his eyes locked on her. Lillian's face burned, and she buried it in her hands until Atlas finished the song.

"A little on the nose, but great job, Atlas." Finn grinned and clapped him on the back as he returned to the table.

Lillian refused to meet Atlas's eyes, the blush still painting her face crimson from the attention.

"Your turn, ice princess," Atlas purred.

Nausea rolled through her, and she was suddenly not opposed to another round with the undead instead of stepping onto that stage. She'd never sung in public. But Lillian straightened her back and flicked her white hair over her shoulder.

"Enjoy the show."

While her steps were steady, her hands shook when she took the stage. She fidgeted with her leather tunic. Lillian knew she could not pull off a show like Atlas had just done, but she could sing her favorite song.

It was one of the old songs that everyone in the tavern would know about a man who wished for a little bit more time to settle his affairs before he died.

Closing her eyes, Lillian cleared her throat and began to sing. Her voice was strong, and she let the emotions from her own fate seep into it, the notes falling and rising as she sang about precious time and leaving loved ones behind.

Drowning out the tavern's sounds, she pretended she was

singing back home in her favorite clearing. When she let the last notes fade away, Lillian opened her eyes.

The tavern had gone quiet.

When Lillian lifted her gaze to her friends, Atlas rose to his feet, clapping. The rest of the tavern followed. She tipped her head forward, covering her crimson face with her hair as she gave them all a slight bow and walked back to the table.

As she went to sit down, receiving compliments and claps on the back from her friends, she glanced around the tavern. Her eyes locked with familiar blue ones. Lillian blinked. But Eli still stood there, his bright blue eyes lined with silver as he watched her.

"You look like you've seen a ghost," Atlas elbowed her.

Lillian shook her head, "Not a ghost."

She rose from the table and stumbled toward Eli. Her friends' eyes burned into her back as she, not very gracefully, flung herself into Eli's arms.

"Hi, Lil," he whispered in her ear.

She swallowed, too emotional to get any words out. Lillian hadn't realized how much she'd missed him, her piece of home.

She pulled him closer, wrapping her hands in his soft auburn hair.

"I can't believe you're here."

Eli hummed in agreement and then pulled back to look at her, cupping her cheek. "You look different. I can't put my finger on it."

Lillian was about to joke about how near-death experiences will do that to you but caught herself. He'd just been crying from her sad song—no need to remind him of how close to death she really was. Instead, she smiled at him, and he pulled her close, brushing his lips against hers.

"Come. I want you to meet my friends."

Lillian dragged Eli to the table where her friends still gawked at them. She quickly introduced them all, pulling up another chair. Lillian's stomach churned when she realized she had placed herself between Atlas and Eli. She straightened her back as the two men sized each other up, the tension rolling off them quieting the table. Atlas studied Eli with a tight face, a furrow between his brows.

"How do you two know each other?" Astrid also eyed Eli, raising an eyebrow as she met Lillian's eyes.

Eli told them how he and Lillian had grown up together, how he was Lillian's father's familiar. Finn eyed her curiously when Eli got to that part. Peeking at him from under her lashes, she shrugged, trying to convey this was also a *later* conversation.

"What are you doing here," Atlas demanded, and Lillian flinched at his harsh tone.

"I'm here to see Lillian," Eli placed a possessive arm around her shoulders and glared at him. "Why are you here."

Lillian almost choked on her drink. Atlas didn't respond, only raised his eyebrows before staring into his drink.

Eli pulled her closer, her wooden chair scraping the floor as he almost pulled her into his lap. While she settled against his chest, she glanced at Finn and immediately wished she hadn't. His eyes glittered as he winked at her.

"Best show of the night," Finn mouthed.

Lillian threw him a murderous glare before returning to sitting in awkward silence between Atlas and Eli.

After listening to Atlas and Eli taking digs at each other for a while, to Finn's immense amusement, the group decided to call it a night. The boys waited a short way from the tavern as Lillian stayed back with Eli.

"Where are you staying?" Atlas would likely have a problem with Eli coming back with them, but if he didn't have another place to stay, she'd make him agree.

"I'm with a friend. Where are *you* staying?" Eli looked pointedly at her when the men strained their necks, clearly trying to eavesdrop on their conversation. Lillian prayed Finn wouldn't hear *everything*.

"It's a long story, but I'm staying with them. They helped me."

Eli narrowed his eyes. "With that commander, Lillian? What are you thinking?"

Not used to this new, possessive version of him, Lillian reached out to grab his hand. "I'd be happy to tell you everything, but we need time. You owe me some explanations as well, it seems there are a few things you haven't told me."

She couldn't bring herself to be angry about the information he'd been withholding; she was too happy that he was here with her. When worry flashed in Eli's eyes, Lillian eyed him questioningly. He shook his head and promised they would speak. They agreed to meet at midday after they'd both had a full night's sleep.

Eli pulled her in for a hug, and she held him tight, relaxing against his familiar chest. A small part of her heart finally pieced itself together at the strong arms that stroked her back, and she nestled her face into his neck, breathing in his scent.

"Let's not be apart again," Lillian whispered.

Eli nodded and pulled back slightly, sliding his hands into her hair before he kissed her.

It wasn't the gentle kisses he usually favored; Eli kissed her firmly, his grip in her hair tightening as she let out a soft sigh. Lillian giggled when Eli nipped her bottom lip before trailing his lips down her face and gently kissing her neck.

"Let's not," he breathed against her skin.

Before joining the men, Lillian turned back momentarily, watching Eli round a corner. There was a reflection of red hair beside him. Lillian squinted to see better, but Eli disappeared into the darkness.

Chapter Thirty-Seven

When they got home, Atlas stalked straight into his room, slamming the wooden door so hard the cups on the kitchen shelves shook. Sam mumbled something about being too tired for this and closed the door to his room as well.

Grinning, Finn turned to her. "What a day! How about a nightcap?" Lillian nodded; she was too jittery to sleep anyway.

They brought a bottle of ale into Lillian's room and sat on the scratched wooden floor, speaking in hushed voices to not wake the other two. Lillian lit a candle on her bedstand that flickered in Finn's amber eyes as he settled with his back against her bed.

Finn demanded that she tell him everything about the research of the Valkyries, so Lillian recounted what they had found out, including her growing suspicions about Astrid being a rebel.

Finn nodded gravely. "I've heard never to trust a redhead."

Lillian shoved him. "Finn! Do you take anything seriously?"

He shoved back but then laid down on the wooden floor with his arms behind his head. "I do. I think she might be onto something."

"You think there actually might be an heir out there?" Lillian wrapped her arms around her legs, glancing at the moon that shone through her small window.

Finn turned his head to look at her. "Would it be so far-fetched? I know it's a children's tale, but they all have some truth to them."

Lillian nodded. Astrid had said the same thing.

"The king *is* collecting children with strong gifts. Either he is looking for something or afraid of someone challenging him. Maybe both," Finn mused. "I also saw ravens when I flew on Hindra. I don't know if they were actually Valkyrie ravens, but they *are* out at night."

She hummed in agreement, tapping her fingers against the wooden floor. Perhaps there was something to it.

"But onto a more important question: what is going on with Atlas and Eli?"

Lillian groaned, hiding her face in her hands as Finn laughed. She wished she knew what Eli was hiding. Atlas's hostility toward Eli must be because of something he had found out, and she only prayed it wasn't bad enough for him to turn them in, even if he hadn't seemed inclined to so far. When she refused to respond, Finn thankfully switched subjects, and they spoke about anything and everything until the gray morning light seeped through the windows.

When Lillian woke, Finn snored softly on the floor. She placed a blanket over him before she sneaked out of the room. The apartment was quiet when she entered the kitchen to get some food. Lillian grabbed an apple and went out in the early morning.

Few people were outside, the day still early, so Lillian didn't worry too much about being seen as she made her way to the rooftop. Even if it was daytime, she needed some time alone, and the roof was becoming her sanctuary. But as she scaled the ladder, there was rustling above her. Lillian debated whether to climb down and find another spot but decided to keep going. Maybe she could get more answers from Atlas before she demanded them from Eli.

Atlas sat on the ledge, his legs hanging down the side of the building and the morning sun reflecting in his black hair. For the first time since she met him, he wasn't wearing the black guard uniform but a green tunic in the same shade as his deep green eyes.

Lillian walked over and took a seat next to him. He didn't seem surprised to find her there, studying her intently as she sat down.

She poked him. "Still in a mood, I see."

Atlas sighed, impatiently brushing a hand through his hair. "Did you ask your friend what he's been hiding?"

Definitely still in a mood. Lillian tilted her head. "Not yet. But maybe you can tell me?"

When he didn't respond, she stuck out her bottom lip. "Please, Atlas." His mouth twitched even as he rolled his eyes. "What am I missing?"

Atlas turned to face her. "Based on your conversation with Finn yesterday, and you guys seriously need a lesson in keeping your voices down, I think you're getting closer to finding it out."

"Do you mean the Valkyries?" She ignored his comment on overhearing them, silently praying he hadn't heard what Finn had asked about him.

"I've been hearing the same things. Wings in the night, and whispers of the Valkyries stirring."

Lillian frowned. If Atlas had also heard about this, Eli would surely be aware.

"So you believe there is an heir out there? But even so, what would it matter?"

Atlas shot her a strange look. "The heir is the rightful Queen of Orios, Lillian. She is the only one who can make the Valkyries and dragons come back."

"So why hasn't she stepped forward?"

Atlas mumbled, "That's what I am also trying to figure out." But then he shook his head. "You need to be careful the next few days and trials, ice princess. I heard you've made some enemies in the novice group."

She winked at him. Ketil and the rest were the least of her worries. "I think they need to be careful, not me."

Atlas huffed, glaring at her, but didn't push it.

They sat in comfortable silence, the sun warming their faces. When the sun was at its highest point in the sky, Lillian realized she needed to go to meet Eli.

She placed a hand on Atlas's shoulder. "Thank you for being honest with me, Atlas."

His face hardened, but he reached out to tuck a stray strand of hair behind her ear. "Don't thank me, ice princess. I told you, I am no hero."

Lillian frowned but didn't have time to ask him what he meant unless she wanted to keep Eli waiting, so she just shrugged and left him on the roof.

Chapter Thirty-Eight

Eli waited for her outside the tavern, and her heart began racing as soon as she met his blue eyes. When a grin spread across his face, Lillian ran the last few steps and threw herself into his waiting arms. She held him tight, and he laughed softly. "I think I prefer this to a broken nose."

Lillian snorted and nestled her face into his warm neck, releasing a breath of release at his familiar scent.

After a while, Lillian reluctantly pulled back and made to walk into the tavern, but Eli grabbed her hand, explaining that he had a safe place for them to talk. He led her through the winding cobblestone streets while they discussed the trials.

His jaw clenched when she told him about Ketil, and she quickly changed the subject, instead filling him in about Finn and the surprise of finding out he was her bonded familiar. Eli didn't question her decision not to accept the bond, only squeezed her hand, perhaps understanding better than anyone why Lillian didn't want to subject Finn to the pain of her death.

When Eli asked her how she was feeling, Lillian cleared her throat. "I'm okay."

Eli nodded, although worry filled his eyes as he studied her face.

She gently brushed his copper hair out of his face. "Eli, something else happened one of the first days." Eli eyed her questioningly, and she continued, lowering her voice. "I saw Harald. They..." Her voice broke.

Eli looked down at his leather boots, nodding. "I know." He gripped her hand tighter. "We'll talk more when we get there."

They fell silent, walking slowly through the sunlit pebbled road.

After a while, they arrived at a small stone house with broken windowsills and a rotting door that was almost falling off its hinges. It was set slightly apart from the rest of the homes surrounding it, although they all seemed abandoned, with dark windows and doors hanging ajar.

Eli knocked, three hard knocks followed by two soft ones, and a man opened the creaking door, quietly waving them inside the murky house. Lillian didn't get a good look at his face before they stepped inside, but once the door closed, she turned to face him.

She couldn't stop herself from flinching. Scarred, burned skin covered almost every inch of the man's face, and his long blonde hair, hanging loosely around his cheeks, did little to cover it.

He offered her a small smile, his blue eyes kind as they met hers. "Don't worry. Most people react the same way."

Lillian forced a smile and waved awkwardly at him. "I'm sorry. I'm Lillian."

"Hi, Lillian, I'm Aksel."

She smiled wider, keeping her eyes on his, knowing all too well what it was like to have people stare at her for being different.

Aksel motioned for them to join him in the small kitchen. They made small talk while Aksel boiled water for tea, placing three large mugs on the table. Lillian sipped it while Eli explained that Aksel was also part of the rebellion. The king had taken him as a child, his gift allowing him to sense what magic others possessed.

"Is that how you were burned?" Lillian hoped he wouldn't take offense to her asking.

Aksel's eyes darkened. "The king has his methods to make you cooperate."

He'd been in the king's service, helping him identify children with magic, for almost eight years before he was able to escape.

Aksel had been working with the rebels ever since, finding and hiding people with those gifts.

"So is that your mission then? Rescuing the children that have been taken?" She looked pointedly at Eli.

He clasped his hands on top of the table. "Yes. Before Harald was caught..." Eli swallowed. "He got the word out that the king probably keeps them somewhere below the castle until he has a large enough group. After that, they're shipped off—but we're not sure where."

Eli went on to explain that they believed the king offered the children a place in his army, but not before they were starved and desperate so that they would be more amenable.

Lillian leaned forward in her chair, studying the two men closely. "So he's not looking for the Valkyrie heir?"

Aksel frowned, but Eli's eyes widened slightly before he furrowed his brows.

"Eli."

Eli drew a deep breath. "Those are just rumors, Lillian. We've heard them too, but we haven't seen anything that points to her existence."

Lillian narrowed her eyes. She wished Astrid was here, as a sinking feeling in her gut told her Eli was lying.

"A Valkyrie heir. That would mean King Ivar and Queen Liv had a child?" Aksel stared at Lillian, who nodded. "I haven't heard these rumors, but I always felt the king was looking for something specific. I thought it was any gift that could pose a threat to him, but what if it was a specific person," he mused.

"It's just a rumor," Eli interrupted. "We need to focus on finding the children. King Alek already has the numbers. We won't stand a chance if he also has every strong magic wielder on his side."

Lillian raised her eyebrows at his cold tone. "Don't we also want to save the children from what sounds like an awful fate?"

"Of course, Lil." Eli waved his hand dismissively. "Aksel, have we heard anything more about the Crown Prince?"

Aksel affirmed the reports that the Crown Prince was indeed on Echo, but no one had been able to confirm where he was or what he was doing. None of the rebels had met him, and they received contradictory information about what he looked like.

They spent the next few hours making a plan for finding the children. Eli tried to stop Lillian from joining, arguing that she needed to focus on the upcoming trial, but when she persisted, he finally agreed to include her. Aksel and Eli would study the guard movements tonight, and tomorrow evening, the three of them would sneak into the castle to search for them. When the room dimmed, Eli suggested it was time to call it a night.

Lillian extended her hand in goodbye to Aksel, but when his hand touched hers, he recoiled, releasing her as if he'd burned himself.

"What *are* you?" he gasped, staring at her with wide eyes.

Lillian narrowed her eyes. "What do you mean?"

"She's sick, Aksel." Eli glared at him, pulling Lillian into his arms.

Mumbling apologies, Aksel let them out the door. Lillian felt his eyes trail her as they walked down the street.

Chapter Thirty-Nine

Lillian woke early, the morning sun shining in through her window. Her stomach growled, and when she rose from the bed, her head spun. The boys snored softly in their rooms, so she decided to make breakfast. She'd never cooked much, but how hard could it be?

"Is something burning?" Finn came out of his room, yawning.

Lillian threw him a dirty look while wiping her sweaty forehead with her sleeve. "I cooked breakfast."

Atlas and Sam also exited their rooms, both sniffing the air suspiciously.

"What *is* this?" Atlas picked up one of the sausages from the table.

It was maybe a little burned, Lillian admitted. But there were so many things to manage she'd forgotten about them for a second.

"Breakfast," she glowered at him and gestured for them to sit at the table.

Sam inspected one of the potatoes. "Is this even cooked?"

Atlas and Finn snickered as Lillian threw a piece of bread at him. She stared at them with narrowed eyes until they began eating. Lillian picked up a piece of bacon and popped it into her mouth. What in Orios? She couldn't stop herself from spitting it out.

"Ugh. What did I do?" The boys howled with laughter.

They threw out everything that she had tried and miserably

failed to cook. Thankfully, the bread came from the baker, and she'd managed to brew a regular pot of tea.

There was a knock on the door when they cleared the plates. They glanced at each other questioningly, but no one was expecting anyone. Atlas went to the door.

Astrid followed him back into the kitchen. Her face turned crimson as she glanced between the males in the room. When no words escaped Astrid, Lillian took pity on her and dragged the girl into her room, closing the door.

"I don't understand how you manage with all these men around you all the time," Astrid winced.

Lillian snorted. "I grew up with only my father and Eli. I'm used to it."

They spoke about the trial briefly, and Lillian was relieved that Astrid's spirits were up despite what they had been through.

A soft knock interrupted their conversation, and Finn poked his head through the door. "We're getting out of here. Atlas knows of a place outside the city where we can swim."

Lillian glanced at Astrid. "Want to go?" She nodded.

Atlas led them through the bustling city, out past the outposts, and after about an hour walking through the forest, he pointed at the thinning tree line ahead. "We're here."

Lillian sucked in a breath when a grassy clearing opened up, a glittering lake in its center, surrounded by tall trees that cast welcome shade from the summer sun. Atlas hadn't mentioned that the place he knew was an oasis.

"How did you find this?" Lillian breathed in the flowery, clean scent of the meadow.

"I stumbled upon it." Atlas winked at her and gestured toward the lake. "Come on, let's get in the water."

The boys ran ahead, and when they all began to undress, Lillian didn't know where to look, a blush creeping up her neck. One look at Astrid's crimson face and wide eyes, and she couldn't stop a small giggle from escaping.

Finn and Sam were the picture of strength and vitality; their golden skin stretched taut over their strong muscles. But Atlas was something else. When he pulled his tunic off, he revealed a muscular upper body covered in swirling black tattoos, like plumes of darkness dancing across his skin. They wound around his body, accentuating his muscles in a pattern Lillian wanted to trace with her fingers. She couldn't tear her eyes away, mesmerized by the intricacy.

Lillian blinked, and when she finally dragged her gaze away, Finn grinned at her from where he already floated in the clear water. She narrowed her eyes and drew a finger across her throat when he opened his mouth. Quickly removing her tunic and trousers, keeping her boned corset and undergarments on, Lillian made her way to the water's edge. She'd drown Finn if she had to.

The water was cool as it washed over her feet, clear enough that she could see the sandy bottom and the small fish swimming around her ankles, their colorful scales reflecting in the sun. Eyes burned on her face, and she lifted her gaze to find Atlas staring at her. His mouth hung slightly open, and his eyes darkened as they traced her body.

Her face heated, and she quickly dove into the water, swimming below the surface for a few strokes. When she finally came up for air, Lillian was thinking clearly again.

They spent the afternoon swimming and playing in the water. Astrid, opting not to swim, sunned in the soft green grass. When her body was as wrinkled as a raisin, Lillian joined her. She lay in the tall grass, letting the sun dry her hair and body as she watched fluffy white clouds trail across the sky above the treetops. The men floated in the water, quietly discussing tomorrow's second trial. Lillian shut them out. She didn't want to think about the trial—she needed to focus on tonight's mission.

Interrupting her thoughts, Astrid propped herself up on her elbow, her red hair spilling out like blood in the green grass. "I found more information about the Valkyrie heir."

Lillian narrowed her eyes. "Why is this so important to you?"

Astrid gave her a pointed look, "Lillian, I know you're clever. I'm sure you've figured it out by now."

Lillian played with a strand of her white hair. She had her suspicions, but the fact that Astrid hadn't been fully trained, her poor archery and swordplay skills, puzzled her. Her father always told her the rebels were the best fighters in Orios. Well, except for the Valkyries, maybe.

Lillian knitted her brow. "Why are you telling me this?"

"Because we want the same thing." Astrid smiled at her, and Lillian couldn't help herself; she grinned back. It was nice to have a female friend and someone on the same side as her.

"Tell me what you've found out." Even if Eli didn't believe in the rumors, Lillian wanted to have as much information as possible. Being in the dark had done her no good.

Astrid had returned to the library and found a book detailing King Alek's attack on the previous royals. Lillian nodded; she was familiar with the story. Too familiar, with her mother being a casualty of the attack. But the book also referenced the curse that Adeon placed on Queen Liv and King Ivar. While Astrid hadn't found any information about the curse itself, it did speak to who it had been placed on—the royal family.

"Do you see? It doesn't only reference Liv and Ivar. It references their *family*." Astrid stared at her expectantly.

Lillian furrowed her brow. It seemed pretty far-fetched to believe an heir existed from what could just be the choice of words of whoever had written the book. But she promised Astrid they would go back together after the second trial to find out more.

It wasn't until after Lillian parted ways with Astrid that she realized she hadn't asked Astrid how she'd known Lillian was a rebel.

Chapter Forty

That night, Lillian waited until the apartment was quiet before she sneaked out. Staying close to the stone homes lining the winding path, she quickly made her way to the castle. Lillian hesitated when she caught her breath at the top of the hill. She ached to stop by the silver dragon, reminding it that she hadn't forgotten about her promise. But Eli was waiting, and she doubted he would agree to her risking their mission for a dragon. With a final glance to the back of the castle, Lillian promised herself she'd go back tomorrow.

Eli and Aksel's shadows betrayed them before she heard them, two dark shapes against the wall surrounding the castle.

"I think you both need a refresher in evading detection," she whispered as she approached.

Pointing at their shadows, she directed them to a more hidden spot. Once she was confident that no sentries would stumble upon them, she asked Eli what they had learned.

"The guards switch rotation one hour past midnight. The one at the main gate enjoys drinking on duty. We bribed one of the maids to offer him a cup of ale, in which we've placed a sleeping aid. Once he has fallen asleep, we'll sneak in," Eli explained.

Lillian tensed; his plan had quite a few pitfalls, too many people who could falter. But they didn't have time to formulate a new one, so she kept her mouth shut. They stood quietly in a dark alleyway opposite the metal gates waiting for the maid to bring out the drink. Aksel kept his distance, staying as far away from Lillian as possible.

"I'm not contagious, you know," she whispered, giving him a pointed look.

Aksel nodded, but his mouth remained tight, and he moved no closer. Lillian raised her eyebrows but didn't push him when Eli shook his head.

The lone guard sat against the stone wall, picking at his nails. His black uniform was rumpled, and he wasn't even armed; his sword leaned against the wall several feet from him.

When the maid finally came out, Lillian held her breath, but Eli was right; the guard downed the ale in one go before he returned the cup to the maid. As the maid walked off, he topped it off with a swig from his flask. A few minutes later, the guard toppled over, snoring a bit too loudly for Lillian's liking. Eli and Aksel shifted his body so that it wasn't blocking the entrance or in sight of anyone who might pass. Then they slipped into the castle.

The dark stone walls that towered so jarringly over Lillian on her first glimpse of the castle were stifling, as if they were keeping the air out of the long hallways. The smell of the smoke that had once filled the long hallways, burning its victims alive, filled Lillian's nostrils, and her hands trembled when she brushed them over her daggers. Shaking her head, she scolded herself. The castle was scary enough without her imagination running wild.

She focused her eyes on the dim hallway in front of them. Luckily, only a handful of lanterns cast soft light on the long corridor, but there were few places to hide should they come across any guards—no doors or alcoves lined the hallway, only gray stone.

The castle remained quiet as they made their way down the long stone halls, their steps softly echoing as they cautiously walked across the marble floor. Unease filled Lillian when they didn't pass a single guard in the hallway or when they found a stairway that led down to the cellar. When they reached the bottom of the stairs, the dark hallway stretched long in both directions.

"Where do we go now?" Lillian whispered, jerking as even her whisper seemed too loud for the empty castle.

"Let's split up," Eli grabbed her hand, squeezing it when she stiffened at a gust of wind blowing through the hallway. "You come with me. Aksel, you take the other way. If you come across anyone, do what needs to be done."

Lillian knew they might need to hurt some of the guards, but there was something in Eli's tone, so cold and calculating, that made a chill snake down her spine.

She followed Eli into the dark, casting nervous glances behind them. They reached a large wooden door that stood slightly ajar.

"Eli." Lillian gripped his hand tighter as he went to open the door. "I don't like this."

She glanced around again, and while there was no one there, not even a whisper breaking through the thick silence around them, the sensation of being watched still pricked her skin.

Eli ignored her, pulling the door open. An ice-cold breeze swept past them, and she shuddered as it ripped at her cloak. Inside there were more doors, a few of them locked, but the last one opened to another dim staircase. She stared at Eli with raised eyebrows. He only shrugged, and so they walked even further down. Lillian whipped her head around as they descended, but only cold stone walls surrounded the spiraling staircase.

Metallic clangs echoed between the walls as they warily took one step at a time. They were soft, rattling, like someone was moving while chained, and Lillian's heart started pounding so hard that she was surprised each beat didn't reverberate through the stairway. A vast rectangular chamber loomed at the bottom of the stairs, only one lantern shining its dim light over the room. Blinking, Lillian adjusted to the darkness.

The room was filled with thick metal bars, dividing the space into several small cells, large enough for one person. The smell of human waste, sweat, and the coppery tang of blood washed over them, making her eyes tear.

There were so many children. Tears burned behind her eyes as Eli and Lillian slowly walked along the cells, and she let them fall freely when scared eyes opened in dirty faces inside the cells. A small boy, who couldn't have been older than twelve, laid on his side, his dark gaze tracking their movements.

Lillian tried approaching the boy's cell door but found herself stuck a few feet away. She pushed forward, but it was like the air itself had formed a wall against her. She tried another cell with the same outcome.

Puzzled, she turned to Eli. "Something is blocking the cells."

Eli stepped forward, but the wall of air also blocked his path. "I've never seen such magic," Eli shook his head.

He picked up a small pebble and cautiously threw it at a cell. It bounced straight through, landing inside the bars.

"Interesting," he mumbled.

"What do you want now?" A boy within one of the closest cells, perhaps a year younger than Lillian, glared at them through the bars.

Lillian's stomach churned at the pale, thin fingers wrapped around the bars and the hollowness of his face. She couldn't even make out the color of his hair because of the dirt and grime that covered him.

Lillian went to pull back her hood, but Eli grabbed her hand.

Shaking his head, he whispered, "You are too easily recognized. What if they find out we were here and torture them for information?"

Clenching her jaw, she stopped. Lillian stepped as close to the bars as she could get.

"We're here to help you." She spoke softly to the boy, trying to keep the unease out of her voice. "What's your name?"

"Emile." He stared skeptically at them. "Are you going to get us out?"

Several other children stirred, standing up and gripping the bars to stare at them.

A young boy started crying. "Please, please help us get out."

A lump formed in her throat at his desperate cries, but she kept her voice steady. "Yes. I promise we are going to get you out. But first, I need you to help us." She turned to Emile again. "How many of you are there?"

Emile glanced between her and Eli. "There are twenty-three of us in this chamber."

Lillian frowned as she yet again tried to push through the magic. "In this chamber?"

"I don't know where they keep the girls or how many there are."

Lillian raked her eyes over the cells again. A chill spread throughout her body as only young boys stared back at her.

Eli gripped her shoulder. "There is nothing we can do right now. We need to regroup and figure out how to get into the cells."

Lillian nodded slowly. She didn't want to leave, but with the magic surrounding the cells, Eli was right.

She turned to Emile once more. "Do you know what kind of magic this is?"

He shook his head, his eyes cast down.

Lillian promised they would be back and that they'd figure out how to get them out. When they walked back up the stairs, the young boy's cries echoed through the staircase, begging them to come back. Lillian gritted her teeth and swore to herself she would keep her promise.

Chapter Forty-One

The halls were still eerily quiet as they slipped through the shadows, and Lillian wondered if they had just gotten really lucky when voices from the hallway above broke the silence. She jerked when Eli swore quietly, staring at her with wide eyes. Shifting her eyes up, she unsheathed her daggers. Eli squeezed her shoulder quickly before drawing his sword.

When two guards descended the stairs and came into the flickering light of the lanterns lining the stone walls, Lillian thought her heart might beat out of her chest. But she drew a soft breath and twisted her dagger, lashing out before the guards could see them. She hit the first guard in the temple with its hilt. He toppled wordlessly down the stairs, but Lillian winced as the sound of his body hitting the steps rumbled in the stairwell.

Eli jumped the other, covering his mouth with his hand and using two fingers to press down on the pressure points in his neck that instantly rendered him unconscious. He gracefully lowered the guard down onto one of the steps.

"I think *you* might need a refresher in evading detection," he winked.

She pouted but quickly spun around again, adrenaline coursing through her veins. "Let's get the hell out of here."

They ran as fast as they could up the rest of the stairs, and

Lillian gritted her teeth when her body slowed with each step. Eli gently pushed her upward, whispering that she'd be able to rest soon. More voices surrounded them now, coming from every direction. Lillian whipped her head back and forth, trying to identify a corridor without guards.

"There! The intruders are over there."

Lillian stole a glance behind her shoulder. Several guards sprinted toward them. She pushed herself to run faster, hissing at Eli to go ahead as he stayed behind her, keeping her pace. In front of them, the hallway branched into two separate passages, both completely veiled in the darkness.

She stared questioningly at Eli, who inclined his head before reaching out and squeezing her hand quickly. "Get out of here. I'll find you tomorrow," Eli whispered.

They separated and chose one passage each. As Lillian sprinted down the dark corridor, three guards were now on her tail. She frantically searched for an open door or somewhere to hide, but there was nothing but stone around her. Swearing to herself, she prayed Eli had better luck.

As the stone walls curved, she picked up the pace further but was met with a dead end. Lillian slammed into the wall, her teeth clattering as her face collided with the hard stone. She flipped around, her head spinning from the impact. The guards stopped running and stalked toward her, laughing quietly. Lillian set her jaw and took up a fighting stance.

"Oh, this one is feisty. Small, but feisty." One of the guards leered at her while unsheathing his sword.

Lillian gripped her daggers tightly after pulling at her hood to secure it around her face. But when she was about to let the first one fly, a blur of black obscured her vision.

She blinked. A cloaked person stood between herself and the guards. Before Lillian could react, the person grabbed her arm, and the vibrations of magic enveloped her. Warm air tightened around her body, and the world whirled before her eyes. A wave of nausea washed over her, forcing her eyes shut. When Lillian opened them again, the air was different.

She fell to her knees, retching as nausea overtook her. When it finally subsided, she took a deep breath of fresh evening air and frowned as she scanned the familiar rooftop. Startled by a noise behind her, Lillian jumped to her feet and spun around. Atlas stood by the ledge, the cloak no longer concealing his face.

She stared at him. "What just happened?"

"I saved you." He closed the distance between them, and his labored breaths blew a strand of her hair out of her face as he leaned in close. Green fire danced in his eyes when he bore them into hers. "Why were you in the castle, Lillian?"

She scowled. "Why were you?" Atlas didn't waver. She glared back at him, lifting her chin.

Keeping his eyes on hers, Atlas closed the final distance between them with one slow, deliberate step. He slowly traced the curve of her cheek with his finger. "*Ice princess.* Why do you keep getting into so much trouble?"

Her breath hitched in her throat. Not trusting her voice, she shrugged. Lillian stepped back and drew a deep breath when he continued staring into her eyes.

She waved her finger at him. "I'm sure that works on most girls, but not me. Commander."

The corners of his mouth twitched. Lillian forced her features to remain neutral, even as a smile pulled at her own lips, and Atlas's eyes sparkled with amusement as he studied her. When she opened her mouth to ask him how he'd found her, dizziness washed over her, her body swaying slightly.

Atlas gripped her arm to steady her, his eyes tracing over her body. "Are you hurt?"

"I'm just tired," she waved her hand in dismissal. "Those awful guards just chased me through the castle." She sucked in a breath. "Did you see Eli in there? We got separated, and I don't know if he made it out."

A pang of guilt shot through her, and Lillian felt like she was losing her mind. Backing up, she approached the ladder to return to the castle when Atlas's fingers gently closed around her wrist.

"He's okay, Lillian. I saw a red fox sneaking out as I rifted in."

Lillian blew out a breath she hadn't realized she was holding. Eli was alive.

She stepped away from Atlas again. "Rifted?"

His eyes tracked her as she continued to move away from him, his arm still outstretched. A shadow flashed across his face, but it was gone the next instant.

"Rifted," he nodded. "My gift is rifting through space. I think about where I want to go, and a few moments later, I am there."

Lillian had never met anyone who could move between places with his mind. He must be quite powerful if he could bring her along as well.

She tilted her head. "That must be very useful as a commander."

Atlas offered her a half-smile. "It is."

He reached out his hand again. When she didn't take it, he shook his head. "I was going to rift us home. You look ready to drop dead and there is still a trial tomorrow."

Sighing, she took his hand. He didn't know how right he was.

Chapter Forty-Two

Lillian could barely keep her eyes open when they arrived at the courtyard in the morning. She'd only gotten a few hours of sleep before Finn came running into her room and poured a glass of water over her head. She nearly gutted him for it.

The castle grounds bustled with activity. Dozens of guards ran in and out of the castle, urgently whispering to each other. Their black uniforms were stark against the sun-drenched stone, and their faces were grim as they passed Lillian on the way out the gates.

Lillian frowned and glanced at Finn, who shrugged, "I have no idea what's happening, but it seems awfully busy for just a trial."

She nodded.

Atlas stood with a group of guards, his shoulders tense as he gave them instructions. Lillian sidled up next to him when they walked off to follow his orders.

"What's going on?"

Atlas stared at her, his mouth tight. "Why were you in the castle, Lillian?" His words dripped of ice.

"Why?" Her voice wavered under his piercing green gaze.

Atlas narrowed his eyes. "Someone blew up the north chambers in the cellars early this morning."

A chill spread throughout her body. "Is that where...Are the children okay?" she whispered, her voice quivering.

"No." Atlas shook his head, a haunted look in his eyes.

Lillian clenched her fists as hot rage flared within her. "The king."

Atlas brushed his hand against hers, and there was pity in his eyes when she met them.

"It wasn't the king, Lillian." He squeezed her hand softly. "We think it was rebels."

Lillian couldn't breathe. She clasped at her chest, trying to force air into her lungs. Shaking her head, she stared at Atlas with wide eyes. There was no way the rebels could have done this. They wanted to save those children.

But Eli's voice echoed in her mind, *"We won't stand a chance if he also has every strong magic wielder on his side."* Bone-chilling cold gripped her from within.

"Everyone, line up for the trial." Commander Eirik's booming voice interrupted her spiraling.

"Lillian," Atlas pulled her close and whispered, "We'll figure this out."

She stared at him, her gray eyes shining from tears.

"You need to focus on the trial. Keep your wits about you. And stay alive with whatever means necessary." Atlas squeezed her hand again, and for a moment, she didn't think he'd let go, but then he stalked off, joining the other commanders.

Commander Eirik stated that the trial would test their astuteness but didn't offer any more details other than that they were to face it alone. Another table with cups stood behind him.

Knowing what to expect, Lillian walked up to the table and downed one, wiping her mouth with her sleeve. She didn't care what the trial would entail; the moment of reprieve the magic liquid would provide from the pain in her chest was welcomed.

Finn and Sam stood on each side of her, grinning as they wished each other good luck. Lillian stared back at them blankly, her insides yet again a black hole.

Bright light blinded her for a second when she opened her eyes. The sun was high in the sky, not a cloud in sight.

Lillian wished it had rained. She couldn't stand the light when the only thing inside her was darkness. Pushing herself up, she glanced around. She was alone, and lush, green hedges surrounded her on each side, casting shade on the narrow path in front of her.

Still reeling from the shock of Atlas's revelation, she took a staggering step but stopped and shook her head, forcing herself to draw deep breaths. She needed to calm down, to stay alive, so that she could confront Eli.

Lillian slowly made her way forward until the hedge-lined path forked in two. One path was dark, a musty smell wafting from it. She shuddered, the other one it was. As she continued walking, there were more forks and dead ends. It was a maze, she realized.

A scream rang to Lillian's left, and her heart skipped a beat. The next fork, she chose the right path, to get as far away from whatever caused the screaming as possible.

When Lillian turned another corner, a man lay on the path before her, blood pooling on the grass beneath him. She ran toward him, her heart thundering in her chest. Familiar brown eyes stared back at her as the man clawed at his throat. A strangled noise escaped her, and Lillian dropped to her knees.

"Father!" Frantically, she put pressure on his wounds, hushing him. "It's okay. It's going to be okay." Her voice broke when her father wheezed, gasping for air.

"Lillian?"

She turned her head. Eli stared at her with an arrow through his chest, his blue eyes wide as he glanced from her to the arrow.

"No!" Lillian rose and sprinted toward him, but her legs wouldn't cooperate, her boots feeling like they were filled with lead. She couldn't get to him in time. Lillian screamed as he fell to his knees, dying in front of her eyes.

"Lillian?"

She spun around, and there was Finn. Beautiful, happy Finn clutched at his gut, a dagger—*her dagger*—embedded in it. She couldn't move, her feet frozen in place. Tears began streaming down her face.

She whirled around again upon seeing a glimpse of black out of the corner of her eye. Atlas's green eyes locked with hers. He was on his knees, King Alek holding a sword above his neck, and Atlas's voice broke when he desperately screamed her name. Lillian fell to the ground and covered her ears as the screams of her friends dying filled them. Sobbing, she cried for it to stop.

Keep your wits about you. Atlas's voice rumbled in her mind.

She made herself draw a shaky breath. This couldn't be real. Her father was dead. Atlas was a commander. Forcing air down her lungs, in and out, she cautiously lifted her gaze. No bodies lay in the path around her. Trembling, she stood up, taking a small step. Nothing held her in place anymore.

She'd heard about magic wielders who could summon people's greatest fear and make them live their worst nightmares. *It wasn't real.* It wasn't real. She repeated the words to herself until she breathed again, her gait steady. Wiping her cheeks with her sleeve, she shivered even as the sun beat down on her. She needed to get out of this maze.

Lillian approached the tallest part of the hedge next to her. It was sturdy but full of thorns. She gritted her teeth and placed her hands on the thick branch above her. Thorns cut into her arms and legs as she scaled it, but she ignored the pain, only focused on getting up, not slowing until she reached the top.

With the shrubbery no longer obstructing her view, the vast expanse of the maze spread out in front of her. It was huge, the tall greenery surrounding her in all directions. But far in the distance stood two beacons, no green hedges behind them, only the clear blue sky.

The fastest way would be following the right-hand wall. Lillian quickly descended the hedge, wiping her bloody hands on her leather trousers. The next few turns were uneventful, but Lillian kept scanning her surroundings, her ears strained for any sound.

As she approached yet another fork, the familiar smell of decay wafted from the right path. Wincing, she prayed she wasn't about to get cozy with the undead again. She unsheathed her sword and hesitantly walked down the path. A woman screamed further down, and Lillian rushed her steps, but the previous test echoed in her mind, keeping her from outright running.

174

When she turned another corner, Thyra, the blonde girl from the first trial, fought a group of undead. Though these were different than in the first trial. They were more animal-like, with dark leathery skin and huge claws instead of hands, their faces contorted into grotesque masks with long snouts, and standing over eight feet tall. A shiver danced down her spine as one of them sniffed the air, turning its head toward her.

Raising her sword, Lillian joined the other girl, her jaw set as she slashed to drive back the attackers. Thyra threw her a grateful look when Lillian cut the head off one coming for her back. Panting, they fought shoulder to shoulder until only one remained.

Lillian bled from her shoulder and chest, where one of the undead had ripped into her with its claw. Thyra shifted to the right beside her, the monstrous creature following, when she lost her footing. Lillian reacted without thinking. Jumping between the undead and Thyra, she met the blow of its claw with her sword, her arm shaking from the impact.

White-hot pain shot through her stomach when its other claw embedded itself in her flesh. She stumbled back, wrapping her arm around her gut. The creature followed, licking its lips as it studied the blood dripping onto the ground. Grimacing, she tried to steady herself as the creature launched itself at her yet again. She met the monster head-on, ducking when its claw swiped at her throat.

When the creature slipped on Lillian's blood, she used the last of her strength to lash out with her sword, delivering the final blow. Falling to her knees, Lillian panted as she examined the injury. It was deep, but not deep enough to cut into her organs. She'd live—at least if she made it out of the maze in time to not bleed to death. Using one of her daggers, she cut off the bottom of her tunic, tying the strip of fabric tight around her waist. Lillian got to her feet once she was sure she wouldn't faint and stared down the sunlit path.

Thyra was nowhere to be found. Violently cursing herself for saving someone who had now left her to die twice, Lillian continued walking. She had to go slow, wincing with every step as pain radiated through her body. Thankfully, she didn't stumble upon any more awful creatures or nightmares.

It was almost too quiet for her liking. Lillian froze when a gust of wind blew through the maze, but as nothing attacked, she continued her slow strides. The glow from the lanterns shone over the tall hedges ahead. When she reached the final fork, she cursed again. The path on the right was pitch-dark.

Chapter Forty-Three

"That was my reaction, too."

Whipping her head around, she found Finn leaning against the hedge, his golden features contrasting with the greenery surrounding them.

"Hello, silver girl." He winked at her.

Lillian's throat tightened. "Hello, golden boy," she got out.

Finn's amber eyes went to her stomach. "You're hurt." He walked up to her, gripping her hand in his.

"It's not that bad. I can walk." She tried to smile when he worriedly searched her face.

Finn nodded slowly. "We're almost there. We'll finish it together."

Finn led the way down the dark pathway with a firm hold on her hand. The hedges closed above them, forming a green tunnel as the sun disappeared behind them. They walked in silence for a few moments until darkness completely enveloped them.

"I can't see anything," Lillian hissed.

Finn squeezed her hand. "I'll lead us."

She'd forgotten about his useful night sight. Lillian squeezed his hand back, grateful she wasn't alone. But her blood ran cold when a snarl broke the silence.

"What was that?" Lillian's voice was barely a whisper.

Finn remained quiet. His body shifted, searching for the source of the sound. "Garm," he breathed.

She sucked in a breath. Garms resembled wolves but were far more blood-thirsty, and their massive fangs could rip a person in two. They were said to guard the gates of death. Hellhounds, her father called them.

"Stand against the wall." Finn nudged her until the thorns from the hedge cut into her back. "I'll cover you."

Lillian shook her head but realized Finn had his back to her. "Don't be ridiculous; we'll need both of us to kill it." Not that she'd ever killed a Garm before.

The snarl rang closer, and Lillian readied her sword. From the clang of metal, she knew Finn did the same. A gust of wind whipped her hair around her face, and Finn cursed as his sword cleaved through the air. A loud whine pierced the darkness following his strike.

"There are two of them," Finn hissed.

Before she could respond, he was slashing again. His sword hit flesh with a sickening thump, and he gasped when he jumped out of the way of its claws. "Watch out!"

How was she going to watch out when *she couldn't see*? Lillian growled to herself, cursing her lack of magic for the umpteenth time. Hot, foul breath brushed against her skin, and she sliced blindly with her sword in the direction where it had come from. Another snarl broke through the darkness, but the foul smell eased slightly.

Lillian gripped her sword tight when the air stilled. Claws ripped through the bandages on her stomach, and she cried out at the surge of pain. Frantically, she lashed out with her sword, finally sensing it slice through thick fur. Clutching her stomach with one hand, the other still wielding the sword in front of her, she took a step back.

Finn's labored breaths brushed her cheek as he stepped in front of her. "Please, lower your sword, or you'll hurt me. I've got this one."

Helplessness filled her as she listened to Finn fight the Garm. Snarling and Finn cursing were the only sounds until it went silent.

"Finn?" Her voice shook as she reached out a hand in the darkness.

When his warm hand found hers, she blew out a breath of relief. Relief that quickly faded when more howling echoed in the distance.

"Lillian." Finn gripped her shoulders. "I know you're stubborn and that you're sick. But please, listen to me. I can share my night sight with you if you accept the bond. We will not make it out here alive unless you can fight."

Lillian started shaking her head, but Finn grabbed her more firmly. "There is no way I am leaving you, so then we both die here today. It's your choice."

Lillian groaned. Searching her mind, she tried to come up with another solution. Any solution. Her mind was blank. She glanced at Finn, at least where she believed him to be.

"You realize it might kill you when I die?"

Finn gently squeezed her shoulders. "It would be my honor to die for you, silver girl."

Tears lined Lillian's eyes when she finally inclined her head. At that moment, she hated herself, and she clenched her fists until her nails drew blood.

"I know what you're thinking. Stop it right now. You are the most wonderful woman I've ever met. You're funny, smart, and unusually violent. Exactly my kind of girl."

Lillian cleared her throat as the sound of howling intensified. "Let's do this."

Finn unsheathed one of her daggers from her thigh and made a small cut in each of their palms—the left ones, the ones closest to their hearts.

"Together," he said quietly.

Finn raised his hand to her mouth at the same time she raised hers. The moment his blood touched her tongue, her body relaxed. The bond hummed within her. She could see it now—gold and silver twirling around each other within her and between them.

Lillian.

She snapped her head up. *Did you just speak in my mind?*

It wasn't as scary as she'd thought it would be. Not an intrusion; instead, his voice was like a soft caress inside her head. And there was a separation between her thoughts and his—she could let him in, but she didn't have to. It was natural.

When she lifted her eyes to Finn, she saw herself standing in the dark. Her white hair had come unbound, and there was blood on her face. Lillian raised a hand, and the version in front of her mirrored the movement.

Her forehead wrinkled. "Finn. I think I'm seeing through your eyes."

"Seriously? That's amazing. Let me try again."

Her gaze switched to her own, and Finn finally stood before her with a familiar grin. She stared at the green hedges surrounding them and the two dead Garms lying a few feet away on the grassy ground.

Lillian tilted her head. "You can *really* see in the dark."

Finn threw his head back and laughed. "Let's explore the other awesome things we can do after we kill some Garms."

When the Garms approached, thankfully only another pair, they cut them down quickly. Even hurt, with her sight back, Lillian was able to take down her own.

Chapter Forty-Four

With Finn's arm wrapped around her shoulders, they finally left the darkness. Before them stood the beacons, casting their soft glow on the end of the lush hedges. Forest spread out outside the exit, and behind it, the flickering lights of the slanted capital shone against the darkening sky. It was quiet when they approached—no groups of novices hovered outside the exit.

Atlas leaned against one of the beacons, scanning the glumly lit path before him. His shoulders relaxed when he met her eyes. When they came closer, Atlas's eyes traced her gut and the arm clutching it. His jaw flexed, and he sprinted to them without waiting for them to cross the finish line.

"How badly are you hurt?"

Lillian started to respond when Finn interrupted her. "She needs a healer."

Protectiveness rolled down the bond, a twinge of worry embedded in it.

She furrowed her brow. *Weird.*

I know. It is weird. Finn winked. *I can feel your pain too, so getting you healed will also help me.*

She'd forgotten about that part, an image of Eli doubling over from pain as the sentries beat her father, flashing through her mind. She buried it quickly.

What was that? Finn looked at her questioningly.

Later. She jerked her head at Atlas, who studied them closely.

"You bonded." Atlas stared at her, and when a blinding smile overtook his face, Lillian nearly choked. Atlas turned to Finn and clapped him on the back. "Finally!"

She furrowed her brow. *Weirder.*

Finn and Atlas both grinned at her. Lillian winced when another jolt of pain seared through her gut and almost missed when Finn inclined his head to Atlas. Atlas promptly scooped her into his arms.

"Let. Me. Down," she hissed as he carried her away from the maze.

"No." Atlas threw her a bored glare and kept on walking.

Lillian glared at him. "I said, let me down. I need to wait for my friends."

"Finn is waiting for your friends. You can check in with him via your bond if you're worried. But you're coming with me to a healer."

Lillian sighed. Squirming, she tried to get out of his hold, but Atlas was too strong. Only because she was hurt, she told herself. Otherwise, she'd have him on the ground. They were silent for a moment. Atlas's strong arms were gentle as they held her, and a battle between unease and safety filled her at their closeness.

She cleared her throat. "So, do you and Finn also mind-speak?"

Atlas met her eyes, one of the corners of his mouth curling up. "No. We just agree on keeping someone we care about alive."

Her face heated, and she quickly averted her eyes.

Atlas's smile widened, his eyes twinkling as he studied her face. "So red. Did I fluster you?"

Lillian violently shook her head. "Absolutely not."

But when her treacherous face turned even more crimson, she groaned. Atlas began shaking, the vibrations sending small jabs of pain through her gut. Peeking at him from under her eyelashes, she realized he was laughing; his beautiful face crinkled with amusement.

Beautiful face, huh? She tensed when Finn's booming laugh vibrated along the bond. Insufferable men. The vibrations came stronger. Lillian pursed her lips to stop the smile that threatened to spread across her face. Stupid bond.

Chapter Forty-Five

Atlas brought her to a healer close to the castle. A bald, older man who only needed to hold her hand as he healed her wounds. When she inspected her stomach, she winced. Four jagged lines now permanently marked her.

"Garms have poison in their claws." Atlas studied her new scars, his face tight.

The healer nodded and explained that while she wouldn't have any permanent damage, she would carry the scars for the rest of her life. Lillian snorted; she wouldn't have to deal with them for long then.

When Atlas curiously searched her face, she winked. "It's fine. You should have seen how I left them."

Shaking his head, Atlas motioned for her to join him.

"Where are we going?"

"To the castle. The surviving novices are to gather there for information about the next trial."

Worry crashed through her.

They're okay. Astrid and Sam are with me.

She sent a soft *thank you* back to Finn.

When they arrived back in the courtyard, Lillian couldn't believe it had been just this morning that she'd learned about the children, that only a few hours had passed. It seemed like it had been years. Atlas slipped away when the others came into view, and she stared after him, a wrinkle forming between her brows.

Finn's amber eyes glittered when she met them.

Hi, golden boy.

He grinned and waved for her to join him. Astrid and Sam stood next to him, and she pulled them both into a tight hug. They were dusty and bloodied, and Sam also had some type of black grime sticking to his skin. Lillian winced but knew she didn't look much better. She was desperate for a bath.

Yeah, you stink.

She narrowed her eyes at Finn, who laughed under his breath and wrapped his arm around her shoulders.

Astrid and Sam quietly told them about their experience. Sam had gotten stuck in black tarry quicksand and nearly drowned. Lillian reached out and squeezed his hand quickly when he shuddered.

"Novices. There are fourteen of you left. Congratulations." Atlas's voice was flat, but there was a twinge of regret in it.

Lillian searched his face, and he shifted his gaze to meet hers. Once their eyes met, his features softened. Lillian's face warmed under his stare, and she quickly glanced down at her bloodied boots.

"In two days, you will have the third and final trial. Five of you will join the esteemed King's Guard." He paused. "Tomorrow is the Summer Solstice. To celebrate, the king will host a ball. You're expected to attend and to dress up. And while you're not there as official guards, you're to study the King's Guard—how they protect the king. Don't embarrass us, and don't be late."

Atlas walked off with Commander Jon and Eirik.

A ball! Lillian had never been to a ball. A surge of excitement shot through her, and she glanced at Finn and Sam, who both grinned. Astrid frowned when Lillian excitedly turned to her.

Lillian approached her friend and touched her arm. "Are you okay?"

Astrid glared at her. "A ball? To celebrate sixteen of us getting

185

killed?" She clenched her fists and hissed, "And after those children."

Guilt and horror at herself washed over Lillian. Astrid was right.

Astrid narrowed her eyes, her blue eyes nearly black. "I need to do something tonight. It seems there is no one we can trust. But tomorrow, after the ball, will you come with me? I think I may have figured out something that could help us."

Lillian nodded and gripped her friend's hand. "I promise. You can trust me, Astrid. We're on the same side."

A shiver ran down her spine, and she felt it then—a rift between rebels. She disagreed with what Eli had done. There must be another way. And if Astrid had found it, Lillian would fight by her side. She only hoped she could convince the boy she loved to do so as well.

Astrid inclined her head and took off, not once glancing back as Lillian stared after her.

Chapter Forty-Six

On the way home, Finn entertained them by practicing sharing his gifts with Lillian. Sam howled with laughter when Finn succeeded in seeing out of Lillian's eyes and then wouldn't stop referring to himself as the most handsome man he'd ever seen. He also shared his heightened hearing, which had Lillian wincing as Sam's laugh boomed through her head. She had to cover her ears until Finn figured out how to stop it.

As soon as they got to the apartment, Lillian drew a bath. She moaned when she slipped into the warm water—it was the best bath she'd ever had. After carefully washing the blood out of her hair, she scrubbed her body and inspected the new scars, now covering most of her stomach. Tracing them with her fingers, she shrugged; while they weren't pretty, at least they made her feel like she was doing something.

When she finally got out, she brushed her white hair until it shone. Even if she had nothing ball-worthy to wear tomorrow, she would at least try to look decent. Dressed only in a soft tunic that went to her mid-thigh, Lillian walked out to the kitchen.

Eli sat on a chair by the kitchen table, bread and cheese laid in front of him, the window behind him open to let the evening breeze in. Finn and Sam were getting ready to leave when she glanced at the door. Finn offered her a small smile.

We'll give you some privacy. I heard what the rebels did. If you agree, I want to tell Sam about your plans. I believe we can trust him, and he's been suspicious for a while.

She shot him a grateful look and nodded. Despite her father and Eli's warnings, she trusted Sam, too. Turning to Eli, she struggled to meet his eyes, fidgeting with a piece of bread she picked up.

"I'm guessing you bonded then," Eli eyed her.

Lillian nodded, "I would have died if he hadn't pushed me to do it."

Wincing, Eli reached out to grab her hand. She pulled out of his grip and backed up, resting her hands on the back of the chair opposite him.

"I'm grateful you have others who care about you, Lillian. I was worried about you today. I wish you would have let me join the trials with you." He paused for a moment. "I don't trust that commander, though. I don't think it's wise to spend so much time with our enemies."

Lillian opened her mouth to explain that while Atlas was a commander, he knew about her and the rebels and hadn't exposed them. But Eli would only worry more, maybe even force her to leave the trials at the risk of Atlas betraying them.

"He wasn't the one who blew up the chamber, though, was he."

It came out harsher than she meant, and Eli flinched at her tone. An overwhelming need to apologize overcame her; she'd never fought with Eli. But she kept quiet, studying his face closely.

Eli's eyes filled with pain when he returned her glare. "No, he wasn't," he said quietly.

He looked so young then, only three years her senior, with the weight of the rebellion on his shoulders.

She softened her gaze. "Tell me why. And no more lies, Eli."

He blew out a breath through his nose, bowing his head so that his auburn hair fell into his eyes.

"Atli had so many plans in place, Lil." The use of his pet name for her made her reach out her hand and grip his over the table. "He made me swear to follow through on them if he wasn't alive to do it himself."

They stared at each other for a moment, pain and understanding shining in their eyes.

"If we couldn't save them, we needed to eliminate them. I'm sorry I didn't tell you, but I knew you couldn't bear it. And I didn't want you to. You're already surrounded by so much death, Lillian." Eli searched her face pleadingly.

She nodded slowly. Eli and her father always tried to protect her, not willing for her to bear more pain than the sickness that ravaged her body.

"If you had told me, we could have discussed it, Eli. I could have helped come up with another plan."

He squeezed her hand. "I promise. I will talk to you about any new plans."

Despite his words, a knot formed in Lillian's stomach. Eli wasn't meeting her eyes. But when he rose and pulled her into his arms, she let him. She nestled her face into his broad chest, breathing in the leathery scent from his tunic while he gently stroked her hair.

"I'm truly sorry, Lillian," he whispered.

She held him tighter and nodded; even if she disagreed, she had to trust Eli believed he did the right thing.

When she released her hold, Eli pulled Lillian onto his lap, and they stayed at the kitchen table, quietly discussing what they'd do next. Lillian would gather as much information as possible about the king and the guards he favored at the ball tomorrow, while Eli would use his fox to sneak around the castle grounds, making sure they knew its layout and guard movements.

When Finn and Sam returned, Finn drunkenly announced their arrival in her mind before slamming the door open. Eli soon bid them goodnight after that. He held Lillian tight before kissing her cheek and slipping out the door. Finn, apparently not drunk enough, convinced them to stay up. Opening a bottle of wine they'd stolen from the tavern they'd sojourned, they talked about the rebel movement, her father, and what Eli had told her today.

Sam wasn't surprised when Finn filled him in and eagerly offered his help. His parents had been caught in the crossfire when

King Alek hunted down the Valkyries and any others loyal to the previous royal family. He'd only joined the trials because his brother was sick, and he needed to support them both.

Lillian's heart ached for him when his brown eyes filled with sorrow. Too familiar with the pain a family member feels when a loved one is sick.

They all reached for their weapons when a hard knock interrupted their conversation. Lillian tiptoed to the door. Kicking it open with her foot, she glanced outside, her heart pounding and daggers clenched in her fists. There was no one there.

Finn peered over her shoulder, "It's a package."

She glanced down. A small, brown package lay on their doorstep.

Do you think it could be dangerous? Lillian studied it.

No, it seems pretty harmless. Finn reached down to grab it and kicked the door close. *It's yours.* He pointed to a note on the package with Lillian's name.

Sam eyed them. "Guys, I know the bond is new and all, but can you speak out loud for the rest of us?"

Lillian offered him a crooked smile. She used to hate it when Eli and her father did exactly that. Nodding, she picked up the note.

"What is it?" Finn made a grab for the paper in her hand. She smacked his hand away.

"It's a dress," Lillian beamed. "From Thyra, the blonde that left me to die during both trials."

"During both trials?" Sam stared at her.

She dismissively waved her hand as she opened the package. A dramatic black dress made from the softest fabric Lillian had ever felt tumbled out. When she lifted it to inspect it more closely, tiny crystals covered the entire dress, making it shimmer in the candlelight. She sucked in a breath. It must have cost a fortune.

"She must be feeling a tad guilty," Finn elbowed her. "But if you plan on wearing that tomorrow, almost dying might be worth it."

Lillian couldn't stop the grin that spread across her face.

Chapter Forty-Seven

In the morning, Lillian made up an excuse for not joining the boys at the lake again, anxiously waiting until they left the apartment. With the final trial taking place the day after tomorrow, today could be her last chance to free the dragon. She'd considered asking Finn or Eli to join her, but her plan was risky, and she doubted either of them would be supportive.

The sunlit courtyard was quiet when she entered; no novices using the training grounds, but the two guards she'd seen the other night stood guard outside the castle doors. Lillian blew out a breath of relief at her luck. She confidently strode through the metal gates, even as her heart hammered in her chest.

Waving to the guards, she called out, "Will any of you gentlemen help me train? I want to be at my best during the final trial."

She held her breath while the guards glanced at each other. One of them finally shrugged and stalked toward her.

He smiled at her as he stepped into the ring, pulling at his black uniform jacket before unsheathing his sword.

"I've seen you fight before. We're all betting on you making it into the ranks."

Lillian made herself smile back. "That's very kind of you. Shall we?" She raised her sword.

The guard was an excellent sparring partner; sweat dripped down her neck as she parried his blows, and he grinned encouragingly when she almost managed to disarm him.

She just needed to get a little closer.

Making herself stumble over a small stone in the fighting ring, she fell right into the guard, the force slamming them both into the ground.

Lillian giggled as she slipped a hand inside his uniform jacket, "Well, that wasn't very graceful."

The guard offered his hand to help her up. She took it, smiling shyly.

"You should probably rest. You're bleeding." The guard pointed to her nose.

When Lillian wiped it with her sleeve, her white tunic returned red. Dread filled her; it appeared to happen more frequently now. But she pushed the fear away—it had at least been good timing.

"You're right. Thank you for training with me." She reached out to shake his hand. "Maybe we can do it again after the trials?"

The guard's face reddened, and he mumbled something incoherent before striding back to the entrance and taking up his post.

Lillian willed her racing heart to calm as she slowly walked out of the courtyard. When she was out of sight, she drew a deep breath. The keys jangled inside her tunic; she gripped them tightly and quickly slipped behind the castle, praying the dragon was still there.

The gods apparently favored her; as soon as she rounded the corner, icy-blue eyes bore into hers, and the dragon glittered in the sunlight. Glancing around, she scanned the small courtyard, but no guards stood around it, and the windows lining the back of the castle were dark. She shook her head; if she'd been on the king's side, she might have told him his security was seriously lacking.

As Lillian approached the dragon, she lifted the keys. "I told you I'd get you out."

The dragon let out a soft whine, whipping its head excitedly. When she reached the gilded cage, she paused.

"Promise that you won't kill me when you're free?" The dragon huffed.

"A girl can't be too sure. There are too many who already want to see me dead." It tilted its head and studied her. "Sorry, less talk, more opening of the cage."

Lillian tried a few keys, her stomach sinking. With shaking hands, she tried the final key, and when it turned with a sharp click, she let out a small quip of relief. Quickly glancing around, she made sure no one had heard her before she swung the door open. The dragon didn't hesitate. It stomped with heavy steps out of the cage, flexing its large wings and tilting its head to the sun. Lillian smiled at the happy purr vibrating in its throat.

"Time to leave, little dragon. I don't know when they're coming to check on you."

The dragon turned and met her eyes, and when it stalked toward her, Lillian forced herself to remain still. It huffed again, nudging her with its snout and blowing its warm breath through her thin tunic. Wary of its long spikes, she stroked its head, blinking as she realized what she was doing. The dragon's silver scales were surprisingly soft, and her hand glided over them effortlessly. The purr in its throat deepened when she gently trailed her fingers across its head.

When she stopped, anxious for the dragon to take off, it stared at her expectantly. Bending its leg, it flipped its head toward its back. Lillian's eyes widened.

"I can't go with you, little dragon. I have something I need to finish."

The dragon growled, and she flinched when the sound echoed between the dark castle walls.

"Hush. I can't come. But you need to leave. Now!"

Steps crunched on the gravel path. The dragon glanced at her again, its eyes lined with silver.

"I'll be alright. Go! Unless you want to go back into that cage?"

With one final huff, the dragon spread its wings and whipped the hair around her face as it took to the sky. Flying with impossible speed, it was soon only a speck on the horizon.

"Shit! She let the beast out!" The guard she'd trained with yelled behind her.

Lillian spun around to find four guards racing toward her. Her stomach flipped, and she quickly unfastened her bow, releasing an arrow. The guard Lillian aimed for dove, the arrow missing his shoulder by an inch. She knocked one more and sent it flying. It pierced the closest guard's arm. But before she could release another, vines from the castle wall wrapped around her arms and legs.

She struggled against them, but the vines only tightened, wrapping around her entire body. Lillian dropped the bow and tried to reach for her daggers, but her arms were bound too tightly. She snarled when the guards surrounded her.

"You're dead," the man wielding the vines hissed.

"No. You are."

Her eyes widened when Atlas appeared behind the man, slitting his throat before he could respond. In a flash, he rifted to the next guard, snapping his neck. The other two tried to escape, but Atlas was too fast. Both lay lifeless before Lillian could free herself from the vines.

Atlas stalked over, using his sword to cut off the vines' hold. "Are you hurt?"

Lillian gaped at him. "Did you have to kill them?"

Atlas shrugged. "They saw you. If I'd left them alive, the king would know you were the one who let out the poor dragon. And they were going to hurt you. I wish I could have taken my time ending their lives." His voice was so cold a chill snaked down Lillian's spine.

Atlas's green eyes burned into hers, and she tensed. "Good work getting her out. A dragon should never be caged. It's a vile crime against nature."

She stared at him with wide eyes. "You don't think it was stupid to risk it? I almost died."

Atlas raised his eyebrows. "No, I think it was brave. And you didn't almost die; I saved you. Again." He winked at her and reached out his hand. "Come on. I'll rift you home so you're not late for the ball, and then I'll take care of this."

Chapter Forty-Eight

Lillian took her time getting ready for the ball. After a long bath, she braided her damp hair. While waiting for it to dry, she picked up her sparse cosmetics pouch. She wanted to go all out for her first, and probably only, ball. Lillian pushed away the guilt at the tiny flame of excitement that burned in her chest. She'd die soon enough. She could have one night.

She added coal around her eyes, the darkness accentuating the gray, and dabbed on a bit of rouge to her pale face. When her hair dried, she unfastened the braid, satisfied with the soft curls that fell to her waist. She added a few smaller braids, in which she weaved in fine silver threads.

After a quick mind conversation with Finn, she took out the dress from her small closet. Finn and the others had gone ahead, complaining that she was taking too long, but Lillian didn't mind.

She planned on making a bit of an entrance, hoping it would attract the king's attention. And maybe because Lillian wanted, just the tiniest bit, to see the attendees' reactions. The time she'd spent in the capital, she'd mainly been covered in blood and grime; tonight, she hoped to intimidate people for a different reason.

The fabric of the dress was thin, showing a hint of the outline of her body through the midnight black, and its boned bodice sucked in her waist. When she laced it up, she was grateful for the long hours of training that had made her lean, her limbs pure muscle. The dress gently clung to her shoulders, held together by two silver clasps, and fell all the way to the ground, dramatically sweeping across the floor when she stepped across the small room.

She stilled when she turned to look at herself in the dusty mirror. Her white hair, the silver bands weaved into it, and the tiny crystals on the dress glittered in the moonlight streaming from the window. Her gray eyes seemed lighter, two full moons in her face accentuated by the coal she'd added. And the deep black dress didn't wash her out. It made her look regal. No ice princess anymore, she thought. She was Queen of the Night.

Nerves fluttered in her stomach when she entered the castle grounds. Hundreds of lanterns lined the courtyard, casting the pebbled path from the metal gates to the large double doors of the castle in soft orange hues.

Lillian raised her eyebrows at the many guards posted by the castle walls, overhearing one mutter about having to work on his day off because of a stupid beast. She smiled slightly as she passed him. The two guards at the door stared at her as they opened it, and one of them staggered when Lillian winked at him. Smirking, she made her way to the ballroom through the long stone hallways.

When she entered the large double doors, Lillian sucked in a breath. She'd never seen such riches. The room was magnificent, with huge red and gold tapestries hanging down the curved stone walls and hundreds of lanterns standing on floor, casting the room in soft light. Golden beams lined the stone ceiling, glistening in the flickering flames of the lanterns. And there was table after table with food and drinks. Lillian's mouth watered as her eyes scanned the delicious dishes, their aromas filling the warmly lit room.

She was late—the room was already full of people. A few novices stood in small groups, looking slightly out of place, but most of the room was filled with the king's court, nobility, and wealthy merchants. Her eyes widened as she took in the women; they wore dresses in every color: exquisite pink, blue, and purple, and even some pure silver and gold ones that sparkled in the light of the lanterns. The men wore black jackets, many adorned with golden medals and rapiers hanging at their waists.

Guards lined every wall, and fifteen or so stood watch around the king, their sharp eyes surveying the room, armed to the teeth with swords and daggers glittering against their black uniforms. King Alek sat on a large marble throne in the back of the room, several members of his court joining him on the tall dais, but his eyes were fixed on a beautiful blonde courtesan seductively dancing in a sheer silver gown in front of him.

A large marble staircase with a plush red carpet led down to the ballroom, and Lillian lifted her chin before slowly descending. Her black dress swept across the wide stairs, shimmering like the stars in the night sky in the firelight's soft glow.

She didn't dare meet anyone's eye, keeping her gaze straight ahead and clenching her fists to stop her hands from shaking. Upon taking the final step, Lillian finally let her eyes sweep across the room. She held back a smile when several men in the king's court stared at her with wide eyes.

A tug on the bond willed her left. Lillian glanced over her shoulder, expecting to find Finn's wide grin, but met Atlas's green eyes. Atlas wore his usual guard uniform, but his jacket was left open, and the white tunic underneath revealed a hint of his broad chest and made his tan skin glisten in the soft light. His lips parted slightly, and his eyes were dark as he swept his gaze over her body. He took a staggering step toward her, his eyes fixed on hers.

Lillian slowly walked over, and when she reached him, she curtsied low.

"Hello, Commander."

When he didn't respond, Lillian's face heated. But then Atlas bowed deep, taking her hand in his and kissing it with a feather-light touch. When he looked up again, the corners of his mouth curved before a wide smile spread across his face.

Lillian's breath hitched—seeing him smile like this was like being blinded. His green eyes danced as they watched her, his smile brightening his every feature. She tried to come up with something to say, but the intensity of his stare made her mind go blank.

"Silver girl, you've really outdone yourself. There are men literally drooling around us."

Finn popped up behind Atlas and pulled her into a tight embrace.

Atlas seems to have lost his ability to function as well.

She frowned, but Finn only laughed and dragged her with him to get some wine. He pressed a large golden flute into her hand, and she took a long sip, trying to clear her mind from the fog that had overtaken it as she met Atlas's eyes.

Atlas's stare burned into her back, but Lillian forced herself to keep her own on Finn. Finn was in high spirits, drinking and gossiping about the noble women who had already tried to bribe him to join their beds. She giggled when Finn imitated an especially persistent woman who had pushed two gold coins into his hand and whispered about a free room in the king's guest wing.

Taking another big mouth of wine, she glanced around the room. Thyra studied her from the other side of the dance floor, dressed in a beautiful silver gown with green embroidery twirling up the skirts. Lillian inclined her head when the blonde winked at her. When the music began, Finn pulled her onto the dance floor.

Lillian didn't think about anything else when the music filled her, and Finn expertly spun her around. She forgot all about her plans to get close to the king. The only things that existed were movement and music. Sam joined them at some point, and the three of them danced and giggled until sweat dripped down her back.

A hand wrapped around her arm mid-dance, and she spun around, her black dress billowing around her. Atlas wasn't smiling anymore.

"Come on, grumpy, dance with us." Lillian tried to pull him into their circle, but Atlas held firm.

"How much wine did you let her have?" He glared at Finn and Sam.

Finn bit his lip, looking down at his feet. "She's had two cups."

Lillian didn't understand what the problem was; she felt amazing. She pouted as she glowered at Atlas. "Don't be a killjoy."

Atlas tightened his grip on her arm and dragged her off the dance floor. She searched his face, snickering as she imitated the scowl he bore.

"Where are we going?"

Atlas didn't respond; he just led her out of the ballroom onto a balcony overlooking the courtyard.

Lillian sighed happily at the evening breeze blowing through her dress. Tilting her head to the large moon and the sparkling stars, she closed her eyes.

"I love the night. It is the only thing that makes me happy."

She opened her eyes and glanced at Atlas. There was something hard in his gaze, and his eyes were still darker than she was used to, the green reminding her of the forest at dusk. She slowly approached him until their bodies were flush, and she could feel his heart pounding through the black guard's uniform.

Lifting her fingers to his face, Lillian traced the frown between his eyebrows.

"Always so serious. I like it more when you smile. You have such a nice smile."

He shuddered at her touch, his eyes trailing her fingers.

"What makes you happy, Atlas?"

She stuck out her bottom lip when he gently removed her hands and looked at him from under her eyelashes.

Atlas squeezed her hand. "Lillian, you drank a lot of enchanted wine. You are not yourself right now."

She frowned. She felt great. Better than great, actually.

"I'll wait with you until it passes."

"Will you dance with me while we wait?" The music drifted through the open windows, and her body wanted to move.

He slowly shook his head.

"*Please*, Atlas?"

Pinching his nose, he sighed deeply. Lillian thought he was about to return inside when his arm circled her waist. Atlas studied her as he hesitantly pulled her closer.

"You're going to regret this."

But when Lillian only tilted her head, he offered her his hand,

and she took it, placing her other hand on his chest. Slowly, he spun her around, leading them in a small circle on the balcony.

Leaning her head on his chest, Lillian listened to his strong heartbeat. Atlas released a deep breath that made his chest rumble, and his hand stroked her back when he leaned down to rest his head on hers.

After a few dances, Lillian's thoughts cleared, and a deep blush crept up her neck. She had *begged* Atlas to dance with her on the balcony, all alone. She stepped out of his arms, her eyes cast down.

"Lillian?" Atlas's voice was soft.

He took a step forward, and Lillian gritted her teeth. She was never drinking again.

Atlas put a finger under her chin and tipped her head up. "Lillian, I know it was the wine."

She shrugged but finally met his eyes. Her body jerked at the intensity of his stare. Atlas cupped her chin. "Lillian," he started but was interrupted by an announcement from the ballroom. The king was making a toast.

Atlas glanced at her and opened his mouth, but then he sighed and motioned for her to join him inside. They slipped into the ballroom. Lillian kept close to the wall, staring daggers at the table with wine.

When the king rose, Lillian realized that she hadn't seen Astrid. She scanned the packed room but didn't find flaming red hair anywhere. Lillian shrugged. Astrid hadn't seen too keen on the ball yesterday, so perhaps she'd decided not to come.

The room quieted when the king began his speech, everyone turning toward the dais. His shrill voice echoed through the ballroom as he welcomed everyone and congratulated the novices on their success in the trials. Lillian stopped listening after a while, bored as the king launched into a lengthy expression of gratitude to Adeon for his support in his rule and the Kingdom of Orios.

Lillian fidgeted with her dress, picking at the tiny crystals and wondering when she could sneak out when her ears pricked at the king mentioning the Crown Prince.

"I am excited to announce Crown Prince Kian has returned from Hindra."

Lillian's eyes wandered around the room. No one in the crowd apart from the king wore a crown. Warmth trailed over her face, and she met Atlas's gaze. He searched her face, his jaw tight. Wincing, she quickly averted her eyes.

"Crown Prince Kian has been aiding me the past few weeks. As you all know, the rebel movement has become an increased threat. We've even found and executed rebels who tried to infiltrate the castle."

Lillian stiffened when she remembered Harald, the smile he'd given her as he was executed.

"I need the utmost loyalty from my closest guards, so I asked the Crown Prince and a few trusted guards to oversee the trials this year. To make sure no rebel forces interfered."

Lillian straightened when she recognized one of the guards beside the king as the one who'd faced Astrid that first day, who'd nearly killed her with whatever his magic was. A wave of apprehension brushed her skin when she accidentally met his dark gaze.

Finn's worry slid across their bond, raising the hair on the back of her neck. *Do you think it's a trap?*

She met his eyes across the room. *I'm not sure.*

Lillian was grateful that she'd strapped her daggers to her thighs under the dress and slowly moved her hands, ready to grip them.

"Since we are down to the final trial, I have released the Crown Prince of these duties so he can take up his rightful place at my side." The king paused. "Everyone, please welcome Crown Prince Kian back to Echo."

King Alek threw out his arms, and everyone in the room cheered. Lillian strained her neck, but there was no sign of the prince anywhere. Atlas slowly approached the dais to protect the Crown Prince as he joined the king.

But Lillian's blood ran cold when he didn't stop below the dais. She didn't move as the king draped his arm over Atlas's shoulders, and everyone in the room dropped to one knee.

Bow, Lillian.

She couldn't move.

Bow, now! They'll kill you for treason! Finn screamed down the bond, fear slithering along the silver and golden twirls.

In a trance, Lillian dropped to one knee, her black dress spreading over the marble floor like the night sky itself spilled onto it. When she glanced at the throne, she met Atlas's—Kian's eyes.

Hers filled with tears, hot, angry tears of betrayal. She clenched her fists hard enough that her nails drew blood to stop them from spilling down her cheeks. Kian's eyes were cold before he shifted them to someone else in the room. As soon as the king told them to rise, Lillian bolted.

Chapter Forty-Nine

Lillian didn't know where she was running. The tears she'd held back fell as soon as she left the room, clouding her vision as she stormed down the glum stone hallways. Finn tried to reach her through the bond, but she shut him out. She angrily wiped at the tears that kept streaming down her cheeks, and when her father's voice rang in her head, she nearly choked on a sob at the truth of them.

You can't trust anyone, Lil.

Lillian aimlessly wandered down hall after hall. She couldn't believe the commander, *her friend*, was the Crown Prince. Had he pretended to care to get close to her so that he could betray them all? Had Lillian signed all of their death sentences? She'd brought Finn and Sam into this. And Astrid. Lillian swallowed as dread coursed through her veins. She'd kill him if he touched them. She might have to kill him anyway. The son of the king she'd come to murder.

Her tears finally made way to anger, and she began noticing her surroundings. It was quiet in this part of the castle. The smell of food wafted through the halls, servants yelling orders to each other as they ran down the long hallway. A few servants passed right by her, barely taking notice. Maybe they were used to women in gowns crying in the hallways.

When she rounded yet another corner, loud voices echoed between the walls. She halted, listening cautiously. They were enraged, several men shouting words she couldn't make out. Tiptoeing, she made her way closer, peeking around a giant marble statue of Adeon. Six guards surrounded someone, taunting them.

"Did you really think you would get away with it?" One of the guards kicked a lifeless person on the ground. "Fucking rebels. They're all as dumb as the next."

Lillian inched closer, her heart pounding in her chest. When one of the guards stepped to the side, clearing the view, Lillian bit back a scream.

Astrid's distinctive red hair spilled across the shiny stone floor before the guards. She wasn't moving. Rage, as she'd only felt when her father was murdered, filled Lillian, and she quickly unsheathed her daggers. Taking a deep breath, she stepped out from behind the statue, ready to kill every last one of the guards.

She leaped forward, but an arm curled around her middle, and a hand covered her mouth. Lillian thrashed as the person pulled her back, biting down as hard as she could. Blood filled her mouth, but they didn't let go. Magic enveloped her, and she screamed as the world whirled.

The night breeze caressed her face when she was finally released. Spinning around, she threw her dagger at Atlas, or Kian, or whatever his name was. It sliced his cheek, drops of blood dripping down onto his black uniform. She readied the other one.

"Stop, Lillian." Kian raised his hands.

"Take me back. Take me back now!" She screamed at him, not caring who heard. "They'll kill her!"

Lillian glanced around. Only stone buildings surrounded her, the dark castle looming over them in the distance—there was no way she'd make it back in time. Kian's eyes narrowed when they met hers, his strong jaw set. She started sobbing.

"Please! Please, take me back."

Astrid couldn't die; she wouldn't allow it.

Lillian flinched when he stepped closer, backing away from him. Kian's face hardened. "It was too late. She was already dead.

Lillian, I am sorry. But you're too important. I won't let you die as well. You can hate me all you like for it, but I won't take you back."

His words didn't register. Lillian threw the other dagger, but tears blinded her, and her aim was off. She snarled when it didn't even nick him.

Kian closed the distance between them, grabbing her shoulders. "Lillian, listen to me."

She met his eyes, but when he reached out to touch her cheek, she slapped him so hard her palm stung from the impact. Kian didn't react, only reached for her again. She punched his chest again and again until her strength wavered, a broken cry leaving her throat. Kian remained still, keeping his hands idle by his sides. Lillian crumpled to the ground when the adrenaline wore off, and Kian lowered himself down next to her, worriedly searching her face.

"You did this." Lillian's voice was hoarse. "You killed her."

Kian sighed. "I didn't betray her. I don't know who did, but I promise you it wasn't me. I've been protecting all of you."

Lillian shook her head. It couldn't be a coincidence that the king released him from his duties the same night they found a rebel who was part of the trials. She stared at him through hazy eyes. Blood still dripped from the cut on his face. She hoped it would scar.

"Astrid was going rogue, Lillian. I knew she was a rebel, but she wasn't following the orders that she was given."

"So it was her own fault?" Lillian hissed.

His face softened. "I'm not saying that. But I couldn't protect her. I didn't know what she was planning."

Lillian started shaking. This isn't what was supposed to happen. She was the one who was supposed to die—no one else.

"Do you know what Astrid was up to?" Kian reached out to wrap his arm around her but pulled back when she snarled at him.

Lillian's head spun. Why had Astrid been in the castle tonight? She hadn't worn a ball gown, so she hadn't planned on attending. It didn't make sense. They'd agreed to meet after the ball.

"Tell me what you know," she demanded quietly.

She didn't owe him any answers. He was the one who had lied to her. Kian should be the one answering questions tonight.

Wrapping his arms around his legs, Kian blew out a breath.

"I have been working against the king, my father, for the past three years. Trying to save as many as possible with my position." He paused, a shadow crossing his face. "Alek murdered my mother. I couldn't just stand by after that."

Lillian glared at him. The grief and betrayal within her left no room for compassion. The official story was that the queen had passed away after a time of sickness. Not that she put it beneath the king to murder his wife. He did not have any qualms about killing children, men, or women whenever it suited him.

"Since then, I have been trying to find rebels and get them to safety. That's what I was planning to do with Atli. But I arrived too late." He shook his head, his inky black hair reflecting the silvery moonlight. "But everything changed that day in the market. When I saw you."

Kian's eyes burned into hers. She averted her gaze, staring intently at the hem of her dirty dress.

"Why?"

"Do you ever wonder what is truly making you sick? Why your hair and skin pale with every year that passes?"

Lillian shook her head slowly. The healers she'd gone to had all been bewildered. They had never been able to work out why her body was wasting away.

"I've seen it once before. In a book, in my father's library." Kian's voice was gentle. "I didn't tell you immediately because I thought you knew—that you were hiding. But after meeting you, seeing how sick you are, and realizing you're completely unaware. I... I don't see how you can be kept oblivious anymore."

Lillian frowned. "What are you trying to tell me?"

"The book was about Queen Liv."

His eyes searched hers. She stared blankly back.

"It was a drawing of her after Adeon placed the curse on her and King Ivar. She, too, had paled, her hair turned snow white."

Pulling at a white strand of her hair, Lillian pondered his words. "So I am cursed?"

"You're her daughter."

Chapter Fifty

Lillian didn't believe him. She drew deep breaths as waves of nausea rolled through her. She couldn't be the daughter of Queen Liv and King Ivar. Her father wouldn't have lied to her for her whole life. *Eli* wouldn't have lied to her all this time.

She rose to her feet and paced back and forth, glaring at the moon that looked back at her. Kian remained on the ground, his eyes trailing her. Lillian ground her teeth at the pity in them.

"It's not possible." She stared at him. "You must have misunderstood."

"Lillian, you're a spitting image of her. Atli was Ivar's right hand; he must have saved you that day eighteen years ago and raised you as his own so my father wouldn't find you. Your parents were already cursed when you were born. They kept you a secret since they couldn't protect you without their magic."

Lillian bit back a growl. If Kian was right, everything in her life was a lie. *She* was a lie.

"Why wouldn't he have told me?" Her voice broke.

"I'm not sure. My guess is that Atli came to love you as his own daughter, and he wanted to find a way to break the curse before he got your hopes up."

Rising to his feet, Kian stepped toward her, his arms out. Lillian backed away. He'd lied to her. Everyone had lied to her.

208

"Do you know how to break the curse?" She forced herself to ask, even if she didn't want his help.

Kian stared at her as she retreated, silver filling his eyes as he slowly shook his head. There was so much pain in them that it hurt Lillian's own heart.

She couldn't take it—couldn't see another person look at her with that pain in their eyes. A strangled noise escaped her, and Lillian spun on her heel and raced up the slanted path to the castle. When Kian called out for her, she gritted her teeth but didn't turn back.

The ball was still in full swing. She clenched and unclenched her fists, trying to dampen the rage coursing through her veins. How dare the world just go on when her friend's life had just ended. She wanted to fight them. Fight the king and his men. Snarling, she realized she'd left her daggers with Kian. At least she was as good with her fists. If anyone came for her, she'd kill them with her bare hands.

It wasn't until she reached the statue of Adeon that Lillian realized she was back where she'd last seen Astrid. There was no one there. No blood on the floor, as if it hadn't even happened.

She made a foul gesture to the stone statue, wishing the god it represented would appear so she could kill him or maybe for him just to end her. She was so tired of all this death—so tired of fighting. Maybe if Adeon just finished what he started she'd finally find peace.

When nothing happened, she slid down with her back against the statue, and more hot tears spilled for her friend. Slamming her hand against the marble floor, she wondered if Astrid had known who she really was.

Finn found her there an hour later. Lillian's tears had dried, her eyes vacant and unseeing. He didn't ask any questions, just scooped her into his arms. A small scrap of paper blew across the floor as he picked her up. She reached out and grabbed it, scrunching it up in her hand. Finn carried her the whole way home, softly humming a children's tune in her ear.

The apartment was dark when they entered, and Lillian blew out a breath of relief. Finn gently placed Lillian on her bed and curled up on the floor beside her. Turning to face the wall, she tried to fall asleep. She was exhausted, but sleep didn't come, her mind racing with everything she'd learned. Finn's breaths were also uneven below her.

Finn, did you... Did you know about Atlas?

No. A sense of betrayal vibrated along the bond. *Will you tell me what happened, Lillian? I know it's not just Atlas.*

She swallowed. *Can I show you instead?*

Finn had been eager to share memories, but she'd been reluctant. It felt too vulnerable to let someone into her past, fully into her mind. But she didn't have words to explain what had happened, how to tell him that Astrid was dead, what Lillian found out about herself.

Yes.

Lillian examined the wall around her mind. It wasn't as rigid as she expected. She didn't have to tear down the whole thing to let Finn in; there was a small door that led to specific memories. Finn carefully brushed against the small opening, and Lillian let her mind replay the events from the evening.

His sadness rippled through her like a shock wave as they watched Astrid die. Wincing, she watched herself attack Kian, how he didn't lift an arm to defend himself, letting Lillian take out her grief and anger on him.

The disbelief rolling down the bond was like white-hot coal as Kian revealed her true identity: that it was a curse that was killing her.

But it was Finn's outrage as Kian confirmed that he didn't know how to break the curse that threatened to make her sick, waves of nausea crashing through her. When they watched Finn find her by the statue, he pulled back, and the door in her mind slammed shut. Lillian didn't dare try to read Finn's emotions.

Do you realize that you're a Valkyrie? That is amazing. I wonder what your wings look like.

Lillian almost snorted. Only Finn would find the one good thing from one of the worst nights of her life.

Unless I break the curse, I guess we'll never know.

Unease filled her. If her father hadn't found out how to do it the past eighteen years, Lillian doubted she'd be able to do it within months.

We will figure it out.

When Lillian finally drifted off to sleep, she thought she heard Finn whisper, "Good night, Valkyrie Queen."

Chapter Fifty-One

Lillian woke up with a gasp. The echo of wings and the feeling of falling through the air had filled her dreams. Shaking her head, she sat up and pushed the sticky covers off, squinting against the sun shining through the window above the bed. Memories from yesterday washed over her, bile rising in her throat at the thought of Astrid. She drew a few deep breaths.

She would not fall apart.

Her mission hadn't changed. She needed to focus on getting through the next few days and taking her place in the King's Guard. She might be the Valkyrie heir but she still needed to kill King Alek. Perhaps even more so now if he found out who she was. Lillian would try to find a way to break the curse once she succeeded. Her stomach churned; she hoped she could hold on that long.

Finn was already up. There was no sign of him on the wooden floor below her. Lillian strained her ears, but the apartment was quiet. She blew out a breath of relief; she wasn't in the mood to talk to anyone.

She'd slept in the dress, so she quickly peeled it off and pulled on her favorite leather trousers and a black tunic. Before Lillian strapped her sword to her back, she paused to study it. The black stone embellishing the pommel glittered in the sunlight.

Which mother had it belonged to?

After tying her hair back in a high ponytail, she left the room. None of the others were around, but her daggers lay on the kitchen table next to a plate of food. Both daggers were cleaned and sharpened.

Lillian pushed the thoughts of what she'd last done with them away and fastened them at her thighs. She tried to eat a few bites of food, but the cold meat tasted like ash on her tongue. Giving up as each bite became more difficult to swallow, she walked through the door. It was time for Eli to answer some questions.

Sweat streamed down her back by the time she arrived at the abandoned-looking stone house. She didn't bother with knocking or the code Eli used last time. When she kicked open the rotting door, its hinges creaked as it threatened to fall off. The anger felt good. She was done, absolutely done, with everyone lying to her. A chair fell over in the kitchen when she strolled through the door into the dusty house.

Eli and Aksel had both drawn their swords, standing with legs wide in a fighting stance. Eli lowered his sword when he recognized Lillian, but Aksel kept his sword raised, watching her with narrowed eyes.

She calmly studied them as she pulled a chair from the table, flipped it around, and sat down, leaning her arms on its back. Clicking her tongue, she threw Aksel a pointed look.

"You're not going to offer me any tea today?"

He narrowed his eyes further.

Smirking, she turned to Eli. "I thought we said no more lies, Eli." Her voice was icy, the rage inside her barely contained.

He sat down, his eyes worriedly scanning her face. "What do you mean? What's happened, Lil?"

His eyes didn't quite meet hers. Again.

She bit her cheek to not snarl at him. "Oh, you know, the usual. I went to a ball, my friend was murdered, and I found out I'm the rightful heir to the throne."

Aksel sucked in a breath while Eli stared at her with wary eyes. Eli waved to Aksel, not once breaking eye contact with Lillian.

"Aksel, can you please leave us for a moment."

Lowering his sword, although tension still lingered in his posture, Aksel quietly left the kitchen. Lillian studied his long blonde hair, almost the same length as her own, as he walked out, remembering how he'd reacted when she'd touched him. "*What are you?*" It made more sense now.

Tilting her head, she glared at Eli. "You knew."

She had to sit down on her hands to keep herself from punching him, breaking his nose yet again. His betrayal hurt the worst. She'd only just met Kian, but Eli was her friend, her lover—the one person she was supposed to trust.

He offered her a sad smile. "I did. I've wanted to tell you for so long."

"So why didn't you," she demanded.

Leaning forward in his chair, he studied her. "Atli convinced me not to."

"Because he didn't want to get my hopes up before he found a way to break the curse?"

It was difficult to keep her voice steady. She was so sick of her father and Eli sheltering her, not trusting her ability to take care of herself.

"Something like that. Please trust me. It was for your own sake."

Shaking her head, she slammed her palms on the table. "How am I supposed to trust you? You've lied to me my whole life and keep doing it."

A lump formed in her throat, and she swallowed hard—she was done being sad. She needed to fuel the rage, or she'd fall into a heap on the floor, broken beyond repair. Rising to his feet, Eli reached for her. Lillian gritted her teeth but didn't move.

Eli's eyes filled with tears.

"I'm sorry," he choked. "Atli was figuring it out. He didn't want you to know, for you to worry. I disagreed with his plan. I didn't want to do it. But he took me in, Lillian. He saved my life when I was living on the streets. I couldn't betray him. I can't betray him, even now."

Lillian had never seen him cry. Not even when her father died. Her heart broke a bit more then, not for herself, but for Eli. He rarely talked about the years before he found them—when her father took him in and raised him. She was only little but remembered him being skin and bones, jumping at the slightest sound.

She finally reached out and wrapped her arms around him. Eli leaned into her embrace, pulling her closer. His tears soaked her tunic as he sobbed into her shoulder. She didn't let herself cry—she wasn't even sure if she had more tears after last night.

Once Eli calmed, she let him pull her into his lap. Playing with the hem of his gray tunic, she said quietly. "I'm still going to kill the king."

Eli nodded. "I didn't expect anything less."

"And you're going to tell me what you're planning next."

Eli called back Aksel, who kept eyeing Lillian suspiciously. She rolled her eyes, it wasn't like she would sprout wings right here. She was still dying.

An informant had told Aksel that the third trial would span three days. While he wasn't sure exactly what it would entail, he knew it would take place away from the capital. On the last day, King Alek would attend to appoint the five new guards. Apparently, it would be some grand finale, to which the king's court and nobles were invited to watch. She clenched her fists. *Of course,* it wasn't enough that twenty-five of them would die in these trials; their deaths needed to serve as entertainment as well.

Eli explained that they believed the king would have less protection than usual since some of his guards would be left behind to protect the castle. The court and nobles would bring their own guards, of course, but even though they technically also served the king, they'd hopefully protect whoever paid their salary. It would be the best opportunity they'd get unless Lillian preferred to wait until she'd joined the guard.

If she *approved*, Eli emphasized the word; he and Aksel, together with a few other trusted rebels, would cause a diversion when the king appointed her to allow Lillian an opportunity to kill him. Lillian studied the worn wooden table, picking at a loose sliver. She could see about a million flaws with this plan, including the king's fire-wielding abilities, but after a while, she nodded. It was worth the risk. She just needed to stay alive long enough to see it through.

When Aksel took off to meet with his informant, Lillian finally dug up the courage to ask Eli the question she dreaded.

"Did you know Astrid?"

She intently studied the table and the sun's rays that glittered in the dust lining it, wincing as a small piece of wood pricked her finger when she pulled at it.

Eli brushed his auburn hair out of his face. "I didn't know her personally, but I knew of her. Atli met her on one of his trips. She was the daughter of one of the other rebel leaders on Echo."

Lillian took a deep breath. "What was she doing here?"

Eli glanced at her, weighing his words. "Atli knew that if something happened to him, you would likely set off right for the capital. He didn't want you to face it alone."

Her stomach dropped, and she punched the table, ignoring the stab of pain as more slivers pierced her hand.

"It's not your fault, Lillian," Eli spoke softly. "She wanted to do this. She knew the risks. The king has her sister, so she had as much reason as you to want the king dead."

Every breath Lillian tried to draw stabbed at her chest, but she cleared her throat, "Did she know what I am?"

Eli shook his head slowly, "At least not initially."

Remembering Astrid's fascination with the Valkyries, how she'd been obsessing over finding out more, and how she'd studied Lillian's face that night in the library, Lillian shuddered. Even Astrid had figured it out before Lillian.

"What do you know of," she swallowed. "Of my parents?"

It was strange referring to the previous king and queen as her parents. She still didn't believe it.

"I don't know much. Alek destroyed most books, so I only know what Atli told me." He studied her. "Liv was one of the most powerful Valkyries ever to have lived, and Ivar was her human match. He wielded the power of the sun, magic like no one had ever seen. When they met, they took one look at each other and knew they were destined to be."

Lillian recalled what she'd read about the Valkyries and their fated mates. Her stomach churned as she wondered if Eli was her mate, and she just didn't know it because of the curse. She shook her head. It wasn't the time to ask.

Eli cupped her cheek. "When we break the curse, you'll be the most powerful person in Orios."

If we break the curse, Lillian thought. But there was another place where she could find more information. After telling Eli she needed to go home to prepare for the final trial and a long lecture on being careful, she slipped out the door.

Chapter Fifty-Two

When she walked down the dark streets, she reached out to Finn. *In the mood to help me break into a house?*

If Finn was surprised by her suggestion, she didn't feel it.

Sounds like fun, silver girl.

She gave him the directions to Astrid's aunt's house and waited for him in the shadows of an alley across the street.

When he arrived, they studied the dark home. The only light was in the kitchen, the servant preparing meals for tomorrow. All the other windows and the tower were dark, only a small lantern shining soft light over the large double doors.

After filling Finn in about the library in the basement, they formulated a plan. Finn would take his owl shape and break a window on the other side of the home, hopefully drawing the servant and anyone else there. Lillian would pick the lock on the front door, and they'd sneak into the library. They didn't have a plan for getting out; they would have to figure it out as they went.

When glass shattering echoed in the quiet night, Lillian leaped out of the shadows and sprinted for the door. Thankfully, the lock was old, and she had no problem picking it without too much damage. They crept into the house once Finn showed up, dressed only in a pair of pants.

Was it too much to ask for you to wear a shirt?

Finn grinned at her in the dark. The night vision was really helpful, she mused. Not that she planned on breaking into houses on
the regular. Lillian had memorized the way the other night, and
without running into anyone, they soon stood outside the painting
of the large bird.

Is it just me, or is it strange that there is a painting of a raven?
Finn examined it closely.

Maybe it's ironic?

Lillian didn't know what to make of it either. If Astrid's uncle
was so close to the king, having a painting of the bird he despised
due to their affiliation with the Valkyries wasn't exactly advisable.
She shrugged; it didn't matter now.

Let's go inside.

Cautiously, Lillian opened the door, wincing as the wood
creaked, and they entered the dark library. It looked exactly as it had
when Lillian was here last. Rows and rows of books lining the
curved walls, with everything in its rightful place. She'd held a small
kernel of hope that there would be a clue to whatever Astrid had
discovered, but no such luck.

As they browsed the shelves, Lillian was once again thankful for
Finn's sharp eyes, as they didn't need to light a lantern to read the
titles. Nothing stood out to her until she came across a small black
book, its back a bit further out than the rest.

She gently pulled it from the shelf and sat in one of the velvet
chairs by the large table in the middle of the room before flipping it
open. Lillian's heart skipped a beat. On the first yellow and fraying
page, in neat handwriting, it said *Liv Volantis*. When Lillian turned
the next page, she realized she was holding her mother's journal. She
tugged on the bond to make Finn come over, and together, they
dove into the life of Queen Liv.

It was difficult to read parts of the journal. Time and wear had
erased paragraphs, even entire pages. But what they could make out
spoke of a woman who loved her people and Hindra, her home. She
wrote of tension between Hindra and Echo, how she and Ivar
worked to unite the people to share the resources between the two
islands. The entry date of her notes jumped, sometimes several

months. When they flipped to the end of the journal, Liv mentioned Adeon for the first time.

He had threatened them; he didn't want Hindra and Echo united and disapproved of Liv and Ivar's union. Adeon gave them a choice: split up and never see each other again, or he would turn on them at the risk of their people. Lillian's heart broke for her mother; the devastation of having to choose between her mate and her people shone through her words. Her parents ultimately chose each other in the end. Lillian struggled to understand it; how could they sacrifice their people for the sake of one person?

But nowhere did it say much about the curse itself, not even when Lillian triple-checked the pages. Her mother had only written one sentence about it. *The curse is killing us, but the alternative is so horrific I can't even put it into words.* A chill snaked down her spine when she realized whatever horror her mother had mentioned was what Lillian would have to face if they figured out how to break the curse.

A thump above them caused them both to jump.

I think it's time we head out. Finn pointed at the door.

Lillian nodded and pocketed the book inside her tunic. When Finn raised his eyebrows, she lifted her chin. *It's my mother's. It belongs to me.*

He didn't argue.

They crept through the dim hallway and up the stairs. Lillian poked her head out from the stairway. *Someone is coming. Get ready.*

She pulled her cloak over her head, cursing Finn through the bond. Lillian knew that him leaving his shirt and cloak would come back to bite them.

She waved at him to get back into the cover of the shadows. *I've got this. I don't want to kill him, so stay back so he doesn't see you.*

Lillian leaped out of the stairway when the soft candlelight fell onto the servant, and before he could scream, she used the hilt of her dagger to knock him on the side of his head. Instantly unconscious, she caught his body and gently rested him against the stone wall.

Whispering, "I'm sorry," she motioned for Finn to hurry up.

As they walked home, thoughts of her mother flooded Lillian's mind. She wondered what she would think of Lillian right now. She wasn't exactly princess material with her bad temper and reckless tendencies. Finn interrupted her thoughts by speaking out loud, albeit in a whisper. She still jerked.

"Have you given any thoughts about what happens after?"

Lillian frowned.

"I mean, once we succeed with your mission and break your curse?" His voice lowered at the end of the sentence.

Lillian shook her head. "Even if I am the rightful heir, why would the people of Orios follow me?"

Finn grabbed her hand and turned to her. Her stomach churned; she hadn't seen such a serious expression on his face before.

"Regardless of what you decide, I will stay by your side. I hope you will consider me for your court."

She almost snorted—*her court*. But Finn's intense stare stopped her from mocking him.

"Always," she said, squeezing his hand.

Outside the apartment, she paused.

He's not there. He told Sam that he was preparing for the trial.

She smiled gratefully at Finn. When she lay in bed that night, mulling over everything they'd learned, she thought she heard wings beating outside the window. But when Lillian glanced at the dark night sky, only the moon shone through the window.

Chapter Fifty-Three

Lillian dressed quickly the following day. Donning her favored fighting leathers and braiding her hair, she studied herself in the mirror. She sighed at the dark circles beneath her eyes, the dull gray looking back at her—even her white hair had lost its shine. As Lillian glanced around the room, making sure she'd not forgotten anything since she wouldn't be returning—regardless of what happened at the trial—the small piece of crumpled paper she'd grabbed from the floor blew across her desk.

Only one sentence was scribbled on it in sloppy handwriting. *What is bound by love, only death can undo.* Lillian flipped the paper over and moved closer to the window to see if there was any invisible ink. But there were only those nine words. Shrugging, she threw the paper back onto her small desk.

Lillian didn't speak as they ate a meal before the trial; she only studied the small apartment and breathed in its calming scent. Sam and Finn were also unusually quiet. Neither engaged in their usual bickering about who would get the second helping of breakfast, both bearing the weight of the final trial.

After almost gagging trying to eat a piece of bacon, Lillian sighed and quietly told them what she knew, that she expected the trial to last three days, urging Finn and Sam to bring their cloaks and fill a light satchel with food. Even if she technically could go three days without food, she preferred to have some energy left to execute the plan Eli and she had agreed on. Lillian filled them in on that, too, making them swear not to breathe a word to Kian. Even if he hadn't betrayed them yet, she was about to kill his father. She didn't believe he would be as supportive.

They arrived early for the trial, to find that most other novices had done the same. There were only thirteen of them left now. Her heart ached as she thought of Astrid. Astrid, who should have been standing next to her, nervously twinning her red hair.

The mongrel who killed so many in the first trial strolled up to them while they waited in the shade under the castle balcony.

"I heard about your redhead friend." He smiled gleefully at Lillian. "Too bad."

She clenched her fists, glaring at him.

"She even put up a bit of a fight. Who knew she had it in her? She screamed like a babe when I almost killed her."

Lillian drew a deep breath, but she couldn't stop herself from responding. "Shut. Up. Or I will kill you before the trial even starts."

Take it easy.

Finn tried to catch her eye, but she didn't look away from the monster, who now smiled broadly at her—a leering, disgusting smile. She bared her teeth in warning.

The mongrel winked at her. "I hope they took their time, played a little before they killed her. They beat her to death, I heard."

Red filled her vision, and she threw herself at the man with a growl. Lillian didn't bother drawing her weapons, using her nails to gouge deep gashes across his fleshy face. As he pushed her off him, she spun, throwing out her leg to throw off his balance. When he wobbled, she kicked him hard in the chest. The man fell backward with a loud thump, dust flying around his large body, and Lillian didn't waste any time before she leaped on top of him, punching his face once, twice. Blood stained her hands, but she didn't care. The pain felt good.

Finn tried to reach her through the bond, but she'd descended into such deep rage that it was easy to block the connection.

She unsheathed one of her daggers, pressed it to the man's throat and hissed, "Those were the last words you'll ever say."

He stared back at her, his watery eyes shining with fear as drops of blood trickled down his neck. Lillian willed herself to finish it—this monster deserved to die. But before she could, someone lifted her off him, and she hissed and spat as she tried to get loose from the strong arms that enveloped her. She'd recognize the smell anywhere, the smell of the nightly wind whipping through the forest. Kian held her tight as she struggled, Finn hovering close by.

"They will disqualify you if you don't follow my lead, Lillian." Kian whispered in her ear, his tone urgent.

She whipped her head up. She couldn't be disqualified. Then, all that happened would have been for nothing. Astrid's and her father's deaths would have been for nothing.

Panting, she slowly let her body go limp in Kian's arms.

"If I let you go, will you attack anyone else?"

She shook her head.

Kian gently set her down, and she spun around, her breathing still labored. Kian and Finn eyed her cautiously—like she was some wounded animal that would attack them at one wrong move.

Rolling her shoulders, she offered them a mocking smirk. "I'm good."

They glanced at each other, then back to her, narrowing their eyes.

Sam stood over the man, a sword to his neck, while the other novices wisely faced another way. With a final glance at her, Kian walked up to the man.

"You will get up and leave right now. Your time in the trials has come to an end. If I see you in the capital again, I will personally kill you." His voice was cold, commanding. A prince talking to his subordinate.

The man didn't argue, quickly scurrying to his feet and leaving the courtyard.

Lillian turned her back and stomped off when Kian walked back toward her. Refusing to meet his eyes, she inspected her split knuckles, wincing as she rubbed her sleeve over them, trying to get rid of the blood. Finn and Sam slipped up by her side. Like two silent bodyguards, they glared at anyone who dared glance in Lillian's direction.

You are insane. But also, that was incredible.

Pride filled the bond as Finn winked at her. She shook her head, a crooked smile on her face.

Sam placed a hand on her shoulder, sorrow lining his eyes as he met hers. Her chest constricted; Sam and Astrid had become close. Lillian had wondered if he felt something more than friends. She put her hand on his and squeezed it.

Finally, the two other commanders entered the courtyard. If they realized they were missing yet another novice, they didn't say anything.

Commander Jon stepped forward.

"The third trial is a trial of perseverance." He gestured to a short, bald man Lillian had never seen before. "Kaspar here will open a portal that will take you each to your own starting point in the northern territory. You will have three days to climb the Skandi. Once you reach the top, there will be a final challenge. Five of you will be then appointed to join the King's Guard."

Goosebumps raced over Lillian's skin. The Skandi. Her father had told her stories about the wild mountain. No one lived close to the Skandi, the rumors of creatures as old as Adeon roaming there discouraging even the bravest of men. She tugged at the hem of her cloak. It was too warm right now, but she'd be grateful for its protection once she was on the mountain. There was snow year-round on the Skandi.

Kian tried to catch her eye, but Lillian kept her gaze straight ahead. She wouldn't be distracted again, and Kian was definitely a distraction. Feeling the warmth of his gaze trail across her face, she inclined her head and focused her eyes on her dusty boots.

Kaspar stepped forward. Lillian eyed him curiously as he closed his eyes and raised his palms. The air vibrated from magic, and slowly, a dark, shimmering portal opened up next to him, glittering like the crystals that covered her ballgown. Her eyes widened; she'd never seen anything like it.

Commander Jon motioned for the novices to get in line, and there was some shuffling as no one wanted to go first. The portal was intimidating. But no point in waiting around here. Lillian stepped forward.

Nodding, Commander Jon asked for her arm. When she offered it, he fastened one of the iron bracelets around it. No magic again. She guessed it made sense; Finn could have just flown to the top otherwise. While she didn't feel any different herself when she tried to communicate with Finn through the bond, there was nothing. A black wall blocked their connection.

Turning around, she caught Finn's eye and mouthed, "Good luck." He inclined his head.

"Novice, time to go through the portal." Commander Jon waved his hand impatiently.

Lillian didn't look back as she stepped through the dark, glittering hole.

Chapter Fifty-Four

Awful. The portal was awful. Lillian's body was compressed, forcing her to curl into herself. The nausea she'd felt when she'd rifted with Kian was nothing, *nothing*, compared to this. Lillian's head spun so fast that there were only swirls of color in front of her eyes. When a bright light finally appeared, she tumbled out of the portal. Falling to her knees on the hard ground, Lillian vomited until there was only bile left. Once the retching finally subsided, she lifted her head.

The landscape took her breath away. The mountain range towered over her, stretching out as far as she could see in both directions, its peaks and valleys forming a beautiful pattern against the clear blue sky. The mountains were clad in colorful green and brown at the base, with snow-white covered tops. The Skandi stood highest of them all, a proud and formidable mountain that seemed to watch her when she took a hesitant step toward it. She drew a deep breath, her lungs chilling as the cold mountain air filled them.

As she walked toward the Skandi's base, she scrambled to remember what her father told her about it. While few lived here, many tried to scale it. But only a handful came back to tell of their feat. The sun's position told her she was approaching the mountain from the north. She sighed—her father once said the easiest route was from the south.

Lillian didn't have time to walk around the mountain to find the easier route. She'd have to make do with the northern side. At least there would be caverns. Her father had talked of caves that went deep into the mountain, most of them accessible from the north.

She gritted her teeth when a strong gust of wind ripped at her clothes, roaring between the mountains and bringing wisps of snow that glittered as they clung to her gray cloak. Lillian shuddered—if it were this cold and only midday, it would be three cold days on the mountain.

The mountainside split into several narrow winding paths from the animals and creatures the mountain was home to. Lillian couldn't see more than fifty yards ahead, so she shrugged, choosing the middle path, praying it wouldn't lead her on a detour. Placing one foot carefully in front of the other, Lillian kept her senses on high alert. She stilled at the slightest movement or sound, barely breathing, hoping she could avoid attracting any of the creatures she'd heard about as a child.

She'd prefer not to stumble upon the Garms and the Fenrirs, another wolf-like creature, but twice the size of Garms and rumored to walk on their hind legs. But most of all, she didn't want to wake the Mungan, a giant serpent said to live in the tunnels beneath the mountain. She winced; she had always hated snakes. Growing up, she'd seen too many children bitten by the vipers that hid in the tall grass in the forests. A Mungan could eat her whole.

A howl pierced the air. Whipping her head in the direction of the sound, Lillian searched the mountainside but couldn't make out much in the dim afternoon light. She cursed softly—she'd already gotten used to the convenience of Finn's night sight; her own appeared even worse now. Lillian chose the right path when she reached another fork, putting as much distance between herself and whatever creature had howled as possible.

She trudged upward, each step becoming increasingly challenging as darkness fell, the mountaintop casting long shadows on the path before her. Stones and rubble made her stumble every other step, and she kept one hand on the grassy mountainside to keep her balance. Lillian wasn't even a third of the way up the mountain, but the drop to her right was still well over a hundred yards. A chill snaked down her spine. There was no way she'd survive if she fell.

Scanning the mountainside, she searched for openings, any indications of a cave where she could find shelter for the night. A few yards above her, the side of the mountain curved slightly. Lillian started toward it, her steps careful, when gravel crunched behind her. She barely had time to whip her head around before a fist connected with her face.

Stars danced in front of Lillian's eyes as she braced herself against the side of the mountain. Holding out an arm to protect her face, she stared at her attacker. Ketil stood in front of her, a vicious smile on his face.

"Not so arrogant, are you, little girl, when the commander isn't here to save your skin?"

Lillian raged at herself. How had she not heard him come up behind her? Thankfully, she stood on higher ground. She needed to use it to her advantage.

"I don't think your mongrel of a friend would dare speak to me like that." She smiled sweetly at him. "To my knowledge, this *little girl* beat him within an inch of his life."

"Oh stupid girl, you actually believe you hurt him? He knew he'd have to deal with those three guard dogs that follow you around if he fought back. My guess is he'd rather pretend you injured him and come after you once you were alone. It seems I'll be the one who'll get that pleasure, though."

Lillian threw her head back and laughed—her guard dogs. Finn would get a kick out of that. She wasn't sure if Kian would like it as much. But she definitely wanted to see his face when she told him to 'sit.'

Ketil glared at her, his body tensing. There was a small crack in the mountainside, and Lillian placed her foot inside it. It would hurt if he pushed her too far, but it would provide some stability. Hopefully, she wouldn't break the foot, but even a broken foot was preferable to falling down the mountain.

Ketil made his decision a split second before his arm swung out. She crouched down, his fist missing her head by a quarter of an inch. Ketil wobbled from the momentum, and Lillian snapped out with a hand, punching his knee. She'd hoped it was all it would take, but Ketil caught himself on the mountainside and swung with his other hand. Lillian wasn't as lucky this time. His fist connected with her stomach, and it took everything in her not to bend over closer to the drop. She gasped for air as she blocked his second swing with her arm.

When Ketil drew his sword, she unsheathed her own and blocked his first blow. She parried the next one when he swung for her side, but she wasn't fast enough. The sword sliced through her upper arm, ripping through her cloak. A glance confirmed it wasn't deep, and Lillian slashed for him next, her sword tearing the bottom of his tunic when he jumped back.

Panting, she realized she hadn't studied Ketil during the first trial—hadn't seen his skill with a sword. But he was good. *Really* good. She could perhaps beat him on the ground, but her weight and size were at a disadvantage on the mountain. She needed more space to move around. Here, strength was key. And Ketil was twice her size.

She glanced around, hoping for anything that might help her, but regretted it the next moment. Ketil put his whole body behind the next blow, and Lillian grasped air as her sword slipped from her grip. It fell a few yards down the mountain and lodged under a branch, glittering in the dim evening light.

Ketil immediately blocked her path to the sword, and Lillian cursed silently when a cold smile spread across his face. But she gritted her teeth and drew her daggers to deflect his next strike. Her arms shook when she pushed with all her strength to try to throw off Ketil's balance. He didn't move an inch. He lunged for her again and again. Lillian growled as she intercepted each blow—she needed to get that sword out of his hands.

A roar echoed between the mountains, and they both whipped their heads up. Lillian froze as a giant black dragon flew into view, its silhouette stark against the darkening sky. The dragon beat its wings and turned mid-air, meeting her eyes for a moment and letting out another roar before disappearing behind a mountaintop. Her eyes widened when two huge ravens appeared behind it, their harsh calls piercing the air as they neared.

"What is happening," Ketil whispered, fear making his voice quiver.

The ravens circled above them, so close that Lillian could see into their intelligent black eyes. It was as if they were staring into her very soul when they glared at her. Their wings must span over twenty feet, and their feathers shimmered under the moon that peeked over the mountaintop.

Unfortunately, Ketil recovered quickly and faced Lillian again. When he lifted his sword to strike, the ravens dove and she could only make out a blur of black shooting through the air.

It happened so fast. The first raven charged Ketil, while the second landed by her side. Lillian recoiled as its wing nudged her. The raven tilted its head and stared at her, and when she locked eyes with it, she stilled. Something in its gaze calmed her; a sense of protectiveness and familiarity emanated from it.

Ketil screamed as the other raven took flight. Blood covered his face, and he awkwardly waved his sword. It reminded Lillian of when she had to fight off the Garms in the dark. Sucking in a breath, Lillian realized the raven had gouged out his eyes.

She glanced from Ketil to the two ravens. They stood by her side now, the one who'd blinded Ketil casually cleaning its wings. The first raven stared at her expectantly, flipping its head between her and Ketil. Lillian took a hesitant step toward him. It was easy to dodge his blows—Ketil was frantic, slashing blindly. If it were her standing there, he wouldn't hesitate, but her stomach churned as she studied the blinded man. The ravens cawed softly as she hesitated.

"I'll still kill you, bitch."

Ketil faced the wrong direction, screaming out over the mountainside. She shook her head. She would not end him this way. Lillian took a step back.

Ketil wasn't in her way; she could still reach the opening above her. Cautiously, Lillian walked back to the ravens perched above her. They parted when she neared, creating a pathway between themselves and the drop to her right. When she passed them, she glanced over her shoulder. The ravens followed her up the mountain.

Lillian didn't dare sheath her daggers, and as she slowly made her way toward what she hoped was a cave, she kept a watchful eye behind her. Even if they hadn't hurt her so far, she didn't want to be caught off guard if they changed their minds. When she finally reached the opening, she scanned the area around them. Ketil still screamed below, but he hadn't moved. There was no way he'd make it up the mountain.

It was a cave. The opening was small, barely big enough for her to squeeze through. When she peered inside, the cave was completely veiled in darkness. Grateful she had brought kindling to start a fire, she found a branch on the ground to use as a torch. Lillian prayed the cave wasn't home to any of the creatures she'd heard lived on the mountain, then took a hesitant step inside.

The cave was oval, its floor adorned with stalagmites that shimmered in the flickering firelight, and the smell of wet stone and grass filled her nostrils. She blew out a breath of relief; it was empty. After searching for any other openings into the mountain and finding none, she ventured back outside. Only one raven sat on the ledge outside the cave, its head tilted to the dark sky. Lillian followed its gaze, but only the night sky and the almost full moon looked back at her.

Strong wings beat the air, and the other raven came into view. She backed up as the raven gracefully landed on the small ledge facing her. When it stepped toward her, its glittering black eyes locked on hers, Lillian forced herself to stand still, although her fingers twitched for the daggers at her thighs. The raven lowered its head as it continued closing the distance between them. When it was only a few feet away, something reflected the moonlight in its black beak.

The raven dropped her sword on the ground and backed up a few steps as Lillian bent down to pick it up. When she grasped the pommel, a tingle danced along her spine. The black stone adorning it was the same color and shape as the black raven's eye.

Lillian studied the two ravens. "Thank you," she said quietly.

They flipped their heads. She stared at them, a wrinkle forming between her brows. The raven who'd dropped the sword unfurled its wing, pointing it toward the cave. Lillian's frown deepened. The raven made the same motion again.

"Do you want me to go in the cave?"

It inclined its head.

"What about you?"

Both ravens crouched lower to the ground, resting on the ledge. Lillian shook her head in disbelief—first, the dragon, now this. One of the ravens opened its mouth in a soft caw. She tentatively smiled back, and its eyes glistened with amusement as it returned her stare.

Lillian found herself yawning and decided to listen to the large bird. The ravens wouldn't fit in the cave anyway, and she doubted anyone would approach the ledge with those two standing guard outside. When Lillian made to turn toward the cave, both ravens dropped one of their legs to the ground, their heads bowed. She stared at them for a moment, then shrugged and offered them a bow of her own. When they straightened, there was approval in their black eyes.

Lillian lit a small fire, counting on the ravens to deter humans and animals alike. It was cold in the cave, and her teeth clattered as she fumbled with the kindling. She laid down as close to the fire as possible without risking setting herself on fire. The gentle, rhythmic rustle of the ravens' wings made her eyelids heavy.

Chapter Fifty-Five

A screech woke her from a deep, dreamless slumber. Lillian bolted up and peeked out of the cave. One of the ravens glared at her, waving its wing impatiently. After scanning the area for danger and finding none, Lillian picked up her things and walked out in the gray morning light, the sun's first rays barely appearing over the horizon.

"I couldn't have gotten a few more hours of sleep?"

She yawned as she waved at the two ravens. They cawed back at her, waving their wings toward the top of the mountain.

Lillian sighed; they were right. She should get going.

"Are you joining me?"

The ravens shook their heads, flicking their heads east. She nodded. Lillian had hoped they might follow her the rest of the way, but they obviously had bird matter to attend to. She snorted, and the ravens tilted their heads.

"Sorry, I am just getting used to this."

Stretching their wings, they gave her one last look before taking off. Their large wings whipped the air around her, making her white hair fly around her face. Lillian watched them until they were just two black dots in the orange-tinted morning sky before continuing her journey up the mountain.

The sun did little to warm her, icy winds blowing straight

through her clothes. Pulling her cloak tighter, she tried to estimate how far she had left. It looked like she'd scaled about one-third of the mountain from where she stood. She should reach the top by mid-afternoon tomorrow if she walked all day. As she scanned the grassy mountainside, she prayed she wouldn't run into any other murderous novices or animals that wanted to eat her.

The morning was quiet, and nothing with weapons or claws approached her, so by midday, she stopped for a break. Her feet ached—her worn boots had given her blisters, and she winced as she pulled them off. She didn't bother with a fire after finding a small crevice in the mountainside that provided some relief from the wind. Sitting inside it, Lillian stared out over the mountains facing her and the white clouds veiling their snow-covered tops.

Lillian ate a few pieces of dried meat and drank a sip of water while watching the sun's rays paint the mountainsides in lush greens and yellows. Her waterskin was half full; she would need to carefully ration it to make it last until tomorrow unless she could melt some snow tonight. But that was only if she reached the snow-covered upper part of the mountain that towered above her.

When she began her trek again, it was still quiet, and she allowed her mind to wander. Finn's question of what she hoped to do after filled her mind. She'd never allowed herself to hope for a future before, believing her early death to be inevitable. But now, there was a kernel of hope, and no matter how hard she tried, she could not squash it.

She could become Queen of Orios. A muffled laugh escaped her lips. She'd never been in a position of authority and had barely joined the rebels. She had no training, no grasp of the responsibilities of a queen. Lillian shook her head. There was no way.

She pondered the fact that she was technically only half-human. She knew very little of the Valkyries, but they carried more primal traits from what she'd read. The Valkyries were known for their possessive nature, fiery temper—apparently, the curse hadn't affected *that*—and ruthless savagery that set them apart from their human cousins.

And the wings. Lillian's stomach fluttered about the prospect of wings. Her whole life, she'd been weak and had to work twice as hard as others to become strong, to survive one more day. With the Valkyrie wings and strength, she'd never again be weak. She smiled at the thought.

Eli said she'd be the most powerful person in Orios if they broke the curse. She wondered if she'd inherited her father's magic. Wielding the sun and Valkyrie traits seemed almost too much for a single person. She sighed. Every fiber inside her hoped she would live to experience it.

In the late afternoon, dark clouds rolled across the sky, casting the mountainside in darkness and making each step more difficult. Icy rain fell, drenching Lillian immediately. She groaned; she was cold to her bones and couldn't feel her hands or feet anymore. She needed to find shelter, even if she hadn't gotten as far as she'd hoped.

There had been a large opening a while back. A gut feeling urged Lillian to walk as far from it as possible, but she turned around when she shivered so hard it felt like her teeth would shatter in her mouth. She'd rather face whatever was in the cave than freeze to death.

A strange smell wafted from the dark cave, and Lillian sniffed the air cautiously as she reached the large, arched entrance. She couldn't put her finger on what it was—the smell pungent but yet not like the scent of magic. At least it wasn't the smell of decay from the undead. Taking a cautious step inside, she peered around the cave. Thankfully, it was empty. Even in the dim light, there was no sign of life. No stalagmites adorned the floor; the black walls were smooth, shining like polished marble.

As she walked further in, the cave curved, a seemingly endless tunnel winding into the mountain, the shining walls gleaming in the dim light from the entrance. Lillian stayed close to the opening —she didn't care to see where the tunnel led. She shuddered as gusts of wind blew through the cave, bringing small drops of ice-cold rain. Staring at the dark sky and the large gray clouds traveling across it, Lillian prayed it would clear soon. She really didn't want to spend the night in this place.

When the rain persisted, she sighed and sat down on the cold ground with her back against the smooth wall, whipping her head back and forth between the opening and the dark tunnel. She shot to her feet at a rustle from deep within the mountain, straining her ears to hear if something was coming for her. But when silence stretched on, and the only sound was the wind whistling through the cave, she slowly sat back down again. The sound of rain and wind was hypnotizing, and Lillian began to feel drowsy. With her hands wrapped around her daggers, she told herself she would rest, just for a little while.

When she woke, the cave was enveloped in darkness, the rain outside relentless. She groaned—she was stuck in here tonight. Lillian lit a small fire, casting the cave in a soft glow, the shiny walls mirroring the flickering light. As she glanced around, the cave was silent. But something was different. She narrowed her eyes and stared at the opening again. The flames reflected in something on the ground in front of it. Cautiously, she rose, daggers in hand, and tiptoed toward it. It was a thick log, glistening in the firelight.

Lillian sucked in a breath. Scales. It was scales that glistened in the glow of the fire. She slowly turned around. The shape curved around the cave, its thick tail covering the entrance. Cursing silently, Lillian realized she had walked right into the Mungan's cave. She clenched her jaw. One step and she could take off running, leaving the monstrous serpent behind. Its tail was still, the serpent hopefully in deep slumber.

Lillian didn't dare put out the fire. Instead, she inched closer to the serpent. When she was near enough to touch it, she stilled, sent a prayer to whoever was listening, and lifted a leg. She held her breath, but the glittering serpent remained still as she swung her other leg over it.

Not risking a glance backward, she took another cautious step to leave the cave when there was a rustle behind her. Giving up on trying to be quiet, Lillian sprinted toward the icy rain that looked much more welcoming than what awaited behind her. When the first drops hit her face, she released a breath.

And was slung back into the cave. The force of the serpent's tail sent her careening into the hard wall. She didn't have time to catch the breath that had been knocked out of her before the tail whipped her again, knocking her to the ground.

A hiss echoed through the cave as the serpent's head snapped around the corner. Panic surged through Lillian when she met its yellow eyes. Black spikes covered its enormous head, similar to the little silver dragon, and black and green scales draped its body. The serpent shimmered in the firelight as it slithered closer to Lillian.

When its tail whipped at her again, she threw herself to the side, and there was a rush of air above her before the tail connected with the wall with a loud crack. The serpent opened its mouth and shrieked so loud in fury that Lillian had to cover her ears.

She sprinted toward the exit, but the tail slammed down before her, forcing her to turn back. Its yellow eyes traced her as she ran in zigzag movements to avoid the vicious tail. Another shriek vibrated through the cave, and Lillian prayed it wouldn't burst her eardrums. As it whipped its head back, preparing to lunge for her, Lillian threw one of her daggers. She growled as it only bounced off the serpent's scales, sliding down on the ground below it.

The serpent lunged, opening its mouth and showing off an impressive row of sharp teeth. Lillian rolled away, its large teeth snapping over where she'd just been standing. Glancing outside, Lillian prayed for the sound of large wings. This would be a great moment for those ravens to show up again. She *really* didn't want to become the Mungan's dinner. But it remained quiet outside, the rain smattering the only sound.

When the serpent lifted its head again, she realized the scales didn't fully cover its underside. Praying for a soft spot, she threw her other dagger. The serpent let out another ear-splitting shriek as the dagger lodged itself in its gut, and it snapped at her in retaliation. Lillian barely had time to throw herself out of the way, the serpent's hot breath grazing her as she yet again rolled away from its vicious teeth.

Unsheathing her sword, she prepared for its next strike. A sharp hiss served as a warning, and Lillian crouched down, slashing at its gut. The serpent's teeth missed her by half an inch, but she wasn't prepared for the tail that followed. A sharp pain seared through her gut as the tail once again flung her into the wall, and a sickening crack echoed through the cave when she slammed head-first into the stone. She shook her head and tried to steady herself, but her vision was blurry.

"You will not touch her."

Lillian and the serpent both jerked their heads in the direction of the voice. Her vision was still blurry, but she'd recognize that black hair and those green eyes anywhere. Kian waved his hands at the serpent, taunting it. The serpent's head snapped back and forth between them but finally made up its mind. It lunged for Lillian again.

She flung herself to the ground. The serpent's head slammed into the wall, and the cave vibrated like the stone itself was breaking. Scrambling to her feet, she stumbled toward Kian. The serpent followed, and she shuddered at the sound of the scales slithering across the stone.

"Get down!"

Lillian threw herself on the ground. Stone and gravel cut into her face and palms as she pressed herself flat against the cave floor. Kian's dagger glinted in the firelight when it flew over her head and hit the serpent's vulnerable underbelly. Lillian rose at the shriek confirming it had hit true, sprinting forward and finally reaching Kian's side. Kian grabbed her hand and dragged her toward the opening, his magic vibrating to rift them away. But the serpent was faster.

Its tail snapped between them, separating them while driving them back into the cave. Lillian stared at Kian with wide eyes. He raised his sword and motioned for her to do the same. They would have to kill it. Lillian didn't let herself consider any other possibility as they stood with swords raised, the serpent's yellow eyes focused on them.

When she met its narrowed eyes, the memory of what the raven had done to Ketil flashed in her mind.

"The eyes," she hissed. "We need to go for the eyes."

Kian inclined his head. When the Mungan launched again, they jumped to the side. Lillian brought her sword down hard, aiming for the large yellow eye, while the serpent snapped its razor-sharp teeth at Kian, who rifted away a second before its jaw closed around him.

The Mungan let out a deafening cry when her sword struck true. It twisted its head up, spraying hot blood over Lillian and Kian. Lillian wiped at her face with her sleeve, keeping her sword readied. Half-blind and furious, the serpent lashed out again. It went after Kian this time; its one intact eye locked on him. When it neared, Lillian took a deep breath and lunged.

Right below its head, with the serpent still focused on Kian, she lifted her sword. The serpent dove, and Lillian angled her sword, driving it straight through the bottom of its jaw. The serpent's body jerked, then went limp, before its head came crashing down on top of her.

Chapter Fifty-Six

Lillian's head pounded. Someone gently touched her forehead, whispering words she couldn't make out. She pried her eyes open. Kian crouched next to her, his green eyes wild. He let out a shaky breath when she met his eyes.

"How are you feeling?"

Lillian's tongue was thick as she opened her mouth to respond. "I feel like a giant snake died on top of me."

Kian let out a strangled laugh. "I see it didn't break your spirit, at least."

Flexing her fingers and toes, Lillian checked every inch of her body. She let out a breath of relief; nothing was broken. Her entire body ached, but she was able to push herself upright. She hissed softly when she touched her head, the pounding intensifying.

"I think you might have a concussion." Kian gently touched her back, helping her to sit up. "You'll need to rest here tonight."

Lillian glanced around the cave. The Mungan's lifeless body lay a few feet away. Goosebumps rippled across her skin, even if she could tell that it was well and truly dead. Her sword and daggers were next to her—not a hint of the serpent's blood on them.

She frowned, the movement sending a sharp pain through her head. "You cleaned my weapons?"

Kian nodded, a sheepish smile overtaking his face. "I went a bit mad waiting for you to wake up."

"What are you doing here?" Lillian tried to soften her voice. He'd helped take down the Mungan, after all.

Kian wiped his bloodied hands on his black uniform jacket. "I sensed you were in danger, so I rifted here."

Lillian's frown deepened. "How did you know where I was?"

Kian reached out to brush a few strands of her hair out of her face.

"I...," he hesitated. "It doesn't matter."

She shook her head slowly. "Are you allowed to help us?"

Kian shrugged, "No."

"Why?" She stared at him.

Kian was quiet for a moment, trailing his gaze up her body. When he met her eyes again, his green eyes blazed.

"You know why."

"Because you have a hero complex?" she joked, trying to lighten the mood.

Kian wasn't smiling; his eyes still watched her intently. Lillian shrugged and began to get up. She could light a fire, inspect the stupid serpent, whatever was needed to defuse what was happening inside his head.

When Kian grabbed her arm, a jolt of electricity shot through her.

"Lillian," he said quietly.

Her body tensed.

"Lillian, look at me."

She shook her head, her gaze fixed on her hands. They shook, and she clenched them quickly, praying Kian hadn't noticed.

"Lillian. Ice princess. The first time I saw you in that market, I knew my life would never be the same." His eyes searched her face. "I'd never seen anyone so beautiful, strong, and vicious."

Lillian shut her eyes. "Kian. Please," she whispered.

"No." His voice was commanding, and he dropped to his knees. "I know you have Eli. I know you love him. But I can't live with myself if I don't tell you how I feel."

Kian placed his hands over her heating cheeks.

"I have loved you since I first laid eyes on you, Lillian. I can't stop thinking about you. Your smell, your face, it's etched into my mind. I can't even stop dreaming about you slapping me. I'd be happy for you to do it every day if it meant I was worthy of your touch."

Kian gently lifted her face. The wild look was back in his eyes, and his warm breath caressed her face as he leaned in.

"Something is drawing us together, Lillian. I know you feel it, too." He sighed. "You're like the air I breathe. I can't function without you."

Lillian wanted to deny it. But deep inside, in that dark place inside her, she knew. Maybe if she'd met Kian first, she'd have let that part of her out. But the thought of Eli wouldn't allow it.

Before she could respond, Kian spoke again. "I don't expect you to choose me. I'm the son of the man who murdered your parents. But I want you to know that you have a choice. And I want you to choose me. I would give you the world, Lillian. Or I'd burn it for you if that's what you want. But please..." His voice broke. "Please, choose me."

Her broken heart shattered into a million pieces at his words. She searched his eyes, truly studying his beautiful face. Lillian wished she was someone else, someone who wouldn't have to crush the hope that burned bright in his eyes. The air charged when Kian leaned forward, so close that their foreheads touched. His thumb slowly stroked her cheek.

Lillian drew a deep breath, forcing her body not to react to his scent, and placed her hands on his hard chest.

"Kian. I love him."

The pain that flashed across his face threatened to break her completely, but she made herself stay strong.

"I won't deny that there is something here. But I love him, Kian. I can't do this to him."

Kian dropped his hands and rose to his feet. Emotions raced across his face as he urged his features back to a neutral expression. He glanced at her.

"I know." He offered her a sad smile. "The worst part is that it makes me love you even more."

Kian turned his back on her, and Lillian let him walk away, even as her heart screamed at her to call him back. She blinked frantically at the tears that welled in her eyes.

Kian lit a small fire, and they ate a meager meal in uncomfortable silence. Lillian tried to come up with something, *anything*, to say. But there were no words.

Intently staring into the flames, Kian finally broke the silence. "I want to say that I can still be your friend, Lillian. But I can't." He met her eyes. "Once this is over, I will be leaving."

She furrowed her brow. "Where will you go?"

"Somewhere far away. Where no one has heard of Crown Prince Kian or King Alek. I think I'd like to go somewhere warm. Maybe someplace with a beach where I can swim every day."

She nodded. That sounded wonderful.

"Maybe I'll also go somewhere far away when all of this is over. Well, if I can break the curse. If I can't, I hope the afterlife has beaches too."

Lillian imagined the afterlife as a sanctuary that fulfilled all of your needs. Unless she'd be sent to hell—she wasn't sure if king killers were welcome in the afterlife.

Kian froze. "I promise you. We will find a way to break the curse." His eyes blazed with that green fire again. "I will not leave until we do. And after that, you will make an amazing queen, Lillian. The people of Orios need you."

Lillian shook her head. She was so tired. So tired of fighting. And the people of Orios needed someone else, someone better to replace King Alek.

"I can't do it." She clenched her fists as her voice shook.

"Look at me, Lillian."

This time, she listened to him.

"You can do anything, ice princess. The beautiful, brave, loyal woman I love will make a great queen. You could destroy this entire wretched world if you wanted. But you won't. You'll protect these lands with your life and make it thrive again. I imagine your parents would be very proud of you."

A lump formed in her throat—she hadn't dared to imagine what her real parents thought of her. Swallowing, she hoped Kian was right. They stayed silent for a while, staring into the dancing flames. When they finally prepared to sleep, Kian extinguished the fire, unwilling to leave it lit to avoid attracting anything with fangs or weapons.

Lillian laid down close to the wall, curling into herself to keep what little heat she had. But even so, her teeth soon began clattering. She clenched her teeth, trying to be quiet, but it only made her whole body shiver. Kian got up from his spot a few feet away. He walked up and laid down behind her.

"What are you doing," she hissed.

"I'm trying to keep you from freezing to death. I'm sure even Eli would agree that me holding you is preferable to you dying."

Lillian started to argue with him, but he only pulled her body close to his and wrapped his arms around her. The heat immediately provided comfort, and Lillian quieted.

Turning around, she nestled her cold face into his chest and listened to his strong heartbeat. Kian blew a soft breath that tickled her scalp, tightened his arms and pulled her closer. Only tonight, she promised herself. The rhythmic thumping of his heart lulled her to sleep, her eyelids heavy as she wondered how she felt so safe in a cave with an ancient monster on the wildest mountain in Orios.

When Kian shifted, Lillian's eyes flew open. His arms were wrapped tightly around her body, her head resting on his chest. Her eyes widened. Had she climbed on top of him while she was sleeping? Wiggling, she tried to shift his arm off her. But when she carefully lifted it, his eyes opened. He glanced at her with a sleepy smile, his black hair tousled from sleep.

"Good morning, ice princess."

"Good morning," she mumbled and quickly got off him.

He laughed softly as she stumbled out of the cave. The skies were clear, and a hint of sunlight sparkled above the horizon. Lillian watched in awe as the sun's first rays cast the snow-covered mountainside in shades of yellow and orange. She sensed Kian before she heard him and spun around as a ray of sunshine hit her.

A smile spread across his face. "Beautiful," he mumbled.

Lillian whipped her head back to the horizon, her face heating.

"I meant the sunrise." Kian walked up to stand beside her, winking when she glanced at him.

Lillian hummed in agreement, trying to make her racing heart calm. They stood quietly for a moment, their eyes on the sun rising higher in the sky.

"I should get going. You will be eliminated if they find out I helped you." Kian nudged her shoulder.

She nodded.

As Kian prepared to rift away, he turned to her once more. "Make sure you get to the top before sundown. Keep to the right path, and you shouldn't run into any trouble."

She nodded again. With a final glance at her, Kian's magic filled the air, and Lillian was alone once more.

Chapter Fifty-Seven

Emptiness filled her when Kian left. Lillian tried telling herself she would have felt the same after anyone's absence, but that dark part of her knew it was a lie. Scolding herself and her stupid feelings, she continued up the mountain.

There, finally, was the top, the snowclad peak glittering in the sunlight. Last night's clouds had veiled it. Lillian was closer than she'd thought; if she continued her pace, she should make it by early afternoon. She drained her waterskin after a few hours and refilled it with some of the fresh snow that now surrounded her. The snow crunched under her feet, but it wasn't icy, so it helped keep her steps steady.

When Lillian faced the next fork, she chose the right path, listening to Kian's advice. After a few steps, the beating of wings filled the air. The ravens' large shadows blocked the sun, and Lillian shivered from the sudden chill. They landed a few feet ahead of her, blocking her path.

"Now you come?" Lillian narrowed her eyes. "I was attacked by a giant snake yesterday. You couldn't have swung by then?" She swore the ravens shrugged.

"I'd love to tell you all about it, but I must get going. I have a trial to finish." Lillian tried to squeeze by them, but they stood firmly planted in her way.

"If you could move, please?" The ravens did no such thing.

She growled. "I need to take the right path. It's the fastest and, from what I've understood, the safest. Move." The ravens just stared at her.

"Please?" Nothing.

The larger raven, the one that retrieved her sword yesterday, pointed its wing behind her.

"No, I need to take the right path." The raven pointed behind her again. "You want me to take the left one?"

When the raven inclined its head, Lillian groaned. But after what they did to Ketil yesterday, she was not about to risk her own eyes picked out for not obeying. Slowly, she turned around, choosing the left path. The ravens followed.

A loud rumble filled the air. Lillian halted when the mountain shifted, the ground beneath her shaking. She fell to her knees after another violent shake, holding on to a snow-covered boulder beside her. The rumble was deafening, echoing between the mountain-tops, and when she glanced behind her, a large mass of snow moved down the mountain. The massive avalanche rushed right down the path Lillian had set out to take.

She stayed on her knees until the mountain calmed. Once she was sure the ground wasn't about to fall beneath her feet, she rose, turning toward the ravens.

Lillian inclined her head. "Thank you."

They'd saved her life again. Lillian was beginning to seriously doubt her own abilities. She could not count how many times she'd now relied on someone else to save her life. The ravens bowed, then spread their wings and dove off the mountainside. Lillian stared after them for a moment, then continued her trek upward.

The path grew steeper, with each winding curve inclining further and the snow covering the path thicker. Cold sweat trickled down Lillian's back when darkness fell. Cursing to herself, she pushed forward. The mountaintop was finally within reach. She didn't let herself rest; Kian said that she needed to arrive before sundown, and while it was too late for that, she prayed they wouldn't eliminate her if she arrived before it was fully dark.

After turning an especially sharp corner, several large beacons appeared, casting the snow-covered mountainside in soft orange light. The mountain flattened into a plateau, maybe two hundred yards wide, and the sound of people milling about broke through the night.

The beacons surrounded the whole plateau, casting their firelight on the small group that stood to the right of a circular enclosure lined with torches—the novices waiting for the grand finale.

Lillian rushed her steps, even as her whole body protested at the movement. The group turned toward her as she approached. Lillian couldn't hear what they were saying over the wind, still seventy yards away, but Kian and Finn stood among them. Her eyes anxiously scanned the rest of the group, and her stomach sank. There was no sign of Sam.

Howling began behind her. Lillian froze, then spun around to face the dark mountainside. But nothing chased her—no creature had scaled the plateau. Turning back toward the group, she took another step. A scream pierced the air. Whipping her head around again, Lillian hesitated.

She glanced at the group and met Kian's eyes. He violently shook his head. Lillian was about to take another step toward them, but when the scream rang again, she spun around and sprinted down the mountain where she'd come from. Stupid, stupid, *stupid*. She repeated the word with each step that she took. This wasn't the time to play hero. There was too much at stake. But she couldn't make herself turn around.

The Garm came into view as she skidded down the mountain, nearly falling with every slippery step. She relaxed slightly; it wasn't pacing around Sam. Another of the novices faced it, his arm shaking as he wielded his sword.

It was a man she'd never spoken to, whom she had paid little attention to. He hadn't stood out in the group. Lillian had honestly forgotten he was still participating. With his mousy blonde hair and lanky body, he hadn't seemed like he would last long.

The arm that wasn't holding the sword curved around his stomach. Bile rose in her throat when she realized his arm was the only thing that stopped his insides from spilling out, blood pooling on the snow beneath him. She couldn't believe the man was still standing.

The Garm hadn't noticed her yet, and Lillian approached the creature slowly, trying to make her steps as silent as possible. She pressed a finger to her lips when she met the man's panicked eyes. Lillian kept his gaze as she slipped up behind the Garm. When it lunged, she let her sword slice through the air.

The Garm jumped slightly more to the left than she'd antici-pated. Instead of her sword cleaving its neck, Lillian slashed its side. The Hellhound let out a vicious snarl and flipped around, glaring at Lillian with its red eyes. She was *so stupid*. Limping in a circle around her, the Garm bared its razor-sharp teeth. She bared her teeth back, some animalistic survival instinct making her snarl at the hound's threat. The other novice fell to the ground, still gripping his stomach. She blew out a soft breath as his chest moved.

Lillian knew she'd only have one chance—the animal was fran-tic, white froth foaming at its mouth. When it launched itself at her, Lillian lunged as well, a feral scream leaving her mouth as she leaped on top of it, driving her sword down its neck. Lillian went down with the Garm, gripping its rough black fur as they slammed into the ground. Thankfully, the Hellhound's body protected her from the hard snow and stone beneath.

The Garm wasn't moving, and she cautiously pushed herself off the still-warm body and ran up to the man. He moaned in the cold snow, barely conscious. *Stupid*, she repeated to herself as she pulled at the arm that wasn't holding the contents of his gut to get him to rise.

"I can't carry you. You need to walk. Lean on me," she hissed through gritted teeth as she braced herself for the man's weight. Even if he wasn't as big as some other novices, he had at least fifty pounds on her.

The man groaned as he stood, leaning heavily on Lillian. Slowly, *so slowly*, they walked up the mountain. The snow was frozen up here, each step more slippery than the next. Lillian tried to keep the man awake by asking him questions. He couldn't die on her now.

His name was Magnus, and he was born in the slums surrounding the capital. But when Lillian asked about his family, he was quiet, his eyelids fluttering.

She shook him with the bit of strength she had left, "Magnus, there is a healer only minutes away. Just a few more steps, and we're there."

He took another step, and Lillian repeated, "Only a few more steps." until they finally stepped onto the plateau.

She groaned when his entire weight collapsed on her shoulder. Magnus finally passed out. Lillian dragged the man, only sheer will moving them toward the group. Finn shifted from one foot to the other, his face tight with worry. When she moved her gaze to Kian, despair lined his eyes. Her stomach sinking, Lillian realized she had to make it across the finish line alone.

Setting her jaw, she used every last bit of strength to drag them both toward the torch-lined circle where she expected the finale to take place. Twenty yards, ten yards. She sucked in a breath, and finally, *finally*, she crossed it, pulling Magnus's lifeless body with her. Finn raced to her side.

"Take him," she panted, and Finn quickly lifted the man into his arms.

Lillian sank to the snow-covered ground, catching her breath. Finn handed the man over to Commander Eirik and sprinted back to her.

"Are you hurt?" He dragged her to her feet.

She shook her head. "Just exhausted. And glad to be done scaling this damn mountain."

Finn tried to flash a grin, but his smile fell as he glanced at the group. Still no Sam.

Quietly, they joined the others. When Kian sought her eyes, she inclined her head, then fixed her gaze on the dark ledge surrounding them. Commander Jon announced that they'd wait another ten minutes. After that, the trial was over, and the finale could begin.

Chapter Fifty-Eight

They were the longest minutes of Lillian's life. She anxiously scanned the darkness around the plateau, praying to see Sam's kind eyes peek over the ridge, the beacons shining their soft light on his blonde hair. When Commander Jon rose, she knew it was too late. But then Finn gasped next to her, and she flipped around to glimpse Sam's grim face as he climbed over the edge.

"Run, Sam!"

Lillian didn't realize she was screaming until her voice rattled her. Sam limped, blood streaming down his face. But he was moving. When Lillian stepped forward, Commander Jon grabbed her arm.

"All novices must finish alone."

Lillian glared at the commander. "What about Magnus?"

He didn't answer.

Sam still walked, painfully slow, toward them. She didn't dare breathe until he finally stumbled over the finish line, just as Commander Jon opened his mouth to speak. Finn and Lillian caught him before he fell to the snow-covered ground. They still held Sam upright when Commander Jon stepped forward.

"Ten of you have made it to the top."

Lillian stole a glance at the other novices, releasing a breath when Ketil was nowhere to be seen.

"It is now time for the final trial." He paused. "All bow to King Alek."

Seven people made their way to them, headed by the king. Six uniformed guards flanked him, a low number compared to the fifteen who had stood at his side during the ball, but they were all heavily armed, with several swords strapped to their backs. The king wore a white fur cloak held together by a thick golden chain, and the crown on his head shimmered in the light from the beacons.

When the king approached, she bowed low. Rage sparkled inside her when he waited a few moments more than necessary before asking them all to rise.

As Lillian rose, she met the king's green eyes. She didn't flinch when his eyes roved over her, letting the rage flow freely through her veins. The king's eyes left her, trailing over each one of the novices before he spoke.

"Congratulations on making it to the final trial." His voice was flat, and the king yawned before he continued. "You will all be paired up to fight. Only swords may be used, and only by the death of your opponent may you win."

The novices stared at each other, and Lillian's nostrils flared. Naturally, the king would ensure they all had blood on their hands at the end of this.

Without another word, the king stalked off and sat by the four long tables in the snow outside the designated circle. Tall candles lined the tables, and the aromas from the steaming food that white-clad servants brought washed over her. His court joined him, and Lillian clenched her fists as they poured wine and laughed, making bets on which novice would win.

Commander Jon walked up to each novice, unfastening their bracelets. When the commander removed her bracelet, she finally sensed the bond with Finn again.

Finn eyed her anxiously. *What are we going to do?*

Let's wait and see.

When Lillian scanned the mountaintop, Eli and his accomplices were nowhere to be seen.

Commander Jon motioned to Thyra, who flicked her blond

hair as she stepped up beside him, and another man Lillian didn't know. She thought his name might be Niels. The king's court cheered when they stepped into the ring, and a wave of nausea rolled through Lillian.

It wasn't a fair fight. Lillian didn't know what magic Thyra possessed, but the man she faced couldn't strike her for his life, his arms flailing as he tried to wield his sword. Thyra carelessly walked up to Niels as the sword tumbled out of his hands and delivered her first and final blow to his heart. Lillian forced herself to watch as his lifeless body crumpled to the ground.

The people around the king clapped, some standing up, as Thyra bowed to them, stepping out of the ring. Commander Jon didn't waste any time. As soon as the body was removed, leaving a pool of blood staining the snow, he waved forward two large men. Both of them had laughed at her that first day.

Lillian regretted her wish to see them dead as soon as the fight began. The men were equaled, relying on no magic, only skill and brute force. More blood stained the ground as both men's swords hit true. They struck the other again and again. In the end, they both limped. One had lost an eye, and the other had no use of his left arm. They circled each other when the slightly larger man kicked the other to the ground and didn't hesitate as he plunged his sword into his heart. More cheers erupted from the crowd.

Commander Jon called two others into the ring. Only Lillian, Sam, Finn, and the tall woman remained. Lillian went cold, and despair flowed freely along the bond. She wasn't sure if it came from her or Finn.

The next fight was over too soon. Lillian didn't even notice who won as Commander Jon stared at her next. And her heart shattered when he pointed to Finn. Lillian didn't move.

Come on, silver girl. Finn already walked toward the ring.

No.

Commander Jon waved impatiently at her. "In the ring, girl."

She didn't spare him a glance.

One more fight, and you can end this.

No.

Lillian shook her head, her feet frozen in place. She would not face Finn in that ring.

Lillian. My Queen. The honor of being your familiar is everything I have asked for in life. Please let me do this for you.

Eyes burned into her back, and she turned her head to meet Kian's stare. Tears filled her gray ones at the shadow that crossed his face.

"No."

Lillian first thought she was the one who had spoken out loud but stiffened when she realized it was Kian.

"No?" Everyone went silent as King Alek spoke. "Prince, what are you saying?"

Kian walked over to Lillian's side, gently brushing his fingers against hers.

"I said no." He stared intently at Lillian. "She will not fight him."

The king laughed. "Does the Crown Prince have a soft spot for a novice?"

Kian only continued staring into Lillian's eyes, and a knot formed in her stomach as she realized what he was doing.

When the king laughed louder, she glared at him. He offered her a cold smile.

"She is an extraordinary beauty. But Prince Kian, would you stoop so low to bed a mere novice? She's probably laid with half of Orios just to get here. You ought to be careful."

Lillian snarled and reached for her sword. Kian subtly shaking his head was the only thing that stopped her from throwing her sword into the king's smug face.

Lillian.

She glanced at Finn. Silver lined his beautiful eyes, and her chest split wide open. She'd do anything to see him with his usual mischievous grin. Desperately, she scanned the mountain, but when there was no sign of Eli, she glanced at Kian again.

The king followed her gaze, and his smile widened.

"Either she fights the novice. Or she can fight you, Kian. The choice is hers."

Lillian stopped breathing. Flicking her eyes between Kian and Finn, for the first time in her life, Lillian didn't know what to do. Kian took a step toward the ring at the same time as Finn spoke to her through the bond.

It's okay, Lillian. I love you.

Hot tears filled her eyes as she shifted her gaze between her friends, and she almost doubled over from the pain that gripped her heart as both men made their way to the ring.

"Please announce your choice. Lillian, was that your name?" The king sneered.

Shaking her head, Lillian backed up. But Commander Eirik stood behind her, urging her forward.

"If you won't choose, I'll execute them both right now."

Lillian stared at the king. He wouldn't execute his son, not in front of an audience.

The king winked and motioned for his guards. "Please seize the Crown Prince."

All six guards grabbed Kian, forcing him down on his knees. Lillian blinked.

"I think beheading is swift enough for a prince, don't you," the king mused.

The crowd was silent, cautiously watching their king. One of the guards raised a sword over Kian's head.

"Finn! I chose Finn!" Her voice broke as she screamed at the king.

She couldn't tear her eyes from the sword hovering over Kian's neck. The king nodded to the guard, who immediately lowered the sword. He laughed again, a hollow, empty laugh, as Lillian blew out a breath of relief.

"Like I would kill my only heir," King Alek smiled at Lillian. "But now we'll at least enjoy a real fight, knowing where your loyalties lie."

She snarled when she realized he'd meant for this to happen.

"Let's get this over with." King Alek waved his hand impatiently at them, turning back to the food on the table.

It's okay, Lillian. There was only unwavering affection vibrating down the bond. *I believe in fate. And I think fate brought me to you —to serve you and help you take your rightful place as queen.*

No. I can't do this, Finn. Not even for Orios. I love you. You're my best friend.

Sucking in a breath, she realized why her parents hadn't been able to choose the people of Orios over each other. Finn wasn't even her mate, and she couldn't do it.

Yes, you can. Lillian caught his eyes again. Finn's beautiful, amber eyes only had love as they met hers. *Step into that ring.*

Commander Eirik nudged her forward. As if watching from the outside, Lillian saw herself take one step, then another, until she stood in the ring. Facing Finn. She thought she was dreaming when he raised his sword.

Let's give them the show of their lifetime.

No. Lillian couldn't unsheathe her sword, her hands shaking by her sides.

Lillian, please. Finn's eyes pleaded with her, begging her to raise her sword.

Lillian lifted her face to the sky, angled to the full moon above. Calm washed over her when she realized she could embrace *this* death. She could go gently for the sake of her friends. She'd found people who loved her and who she fiercely loved back. They would continue this fight without her; she was sure of it. The world needed people like Finn, like Kian, who loved so effortlessly. Who would stand up for their beliefs, no matter what.

Lillian stepped out of the ring.

"I won't do it." She stared directly at the king as she spoke, her voice clear.

The king's nostrils flared when he met her gaze. He waved lazily at his guards, and his voice was cold as he commanded, "Kill her."

Lillian didn't have time to react before the guards seized her. Four of them held her down, her arms locked against her body as they disarmed her. Screams rose around her, and more guards emerged from the mountainside, grabbing Finn and Kian when they lunged for her.

It's okay. Lillian willed herself to calm. *I'm so grateful I met you,*

Finn. Please tell Sam thank you. His compassion made me a better person. And tell Kian. She swallowed. *Tell him I wished I met him first. And I hope he finds that beach one day.*

Lillian shut out Finn's response. She wouldn't break in front of the king.

The crowd roared, crazed from the excitement of a novice betraying the crown. A guard stalked up to her, his raised sword glistening in the moonlight.

She glanced at Kian. He fought the six guards restraining him, punching one in the face before two more appeared to subdue him.

"Lillian! No!"

Kian screamed her name, the sound of his broken voice shattering every piece of the broken heart inside her. But when she met those beautiful green eyes, she willed herself to smile. The first and final smile she'd ever offered him. His face crumbled.

She closed her eyes when the guard readied the sword above her neck.

Chapter Fifty-Nine

A deafening crash echoed through the air, and the world plunged into darkness. Lillian's eyes teared when she squinted through the thick, dark smoke. Clangs of swords and screams surrounded her.

Praying that the rebels had come at last, Lillian pushed herself off the ground. The guards who had been holding her down were nowhere to be seen. Stumbling in the darkness, she reached out through the bond.

Finn! He didn't answer.

Where are you? Lillian screamed down the bond.

Nothing.

Her heart pounding in her chest, she frantically reached for her weapons, only to remember that the guards had disarmed her moments before. Dropping to the ground, Lillian searched for her sword and her daggers. When she didn't feel them, she grabbed for anything that could help. There was nothing but boulders on the ground.

She picked up a large rock. When she stepped in the direction where she'd last seen Kian and Finn, Lillian slammed into someone, the person manic as they pushed to get away from her. It was a young woman who had been part of the crowd surrounding the King. They locked eyes for a moment before the woman took off, terror filling her wide eyes and her white dress billowing behind her before she disappeared in the thick smoke. The metallic echo of swords filled the air, but the smoke was so thick Lillian couldn't make out who was fighting.

Clenching the rock, she continued walking toward where she hoped to find her friends. A glimpse of metal flickered through the smoke, and Lillian darted to the side at the last moment. A sword cleaved the air where she'd just been standing, and the guard wielding it turned to glare at her, his breathing ragged.

When he lifted the sword to strike again, Lillian threw the rock as hard as she could. It hit the man's head with a revolting crack, his body lifeless as it crumbled to the ground. Lillian winced but didn't allow herself to check if he was alive when she grabbed his sword and a dagger that hung at his waist.

Sheathing the dagger at her thigh, Lillian weighed the sword in her hand. It was heavier than her own, a little off balance, but it would have to do. At least it was better than a rock. Stalking toward where she believed most of the fighting was happening, the smoke still lingering like a blanket over the plateau, she fought off two more guards.

"Sam!"

Sam fought a guard before her, panting as she reached him. Together, they quickly took him down, with Sam delivering a devastating blow to the guard's gut that made the man topple over. He didn't rise again.

"The others?"

Lillian glanced around the plateau, the smoke finally lifting and the beacons' light breaking through the shadows. Rebels surrounded them, dressed in black and wearing white bands with raven wings tied around their arms. They fought an impossible number of guards while screaming orders at each other.

Sam shook his head. "I haven't seen them. I must have been unconscious for a moment; I woke up to this hell."

Sam's face was tight from pain. Grabbing his arm, she pulled him from the midst of the fighting.

"Come on, you won't be able to fight much longer. We need to get you out."

Sam tried to protest, but Lillian ignored him and continued dragging him toward the mountain's slope—there were small ledges on the mountainside where he could hide.

Lillian stumbled when her vision changed, the clear night sky in front of her instead of the suffocating smoke.

"What happened?" Sam's worried face was in front of her again.

Lillian shook her head. "I'm not sure. I..."

Her vision flipped to the night sky again. *Finn?*

She could sense he was injured, pain shooting through her own legs. He was alive but unable to move. Lillian tried to walk; she needed to find him, but seeing through Finn's eyes made her clumsy. She blindly stumbled forward while Sam grabbed her arm. Sam's concerned voice sounded as if from far away.

She watched the snow-covered mountainside through Finn's eyes and heard the fighting in the distance through his ears. Snow crunched to the left of her, and she whipped her head toward the sound. No. Finn turned his head to the side. A dark-clad figure approached him, and Lillian and Finn held their breath together as the man removed his hood. When Eli's familiar blue eyes locked with Finn's, Lillian relaxed.

"Hello, Finn," Eli said quietly, and Lillian jerked at the coldness in his voice.

Eli's eyes narrowed as he swept them over Finn's broken body, and apprehension shivered along the bond. Eli pulled out a dagger from the inside of his cloak. Flipping it from hand to hand, he stared at Finn intently.

Finn cleared his throat. "Funny seeing you here. I'd get up to shake your hand, but it seems I've broken both my legs."

The worry that rolled down the bond sent a wave of nausea over Lillian.

"Yes. I'm sorry about that. I thought you would die when I pushed you over the ledge, but you are apparently more durable than I thought."

Lillian started shaking. Sam still held on to her, squeezing her arm. His voice was distant as he worriedly asked what was happening.

"Finn," she got out. She wasn't sure if the shock that rolled along the bond came from her or Finn. Maybe both.

Finn laughed hoarsely. "It's the ladies' favorite thing about me."

Eli snorted. "I'm sure."

His dagger glinted in the moonlight when he crouched down next to Finn.

Keep him talking, Finn!

Lillian blindly pulled at Sam. "He's going to kill him." Her voice broke. "We need to find him. You have to lead, I can't see."

Finn! Look around you. I need to see where you are.

Finn's eyes were locked on Eli, watching the dagger he held.

Look around you!

Finn quickly glanced around the area. Snow surrounded them, smoke billowing above their heads.

"Why are you doing this?" Finn's voice was soft as he addressed Eli.

Look again.

Lillian desperately stumbled forward; they didn't have time to walk around the mountain. When Finn scanned the area again, there was a large formation of stones to his left.

"East," she hissed at Sam. Lillian strained her ears as Sam growled that they needed to walk around. They were on the west side of the plateau.

When Eli spoke again, the rest of Sam's words drowned out, and she blindly stumbled after him, his hand tight on hers.

"Because everything in my life has led up to this moment." Eli ran his fingers through his hair, shifting it out of his face. Lillian's chest constricted at the crazed look in his blue eyes.

"What do you mean?" Finn strained to keep his voice calm.

Good. Keep him talking.

"It was all going to plan. And then you and the rest of your group couldn't leave her alone." Eli's lips curled into a sneer. "You, the commander, or should I say the *Crown Prince*? And that stupid girl, Astrid. She almost ruined everything."

Bile rose in Lillian's throat.

"What did Astrid do?" Finn kept his gaze on the dagger—so close to his neck.

"She figured it out. She was going to tell Lillian." Eli sighed. "I had to take care of her after that." He flicked the dagger in his hand. "It was easy. A note to the king, signed by his precious Commander Atlas, confirming his suspicions that Astrid was a rebel. I'd hoped it would take care of the commander too, that she'd believe he had betrayed her, but alas, no such luck."

Lillian's heart stopped. Eli had betrayed Astrid. She almost doubled over from the pain of his words.

"Quick," she grunted at Sam, and he dragged her faster, distant sounds of metal clashing around them.

Finn glanced from the dagger to Eli's face. "What did she figure out?"

Eli frowned, impatiently flicking his hair again.

"How to break the curse, of course. Orios, are you always this slow?" He glared at Finn. "We've known how to break it since her birth. Everything we did was to prepare her for it, carefully shaping all parts of her life to lead her here. We couldn't risk her failing like her parents did."

Lillian shook her head, her heart beating out of her chest.

Shifting his dagger once more, Eli continued. "Astrid was worried that breaking the curse would break *her*. But Lillian's strong. We *made* her strong. Atli sacrificed himself to set the plan in motion. Now it's my turn to finish it."

When Eli lifted the dagger, Lillian screamed, the desperate sound echoing between the mountaintops. Sam frantically spoke in her ear, trying to reach her. She forced herself to quiet, to listen to him.

"I see them. They're down there."

Finn, you have to give me my sight back.

Lillian almost couldn't bear it when she finally saw out of her own eyes. Sprinting, she threw herself over the ledge.

"Stop!" She screamed as she fell, and Eli whipped his head up just in time to watch her roll as she hit the mountainside.

263

She ignored the pain from the sharp rocks that cut her and rose to her feet. "Stop, Eli."

When she met her lover's blue eyes, her heart shattered. The person looking back wasn't the boy she loved. The person in front of her was mad, his gaze frenzied as he brought the knife closer to Finn's throat.

"Please. You don't have to do this." Lillian begged him, her voice breaking.

Eli narrowed his eyes. "Yes. I do."

"*Please*, Eli," she choked as tears streamed down her face.

"You don't understand. I am giving up everything, *everything*, for this, Lillian. *I have to.*"

Tears formed in Eli's eyes as well. He sucked in a breath, set his jaw, and raised the dagger.

"*No!*"

Lillian didn't know how her own dagger ended up in her hand. Tears clouded her vision as she aimed it at the boy she loved.

When she let the dagger fly, Lillian closed her eyes.

Chapter Sixty

The world was silent. With only the wind ringing in her ears, Lillian sprinted to the men she loved, falling to her knees in the bloodied snow as she reached them. Neither of them moved. Her dagger was lodged in Eli's chest. His eyes were closed, and blood trickled from his mouth down his chin.

"I'm sorry. *I'm so sorry*," she sobbed, laying her head on his chest.

There was no heartbeat.

A blood-curdling cry filled the air. Lillian jerked when she realized it was her own. "This isn't happening, this isn't happening," she mumbled frantically. It must be a dream—a nightmare.

Lillian?

She lifted her head. Finn slowly opened his eyes to look at her. Lillian's sobs intensified as she crawled over to him.

"You're okay," she got out. Finn nodded, lifting a hand to wipe away a tear spilling down her cheek.

"He didn't have time." Finn glanced at Eli's lifeless body. "You saved my life, silver girl."

No feeling of joy filled her at the sound of his words. There was only sorrow. Eli was dead. Because of her.

"Lillian," Sam's gentle voice sounded behind her. "I can heal him if you step aside."

Nodding, she slowly rose, using her sleeve to wipe at her face. She hiccupped when another wave of sobs overcame her.

"We need to get out of here. The rebels are losing. The king had more guards hiding in a cavern on the mountainside. They're over-run." Sam spoke urgently as he worked on Finn.

His words were like a knife, sharp pain slicing clean through Lillian. She had failed. The king was alive. And the boy she loved was dead.

The pain intensified. Her muscles spasmed involuntarily, and the pain of a thousand knives cutting her permeated her whole body.

"Lillian? What's happening?"

She barely heard Finn through the haze of agony.

Another wave of pain sliced through her. Panting, she tried to respond, but no words left her lips. Every breath was a torment. Her nerves were on fire, and her back was splitting wide open. She tried to scream as pain consumed her.

Finn gasped. Her vision went black for a moment before she was thrust into Finn's mind, watching herself through his eyes. Huge black wings grew from her back, glittering as the moonlight reflected in them, casting long shadows on the snow-covered mountain. Her hair turned darker, the white shifting into the darkest of black. Her pale skin shimmered as it turned into a golden tan. When the pain subsided and Lillian straightened, only her light gray eyes remained the same.

"*Valkyrie*," Finn breathed in awe.

Lillian pulled out of his mind, slamming back into her own. How had she broken the curse? The question echoed in her mind as she lifted a strand of black hair. Eli said they'd worked for this her whole life.

Realization dawned on her. She glanced at Eli's body while a fresh wave of pain shot through her. Lillian whimpered—her father and Eli couldn't have been so cruel. But the words on Astrid's note rang in her mind. *What is bound by love, only death can undo.* Astrid had figured it out before Eli betrayed her. And Liv spoke of a horrific price to break the curse.

266

A wave of memories washed over her. Eli courting her, so persistent, until she finally caved. Her father encouraging her to let him in. How they kept her sheltered from all others. Eli flirting with other women when he believed she wasn't watching. Eli's tears when she sang the song about the man who had so little time left. Eli's possessive arm around her shoulder only when he noticed how Kian looked at her. His crazed eyes as he told her he was giving up everything for this.

It wasn't real. Their love wasn't real. Lillian scratched at her throat. She couldn't breathe. Eli made her fall in love with him just for her to kill him. Just for her to break the curse. Her mind went blank, black spots dancing in front of her eyes. She forced the memories away and locked them up deep inside her.

Blinding rage overtook her. She was mesmerized by it. It was as if her magic itself was furious at having been bound, needing release. She could easily kill the two men in front of her. Using just one of her hands, she would snap their fragile necks.

The weight on her back threw her off when she stepped toward them. She glanced over her shoulder, watching her glittering wings stretch out behind her. Lillian tried to curl them in, but instead spread them wider, the feathers blowing softly in the wind whipping around the mountain. She stumbled as the motion made her lose her balance. It snapped her out of her trance, and her eyes widened as she realized what she'd almost done.

Taking a deep breath, she tried calming the simmering rage. It seemed the Valkyrie emotions were volatile indeed. She'd have to be careful with her temper. Sam and Finn watched her quietly, and when she stared back at them, Finn dropped a knee to the ground, his head facing the ground.

My Queen. Finn's voice wasn't the amused one she'd gotten so used to, but serious, awestruck.

"Please get up." Lillian stiffed as even her voice was different, stronger somehow. She flexed her fingers. She had never felt so alive, energy bristling like wildfire under her skin.

"Over there!" A loud voice sounded above the ledge. "Get them!"

Two guards ran toward them, knocking arrows into their bows. Their steps faltered when they noticed her wings, but they quickly recovered, aiming the sharp points of the arrows at their hearts.

She snarled at them, a primal warning vibrating in her throat. Her wings twitched as rage once again flushed her veins. She welcomed it. Let all that pain and sorrow turn into burning flames within her.

Stepping in front of Sam and Finn, she growled, "Put away the bows, and I will spare your lives."

No more of her friends would die today.

When the guards took another step, Lillian erupted. Darkness shot out from her hands, enveloping the two men. Their screams lasted only a second. She felt their deaths in the darkness, two lights going out within her magic. A cold smile spread across her face as the dark plumes curled back to her, caressing her face before vanishing. Power. That was what she was feeling.

Finn's eyes were wide as they met hers. "What *was* that?"

Lillian tilted her head. "I'm guessing my magic."

"I understood that much, but what *is* it?"

Lillian shook her head. It felt like the night sky itself had touched her cheek. Looking down at her hands, she willed it out again, strands of darkness wrapping around her wrists playfully. When they twirled toward Finn, she willed them back. She wasn't sure if they wanted to kill him yet.

"Eli's death broke the curse, didn't it?" Sam backed up a few steps, eyeing her cautiously.

Lillian's face fell, the rage that had absorbed the pain fading away. Finn was instantly at her side, wrapping his hand around hers. His despair hummed through the bond. She nodded but couldn't utter the words to tell them what she suspected, what her father and Eli had done.

"We should go," she said gruffly, her voice thick with emotion.

"Where?" Sam and Finn spoke in unison.

Lillian glanced around them. The smoke above them had finally cleared, and the fighting quieted. A tug pulled her toward the plateau.

"To kill Alek."

She'd made up her mind as soon as the darkness emerged from her. She was strong now. Strong enough to kill the fire-wielding king even without the element of surprise. Darkness would extinguish the flame.

Chapter Sixty-One

Finn and Sam gaped at her.

"The king has hundreds of guards up there. It's like he knew there would be an ambush." Sam shook his head. "We need to wait. You don't know how to control that power of yours yet."

Lillian snarled at him. "I will kill them all."

"And then what? You'll do exactly what Alek did to take power. Kill and destroy. That's not the Lillian I know."

Sam stared at her, challenge in his brown eyes. Finn's agreement echoed along their bond.

A sound rumbled in her throat, a vicious growl leaving her as she glared at them. But deep inside her, something woke. *He is right*, it whispered. Lillian focused on the small voice. *You're not human anymore. The Valkyrie emotions are strong. You need to control them before they control you.* Forcing the anger deep down inside herself, the fog of emotions lifted slightly.

She cleared her throat. "You're right."

"Actually, maybe we're not." Finn stared behind her, dread filling his eyes.

Lillian whipped around, wobbling slightly, still not used to the weight of her wings. Hundreds of guards stood on top of the ledge, the beacons' light flickering on their black uniforms and contorting their faces into cruel masks. King Alek stood in the middle, his gaze transfixed on her, with fire dancing over his palms.

The tug toward the plateau intensified. Her feet tried to carry her to the king, but she held still. Lillian willed the darkness forward, wisps of black swirling around her like a dark cape. King Alek's lips curled into a smile.

Lillian bared her teeth at him, her wings flaring. As the king lifted his hands, there was a sharp tug behind her, and the pull was so strong that she trembled when she tried to keep her feet planted.

The smell of night filled her nostrils, and a jolt went through her when a warm hand wrapped around her arm, and Kian rifted them away.

Lillian fell to her knees and retched when solid ground was finally under her feet. Apparently, her Valkyrie body didn't react well to rifting either.

A cool breeze brushed against her face, bringing the smell of salt water. Lifting her head, she glanced around. She was on a beach. Massive black cliffs towered over them, the vast ocean at their backs. Finn and Sam were also on their knees, and a small part of Lillian was glad she wasn't the only one who struggled with rifting.

Kian faced the wild dark ocean, his back to her. In trance, her hands pushed into the soft sand. Her feet took one step, then another. The tug was so strong she almost stumbled. Hearing her approach, Kian turned, and gray eyes met green.

A song bloomed inside her. *Mine*, it sang. *Mine, mine, mine.* It was as if gravity itself pulled her to him. Kian remained still as she walked up to him, their eyes locked. There was only him. Her soul sang to his, the light to the darkness within her. His eyes darkened when she closed the distance between them.

Lillian reached out and placed a hand on his chest. His heart thundered. *Mine.*

He inclined his head. *Yours.*

Mate. Kian was her mate. His forest-green eyes mesmerized her. It was as if she saw his face for the first time. The high cheekbones, the strong jaw, the proud nose. The black hair that she burned to run her fingers through. *Mine.*

"Please don't kill me for interrupting whatever is happening, but we have company."

Lillian whirled around, a low growl leaving her throat as an overwhelming urge to protect what was hers filled her. Finn backed up, his hands in the air. She shook her head, forcing her mind to clear. Red stained her cheeks when she realized what she was doing.

"Sorry," she winced as she met Finn's eyes.

Kian let out a low laugh while Finn tried to wink at her, a ghost of his old self.

"I'm praying those are friends because they look deadly." Finn gestured behind him.

Lillian lifted her eyes, her body going unnaturally still as she beheld the three winged-women approaching them.

Family. Her Valkyrie senses hummed with pleasure. They were so beautiful. Flanking a tall brunette were two identical blondes, twins, Lillian thought, all three with large black wings. The wings' feathers shifted gently in the breeze, shimmering in the moonlight.

Several swords and bows were strapped to their backs, and they wore golden metal bands over their brows. Finn was right. They did look deadly—three lethal weapons. Lillian couldn't tear her eyes from them.

The women kept their eyes on Lillian as they drew nearer. A few feet away from her, they stopped. The three women dropped a knee in one fluid motion, bowing their heads. Lillian met the brunette's intelligent blue eyes as she looked back up.

"We've been looking for you, Your Majesty."

272

Acknowledgments

I have to start by thanking Michael, my husband. Your unwavering support, even while you were away actually fighting a war, made this book happen. To Josephine, my sister, who shares my love for fantasy. Thank you for brainstorming with me and for always picking up the phone when I get stuck.

To my Beta readers, the first ones outside my family who ever read anything of mine. Thank you for being so kind, supportive and providing invaluable input. To Aimee, my editor. Thank you for helping me bring Echo of Wings to the next level.

And to you, the reader. Thank you for believing in a debut author, and for believing in Echo of Wings.